Dedicated to my good friend Paul Milenski, who was intrigued by the fact that my little second graders would line up eagerly in the morning just to catch a glimpse of my colorful and impractical shoes.

"There's a story in this," he said.

And so, because of him, I wrote it.

D1497447

ONE

"STARLIGHT IS A GENIUS. Even her teacher told me that she's reading on fourth grade level."

"Yes, Miss Mooney," Father Felix said. "Starlight is a wonderful student, the brightest little girl in the second grade. But I still cannot readmit her to Saint Polycarp as long as her hair is crawling with lice."

"I washed her hair. I washed her hair over and over again." Miss Mooney flicked her pierced tongue.

"It is not just a matter of washing her hair," Father Felix tried to explain. "She needs a special shampoo and a fine tooth comb to get rid of the eggs."

The young woman's face crunched in confusion. "Eggs? What eggs?"

"They're little...white things. If you want to speak to Nurse Abby—"

"My daughter doesn't have eggs in her head. That's absurd. And, besides, she caught those bugs from Cupid, that girl who has been tormenting her. I told Mrs. Hopwood to change her seat but Mrs. Hopwood, she doesn't care. She's a horrible teacher."

Father Felix drew a deep breath. "As soon as Starlight's hair is clean, we will welcome her back with open arms."

Miss Mooney stamped her foot on the floor, startling Father Felix and a kindergarten student, who was on his way to the water fountain. "Starlight will not be returning to your school."

"Miss Mooney..." Father Felix tried in vain to reason with her.

"You're evil, do you know that? You call yourself a priest? You making Starlight feel dirty."

"No, it's not—"

But before Father Felix could utter another word, Miss Mooney pointed her purple sequinned nail in his direction. "I curse this school," she screamed, "I curse the building, I curse the teachers—"

The kindergarten student started to wail.

"You're going to have to leave," Father Felix said firmly but Miss Mooney was already making her way down the corridor, cursing everything in sight, the statue of St. Polycarp, the art projects on the wall, the bulletin board papers, and the poor kindergarten student.

Her ranting brought Mrs. Hopwood to the classroom door. "I'm afraid that you've lost another student," Father Felix said. "But really, that woman is a lunatic."

"Welcome to Saint Polycarp," Mrs. Hopwood muttered.

TWO

MILDRED PINKERTON, the seventh grade teacher at St. Polycarp, began the morning of Monday, October 13th doing the same things she had done for the last twenty-eight years of her life.

She entered the faculty room, feeling rather prickly. This irritated feeling continued as she read the morning messages typed neatly by her principal, Father Felix.

Bonnie Crossover had called in sick again. That meant that the fourth grade would have to be split up, herding the children into other classrooms, with busy work that they never did, but that hardly mattered since it was never collected. Everyone knew that Miss Crossover was always sick on Mondays because she spent her entire weekend on one shopping binge after another, and by the time Sunday night rolled around she was plumb exhausted.

The rain lashing against the window meant that there would be no recess for the children. But Miss Pinkerton wouldn't be having a lunch break anyway, since Father Felix had called an Educational Evaluation meeting. Father Felix had asked Miss Pinkerton to chair the committee (well, really, when all was said and done, he had demanded). Because of her years of experience, he had said, and her great leadership ability, she would be able to obtain the state certification for St. Polycarp. This accreditation would lend to the school's creditability and also make it eligible for all sorts of grants.

It was a good thing Father Felix had chosen Miss Pinkerton because, while reading through the committee reports last night, tucked into her warm, cozy bed, Miss Pinkerton had discovered a rather disturbing inconsistency.

She continued to read the morning messages—no gym today. The gym teacher was out again with a strained muscle. He was training for an Ironman competition and was proving to be utterly useless.

And then there were a series of reminders—update bulletin boards, progress reports due by Friday, no beverages at teacher's desk, no sitting at teacher's desk, no cell phones during class hours, no socializing in the halls.

Miss Pinkerton knew all the rules and she was quite fastidious about obeying them. The younger teachers did as they pleased.

She went over to the water cooler and filled the coffeepot, and then after pouring the water into the coffeemaker, carefully spooned out eight teaspoons of hazelnut coffee. That was all she was making—she didn't care. Only five teachers had actually chipped in for the beans and the filters, the others helped themselves to a generous cup and swore that they would throw in fifty cents when they had the change. They never did.

Miss Pinkerton grabbed her coffee mug, opened the small refrigerator and poured a little milk at the bottom of her cup. While the coffee brewed, she went to the ladies' room.

The cubicle was chilly, and as she sat on the ice cold toilet bowl, studying the chipped tiles and wondering if the dirt in the corner were mouse turds or something worse, she told herself—two more years, two more years and then she'd be able to retire, move to the small sleepy town in Maine, and live with her younger sister, be a grand aunt to her nephew's babies.

She washed her hands with frigid water and headed back to the faculty room. She was halfway down the corridor when she noticed that the door to the teachers' lounge was wide open, even though she had shut it tightly. Another teacher must have come in. She hoped it wasn't Julia Hopwood, the second grade teacher. Mrs. Hopwood behaved in a most inappropriate manner, she was past forty and still wearing brightly colored mini skirts, her bulletin boards were always one season behind and her classroom was noisy and disorganized.

And she was always complaining.

But Miss Pinkerton soon discovered that it wasn't Mrs. Hopwood who had left the door open, it wasn't anyone, at least anyone whom she could see.

Except…except Miss Pinkerton could tell that her coffee mug had been moved.

Now some other teacher might not have noticed if her cup had been moved a millimeter to the right or left but Miss Pinkerton was a very precise woman and she knew exactly where she had left the mug, in her usual place, at the head of the long, narrow table. And now it was several spots down.

It was rather concerning and a wee bit ominous.

Nevertheless, she could hardly face the angry, rambunctious mob that was her seventh grade class without her breakfast so she reached inside her Lillian Vernon tote and removed her seven grain bread, which had been smoothed with natural peanut butter. And she poured herself a large helping of coffee. (There was no need to stir it, the milk on the bottom mixed instantly.)

Except the coffee had a peculiar aftertaste, rather metallic. At first Miss Pinkerton suspected that the milk had gone sour, so she actually opened the refrigerator and took a whiff. But no, it seemed quite all right and the expiration date was several days away.

She wouldn't even have finished the coffee but she had to wash down her multivitamin and her large calcium capsule and without enough liquid they would be ineffective.

She took out the folder labeled *Educational Evaluation,* and flipped through the pages. She was on the financial section when her vision began to blur. Miss Pinkerton's vision had never blurred, not in her entire life, so she was quite frightened.

She was thinking about going for help, but she knew she'd never make it down the stairs to the main office. *The phone,* she thought, as she reached her hand out. But then her stomach started to cramp, almost as though there were a furry animal trapped inside, punching her, trying to break free.

She rose slowly but slumped down again. Her elbow knocked her coffee cup clear across the room, where it smacked on the concrete floor and shattered into a dozen pieces. In her desperation, she clutched the Educational Evaluation papers in her hand and then collapsed to the floor in the most graceful manner possible.

Her last thoughts as she sank into oblivion were of her dear sister and the little cottage in Maine.

THREE

JULIA HOPWOOD THREW open the door of her second grade classroom, snapped on the lights and rolled up the blinds (the ones that weren't broken). She sat at her desk, dreading the day ahead.

No recess, a horrid Educational Evaluation meeting, probably canceled gym. The only good part about the rain was that it kept some of the students at home. Usually though, it was the good kids, the quiet ones, who didn't come in. The troublemakers always appeared.

If only Jim's business would pick up, she'd quit teaching, and get a nice job as a school librarian. Part-time.

Mrs. Hopwood was planning to head up to the teachers' room, read the morning messages, grab a cup of coffee (she couldn't remember whether or not she paid this month but Miss Pinkerton certainly would), return to her classroom and write the homework assignment on the board. If Amelia Johnston, the eighth grade teacher, was in, Mrs. Hopwood would stop at her classroom, where they would both commiserate about their miserable lives.

Mrs. Hopwood trudged up the stairs. The halls were silent and shadowy and the light in the seventh grade classroom wasn't on yet. Was it possible that Mrs. Hopwood beat Miss Pinkerton to school? Or less likely, that Miss Pinkerton was actually sick?

But even with her overactive imagination, Mrs. Hopwood could have never guessed the scenario that was about to follow. For when she approached the teachers' room and threw open the door, she discovered Miss Pinkerton on the floor underneath the faculty dining room table. Her first thought was that the teacher had crawled there to retrieve something, perhaps one of those horrible old fashioned clip-on earrings that she always wore. And Mrs. Hopwood actually approached Miss Pinkerton to ask if she could help. But before Mrs. Hopwood had a chance to open her mouth, she noticed the shattered coffee mug on the floor and the scattered papers oozing from the folder.

Mrs. Hopwood knew that Miss Pinkerton would never allow such a mess to exist—if she could help it.

But Miss Pinkerton couldn't help it because she was…Mrs. Hopwood swallowed…she was probably dead.

And because Mrs. Hopwood was a most dramatic woman, her first impulse was not to help Miss Pinkerton (whom she really believed was beyond all help), or even to run out of the room, but to release a bloodcurdling scream.

Before she had paused for breath, Mr. Ironweed, the janitor, appeared in the doorway. He surveyed Mrs. Hopwood and the stretched out Miss Pinkerton and then asked in a most cantankerous voice, "What did you do to her?"

In a million years it would never have occurred to Mrs. Hopwood that she would be blamed for the demise of Miss Pinkerton, although it was a well-known fact that the ladies did not get along.

"I found…her like this," Mrs. Hopwood stuttered.

"I just saw Nurse Abby in her office. I'll get her." Mr. Ironweed left the teachers' room, leaving Mrs. Hopwood to wonder if he had indeed seen Nurse Abby, because Mr. Ironweed was getting along in years (he was seventy if he were a day) and it was rumored that he suffered from dementia.

At any rate, Mrs. Hopwood was not about to stay with the deceased Miss Pinkerton, not for all the cute outfits in the Chadwick's catalog, so she immediately vacated the room and ran straight into Amelia Johnston.

Mrs. Johnston, who was often described as big, black and beautiful, was slightly shocked by Mrs. Hopwood's attempt to flee, because, if there was one thing Mrs. Hopwood wasn't, it was fast on her feet. Especially when she was wearing three inch bright yellow spike heels.

Mrs. Hopwood immediately pointed to the teachers' room, as though she had lost her voice, and Mrs. Johnston entered and did the most sensible thing. She actually attempted to help poor Miss Pinkerton, by going over to the body and pulling it from under the table.

And that's when Mrs. Hopwood noticed that Miss Pinkerton was grasping something in her hand. Something written with big, bold, black letters. An Educational Evaluation folder.

But before Mrs. Hopwood could even think about getting closer, Father Felix came marching up the stairs with Nurse Abby. He roughly pushed Mrs. Hopwood aside, who was watching from the doorway, and even managed a brief jab at Mrs. Johnston, who was just trying to help.

Nurse Abby felt for a pulse. Father Felix knelt down beside the body and, for one moment, Mrs. Hopwood thought that he was going to administer last rites. But instead he murmured, "What do you think the problem is?"

And all Julia could think of was now they were going to have to cancel the Educational Evaluation meeting at lunch and for the first time since September, she would actually have a half of a lunch hour all to herself.

"I'm afraid Miss Pinkerton has passed to the other side," Nurse Abby said in a rather grim voice.

"And she took such excellent care of herself." Mrs. Johnston shook her head.

Father Felix sprang up like a piece of burnt toast. "Mrs. Hopwood and Mrs. Johnston, please go immediately to the cafeteria. Mrs. Johnston, you are to conduct Morning Prayer." Mrs. Hopwood knew why she had not been chosen. She had been reprimanded on several occasions for embellishing the Bible stories, in order to make them more gruesome. He stared at both of them, his large black eyes boring into theirs. His expression was one that reduced many students to tears and, on occasion, some of the more sensitive teachers. (Neither Mrs. Hopwood nor Mrs. Johnston fell into this category.) "You are not to say one word about this matter. I will make a formal announcement later in the day. I don't want to panic the students or their parents."

But Mr. Ironweed had not been warned and it wouldn't have mattered if he had, because he most likely would have forgotten. So by the time Mrs. Hopwood and Mrs. Johnston had actually reached the cafeteria (Mrs. Johnston munching on her breakfast, a Whoopie pie), the news had spread as quickly as the lice which had recently plagued the second grade.

Mrs. Hopwood made her way to her class table, where she was surrounded by students, swarming like pesky mosquitoes.

"Is it true that Miss Pinkerton had a seizure?"

"She had a fight with Mrs. Johnston over the eighth grade cookies and Mrs. Johnston slugged her one."

Mrs. Hopwood looked around at the stunned group of parents.

"Is she dead?"

"Are we getting a substitute?"

"Mrs. Hopwood." Linda Lou, a second grader, pulled on Mrs. Hopwood's brand-new marigold cardigan.

"You know what I heard?" an audacious seventh grader shouted out. "Miss Pinkerton is dead!"

The room grew relatively quiet with this outburst. Mrs. Hopwood looked at Mrs. Johnston, who was just finishing her Whoopie pie. She wondered where the rest of the teachers were and why she and Mrs. Johnston had to be the ones stuck in the cafeteria with the unruly students while the other teachers were, no doubt, holed up in their classrooms, gossiping gleefully.

"Is it true?" a parent holding a small pit bull asked.

"She's dead, all right," Adam Ashton, the boldest boy in the eighth grade confirmed.

"She's been murdered!" Marlene Rodriquez shouted out.

"Someone got her with a coffee cup!" Lori Landon added.

Mrs. Johnston walked up to the podium. She grabbed the microphone, then looked down at her sticky hands. She rubbed them together and turned the microphone on. While she was doing this, the murmuring increased.

"Quiet!" she bellowed, holding up two fingers in the peace sign. Instantly two hundred and thirty-three students (minus the absent ones) and a score of parents leaned forward. "We will have no more talk of Miss Pinkerton at this time!"

A collective groan broke from the crowd.

Mrs. Johnston, who was as tough as nails and as mean as spit, began to pray. "In the name of the Father and of the Son and of the Holy Ghost."

It wasn't until weeks later, when Mrs. Hopwood had been appointed to chair the Education Evaluation committee herself, that she began to suspect that Marlene Rodriquez was right.

FOUR

FATHER FELIX SAT IN his office and washed down two extra strength Tylenols with a diet peach Snapple. He had just returned from church where a service had been held for poor Mildred Pinkerton. An autopsy had determined that the seventh grade teacher had died of a heart attack, pure and simple.

That didn't stop the rumors from flourishing.

These rumors, Father Felix suspected, were coming from Amelia Johnston. Father Felix liked Mrs. Johnston quite a bit, and actually considered her to be a friend. But Mrs. Johnston loved trouble and frequently manufactured it. She phoned other teachers at night with the hopes of firing them up (which was really a rather difficult task, since most of the teachers at St. Polycarp were lethargic at best). The exception was Mrs. Hopwood, who also loved trouble and had a definite flair for the dramatic. At one point of her life, Mrs. Hopwood had hoped to go on stage, but she got married instead, and when her husband's business started to spiral downhill and her son needed private school tuition, Mrs. Hopwood came to teach second grade. Now the classroom was her stage and her students were her audience.

Father Felix would have to speak to Amelia Johnston, who would, no doubt, argue with him and then, when he reminded her that he was the one in charge after all, she would sulk for days.

But really, he could not have her going around claiming that Miss Pinkerton's heart attack was the result of being overburdened with the Educational Evaluation task.

Especially when Father Felix intended to ask Mrs. Hopwood to take Miss Pinkerton's place. Mrs. Hopwood was flaky and disorganized but she was reliable, always came in on time and her students loved her because she gave them candy and wore bright colors and matching outfits.

Now and then the parents would complain that their children weren't really learning anything, but honestly, how much could you expect from a teacher in this day and age? At least she showed up.

Something was gnawing at his mind, though. Giving him an unpleasant, constricted feeling in the pit of his stomach. Before Miss Pinkerton had succumbed to her heart attack, she had left a note for Father Felix. She had wanted to request a meeting with him, something of great importance. Father Felix wondered what it was and was quite frustrated because now he would never find out.

A beep interrupted his thoughts, which was just as well, because his head was aching from the burden of running an elementary school, which the diocese kept threatening to close, and why didn't they already? So he could go back to his nice cushy job counseling priests who were having trouble with their vows.

"Mr. Alabaster is here to see you," Lily Morningstar, the school secretary, announced in a slow, deliberate voice, as though she were talking to Mr. Ironweed. "The diocese sent him to replace poor Mildred Pinkerton."

"Send him in." Father Felix quickly looked through the papers on his desk, hoping Mr. Alabaster's resume (which had been faxed to him) would suddenly appear. But all he found were Educational Evaluation drafts, community service, population studies, mission statement—

The door burst open. In stepped a man who had to be well over six feet tall. His blond hair was neatly combed and his very blue eyes sparkled behind rimless glasses. He was dressed nicely in a suit and Father Felix's initial impression was that this man would scare the seventh graders, a task he himself had been unable to accomplish.

"Father Felix." Mr. Alabaster stuck out his hand and gave Father Felix a hard shake, so hard that Father Felix had some difficulty disengaging his hand. "I am the answer to your problems."

And then Mr. Alabaster did quite a bold thing. He removed the folders from the chair opposite Father Felix and placed them on the floor. He sat down and crossed one leg over another, fiddling with the perfect crease in his pant leg. He smiled with perfect teeth.

Had he been a student, Father Felix would have reprimanded him. He would have demanded to know who had invited Mr. Alabaster to sit down and to remove personal papers. There was no doubt that this man was quite nervy and Father Felix hated nervy people, especially when he was in charge of two hundred and thirty-three students, most of them quite bold themselves.

"Tell me about your background," was all Father Felix could manage to utter.

"Okay." Mr. Alabaster sighed and then began at a breakneck speed. "I graduated from Holy Cross College ten years ago. I took a teaching job in North Carolina at a charter school. I loved the students, I loved the faculty and I was quite happy there. But then the school ran out of money and closed. I returned home, worked for my father in his deli, dabbled in real estate a bit, started my own website business, but I realized that my first love is teaching. I'm a great teacher. It comes natural to me. I'm able to be firm and fair. And I have a great love for math."

Father Felix merely nodded. Then he asked a question he asked all possible recruits. A telling question. "What makes you laugh?"

"Nothing," Mr. Alabaster responded.

"Nothing?" Father Felix had never heard that response before. Mrs. Hopwood had said "everything" and Mrs.

Johnston had said "my twin boys." Everyone said something, if nothing else to be polite.

"I'm a very serious person," Mr. Alabaster explained as he perched on the edge of the chair. "We are put on this earth to make a difference. I intend to do just that." He clapped his hands together and rubbed them with vigor.

There was no doubt in Father Felix's mind that Mr. Alabaster was a man with a rather strong personality and the truth of the matter was that Father Felix did not really like strong personalities. And he didn't like Mr. Alabaster. But it was equally true that it was nearly impossible to find a seventh grade teacher in October (when the competent ones had been snatched up by September) and finding a math teacher was even a more daunting task. The fact that Mr. Alabaster was a man instead of a woman (some ladies could easily be pushed over by manipulative students, which certainly wasn't true in Amelia Johnston's case but that was rare) was an asset. Still there was something off-putting about him…

"I'll tell you what," Father Felix said. "I'd like to keep interviewing for a bit, but in the meantime, I am willing to give you a trial run. Why don't we say a week or two? At that time, you'll be able to determine whether or not you're happy at St. Polycarp—"

"I'm happy already."

"When would you like to start?"

With a great deal of flourish, Mr. Alabaster stood. "How about right now?" He pointed to his briefcase. "I am fully prepared."

Rather than impressed, Father Felix found that he was suspicious. Besides, it was already Friday, the children had been divided between grades and rounding them up would only cause more confusion.

"Monday," Father Felix said. "If you could be here by eight—"

"I'll be here by seven-thirty." Mr. Alabaster extended his hand once again but Father Felix did not grasp it. His shoulder was still sore from the last shake. "You won't be sorry," Mr. Alabaster said, his eyes glittering as he exited Father Felix's office.

I'm already sorry, Father Felix thought. He rose from the chair and realized that he had been sitting on a group of faxes, Mr. Alabaster's among them. He scanned the paper quickly, which confirmed most of what Mr. Alabaster had already told him. At the bottom, there were three references, one of them from a priest.

Still, people had been known to lie. But then again, if the diocese had already checked Mr. Alabaster out...

"I'm going to the store," Nurse Abby said, "for some tea and pretzels. Would you like anything?"

Father Felix reached inside his robe and produced two wrinkled bills. "Regular coffee and a chocolate muffin." He didn't miss Nurse Abby's scowl. She was an advocate against sugar, especially for children, whom she swore had lower resistance as a result of all the sweets thrown at them (especially by Mrs. Hopwood). Lower resistance meant that the pupils were in her office more often, which was a great inconvenience to her as she tried to finish reading the morning paper.

Father Felix picked up Mr. Alabaster's resume and threw it on Ms. Morningstar's desk. Ms. Morningstar, who was deep in a whispered conversation, jerked up and put her hand over the phone.

"When you have a free moment," Father Felix said sarcastically, for as far as he was concerned, Ms. Morningstar had a lot of free moments, "could you please check his references?"

Ms. Morningstar nodded and went back to her phone call. She placed the resume in her to do list, but later that morning there was an unexpected fire drill and in the interim someone had spilled apple juice on her desk and someone else inadvertently threw away the folder and by the time Ms. Morningstar realized that it was missing, Mr. Alabaster had a firm foothold at St. Polycarp.

FIVE

AMELIA JOHNSTON WAS spitting mad. For one thing, her twin boys had kept her up all night, crying, whining. She would no sooner put one down than the other would pop up, whooping and hollering. They didn't call it the terrible twos for nothing, Mrs. Johnston thought, and no one had told her the truth about being a mother. No one told her that once you gave birth, your life was never the same. You worried when you were pregnant, and then you worried that something would go wrong with the birth. Then you worried about crib death, and as soon as they could chew, you worried that your kids would choke. You worried about kidnapping and then according to Mrs. Hopwood, whose own son was a teenager, you worried about drugs and dangerous peers. Mrs. Johnston did not like to worry, it went against her nature.

Which is why she worked. People thought she was crazy to return to teaching so soon (her twins were barely six weeks old and she was right back in the classroom). But she knew that being home with them was one step away from a cell at Sing Sing or a cubicle at Bellevue Mental Hospital. Mrs. Johnston was used to being in control and there was no way she could control two baby boys.

She hired a housekeeper and flew back to St. Polycarp. It wasn't perfect, but at least she was out of the house.

Her first stop on Monday morning was Mrs. Hopwood's second grade classroom. Mrs. Hopwood was already in, drinking coffee, eating a buttered bialy, and writing her morning assignment on the board.

Mrs. Hopwood's printing wasn't so good and her handwriting was even worse, so she spent a lot of time erasing.

Mrs. Johnston collapsed on one of the little second grade chairs and the chair rocked under her ample weight. "I'm mad," she said.

Mrs. Hopwood, who was used to Mrs. Johnston being mad, barely looked up.

"At you."

Mrs. Hopwood dropped the chalk, her face registering surprise. Mrs. Johnston knew that Mrs. Hopwood didn't like people to be angry with her. She had this need for everyone to like her (even people that *she* didn't like—something which made absolutely no sense to Mrs. Johnston.)

"What did I do?"

"Father Felix asked you to head the Educational Evaluation process."

Mrs. Hopwood collapsed in her teacher's chair. "Do you think—" she took a gulp of her coffee "—that I *want* to head the Educational Evaluation process? What are you? Nuts? You want to do it? You do it. I'll march right into Father Felix's office and tell him. Everyone is going to hate me, because no one, and I mean no one, from the teachers, to Ms. Morningstar, to Mr. Ironweed, wants this stupid certification and I'm the one who's going to have to assign them to committees and then push them to do the work. And in the end, guess what? I'm going to end up doing the damn work myself."

"You could have told him no." Mrs. Johnston took out a Snickers candy bar.

"Yeah, sure." Mrs. Hopwood stuffed the bialy into her mouth. "He starts the conversation by telling me how disappointed he is in my bulletin board this month because the letters are crooked and maybe I should get my eyes checked. And then he tells me that my blinds are never even."

Mrs. Johnston looked at the long, narrow windows decorated with ghosts and goblins. The blinds were definitely askew.

"They're broken!" Mrs. Hopwood insisted. "He made me feel inadequate. Oh, and he threw in that the PTA was complaining about me."

"Really?" Mrs. Johnston leaned forward, because this was definitely interesting. "What did they say?"

"It was about homework. I give too much or too little, Father Felix couldn't remember which. When he started all that, I was afraid he was going to write me up and put it in my record. And I'd never work in this town again. So I had to say yes when he asked me about the Educational Evaluation. What else could I do? But if you want to head it, be my guest." Mrs. Hopwood opened her desk drawer and pulled out a wad of papers.

"If he wanted me to do it, he would have asked me. He didn't ask me because he hates me."

"That's crazy. And you know it. He hates me. That's why he's making me do this." Mrs. Hopwood paused for a moment. "Do you want to do it?"

"No. But I just wanted to be asked. You know another reason why I'm pissed?"

Mrs. Hopwood shook her head and looked at the chalkboard.

"Because he hired that horrible teacher for the seventh grade and didn't even ask my opinion. I am the senior teacher and since we have intradepartmental upstairs and I have to work with Mr. Alabaster, he should have asked me what I thought. Well, I'll tell you what I think. He's a crazy person."

"There are a lot of crazy people around here." Mrs. Hopwood shrugged.

"No, I mean really crazy. I went into his classroom yesterday and do you know what he was doing? He was teaching the kids gambling odds. Using dice and everything. I know that's not in the curriculum."

Mrs. Hopwood rose and went back to writing her morning message.

"And another thing," Mrs. Johnston raged on, even though she suspected that Mrs. Hopwood wasn't really paying attention, "I'd like to know what happened to my cookies."

"You mean your white chocolate covered Oreos that you bring in for lunch?" Mrs. Hopwood was now writing out simple addition problems.

"Those too." Mrs. Johnston had finished her candy bar and was still hungry. She was eyeing Mrs. Hopwood's lightly toasted bialy, which was swimming in butter. "But what I'm really referring to are the cookies which the eighth graders are supposed to sell so that we can go on our class trip in June. Do you remember the same thing happened last year?"

Mrs. Hopwood nodded although Mrs. Johnston suspected that she didn't remember at all.

"The cookies arrive every Friday, according to Nurse Abby, whom we all know disapproves of the cookie selling, which is why she is always in a sour mood. The woman has no treats to look forward to, except her power bars and pretzels. Anyway, where are those cookies? That's what I'd like to know. We paid for cartons and cartons. I spoke to Father Felix about it."

"And what did he say?" Mrs. Hopwood gobbled down the rest of her bialy and glanced at the clock.

"Nothing. He had no explanation. He's supposed to be looking into it and we all know what that means. It means that the issue is as dead as poor Mildred Pinkerton."

"We better go downstairs," Mrs. Hopwood said. "We'll be late for morning prayer."

"Do you know what I think?" Mrs. Johnston whispered as they made their way down the long dim corridor. "I think that someone is stealing the cookies and eating them."

"That's a lot of cookies to consume," Mrs. Hopwood said, rather dubiously.

"I know who's doing it too." Mrs. Johnston was rather

irritated by Mrs. Hopwood's refusal to empathize. What good were friends who weren't sympathetic? "Did you ever see those cafeteria ladies? They're obese, especially Myrtle." Mrs. Johnston said this as though she herself were a skinny minny. "I think they steal the cookies and pass them out to their extended families. Or maybe they sell them. Well, I'm going to get to the bottom of this." Mr. Alabaster passed quickly in front of the ladies, almost knocking down Mrs. Johnston, which was quite a feat. "And I'll tell you something else," she said when Mr. Alabaster was out of earshot. "He's outta here."

"But who else can Father Felix get on such short notice?" Mrs. Hopwood asked in a worried tone.

"He can put the seventh and eighth grades together," Mrs. Johnston said, "and I'll teach them all, math and language arts. I'd rather do that than work with that horrid man. You know me, I'm not afraid of hard work."

"I'm glad you feel like that," Mrs. Hopwood said, which immediately raised a red flag for Mrs. Johnston, "because I'm going to have to ask you to head a committee for the Educational Evaluation."

Mrs. Johnston hissed.

"And I'm going to give you first choice. You can do finance or personnel—"

"I'll do personnel," Mrs. Johnston said. "But I'm not happy about it. I just don't understand—"

But Mrs. Hopwood had already left, making her way to the second grade table where a bevy of cute little children waited, eager to admire her polka dotted shoes.

"Mrs. Johnston." Ethan Rosario blocked her path. "Matthew Lupus went into my backpack when I wasn't looking and ate the bag of Cheez Doodles my mother packed for my afternoon snack. He has to pay for them. Right?"

"Sit down." Mrs. Johnston almost pushed the stout student into a chair. "You don't need any Cheez Doodles. He did you a favor." Although Mrs. Johnston wouldn't mind some Cheez Doodles herself.

She had lunch duty and then after school tutoring. It was going to be a long day.

SIX

S<small>HE WAS SUCH A PRETTY GIRL</small>, with her dark hair and her bright blue eyes. She had a nice figure too, reminded him a lot of Millie. Millie had been dead and buried for over twenty years but that didn't stop him from talking to her every night. He'd sit down and hold her photograph and tell her all about his day and she'd listen real good, not even having a chance to interrupt him.

He didn't like to be interrupted.

Millie was a good wife. At least she was at first. But then she insisted on going to work as a cleaning woman of all things. It wasn't enough to keep her own home spotless, she had to do it for others and he resented that. Millie was his wife. He didn't want her picking up other people's dirt. It was bad enough that *he* had to do that.

Then Millie made friends.

With other cleaning women who also worked in the apartment building, people who weren't in her class at all. They gave her ideas on how to manage her own finances, on how a woman should have a life outside of her husband and marriage, like friends and clubs. Millie grew dissatisfied and her skirts kept getting shorter and her blouses tighter.

And then she had that awful accident in the bathtub.

He thought she had it coming, that she was being punished, trying to be something she wasn't. He could have told her that God took revenge on those who hurt innocent people. Although he didn't really blame Millie. It was those horrible women who had led her astray.

He could see it happening here at St. Polycarp. Bonnie

Crossover was a sweet woman. But she was spending too much time around that horrid Julia Hopwood and that judgmental Amelia Johnston. Even the way she dressed was changing. She was such a classy dresser, anyone could see that her clothes were real expensive. But yesterday for Miss Pinkerton's Mass, Miss Crossover had worn a pair of trousers and a fitted sweater instead of her usual long skirt and cardigan with those nice white pearls.

Besides, there was an evil presence in that school. He had felt it when Miss Pinkerton died, real sudden-like. A lot of nasty people on staff who'd just as soon poison your coffee as offer you a homemade cookie. And this in a Catholic school of all places. It wouldn't have happened like this in the old days.

Nobody was looking out for Miss Crossover.

No one except Mr. Ironweed.

SEVEN

Mrs. Hopwood had a well deserved break. Her children were in art, which meant that she had thirty-five minutes all to herself. Unaccustomed to free time, at first Mrs. Hopwood did not know how to spend it.

Should she fix the bulletin board? That seemed rather silly. It was the middle of October and she'd soon be taking down the candy corn and witches and substituting turkeys and veterans. She could work on her lesson plans but that was something she did at night while she watched mindless television. She decided to try and make sense of all the papers she had accumulated for the Educational Evaluation. In the teachers' room, with a cup of coffee, and a Dunkin' Donut (a happy parent, which was a rarity, had graciously donated a box).

But Mrs. Hopwood wasn't too comfortable in the deserted faculty room. Since this was the place where poor Mildred Pinkerton had met her demise (actually Mrs. Hopwood was standing on the exact spot where her legs had been gracefully splayed), Mrs. Hopwood felt spooked as though a restless Miss Pinkerton had come back to haunt the premises. And from everything Mrs. Hopwood knew about Miss Pinkerton, that was exactly what she would do.

Mrs. Hopwood decided to work in her classroom.

But she was carrying too much—all those folders, and a cup of steaming hazelnut coffee, and two chocolate cream donuts. So when she attempted to open the door (her first mistake was actually closing the door), several of the papers flew right out of her hand, as though they had a life of their own and, as though bad luck was following her, they fell behind the couch in the corner.

Mrs. Hopwood did not care to retrieve the papers. She was wearing a brand-new tangerine blazer and she didn't want it to get dusty. As far as she was concerned, those papers could stay lost forever, along with everything else that might be hiding behind that massive piece of furniture. The problem was that she was uncertain as to what information those papers contained so she could not judge their importance.

She cursed under her breath, went to the table, put down what she had been holding and opened the door to the teachers' room. She was not moving that couch by herself. She waited until she heard footsteps. Several first grade girls whizzed by, greeting her politely. They would not do.

Several minutes went by and she heard heavy footsteps. A sixth grader, a troublesome boy by the name of Bruce Brewer, was strolling in the hall and by the look on his full, flat face, it was obvious to Mrs. Hopwood he was looking for trouble. But that wasn't her problem.

"Bruce," she called out to him. "I need you to do me a favor."

He scooted over.

"Could you help me move the couch, please? I'm afraid I lost some papers behind it and it's rather heavy."

"Sure thing." He smiled, confirming Mrs. Hopwood's firm conviction that even the worst behaved children long to be good, to be helpful.

As it turned out, he did it all by himself and even bent behind it to gather the papers. "It's awful dirty back there," he said, which she already knew, which was why she didn't want to get the papers herself.

"Is that it?" she asked him.

He was seated on the couch with his head bent over and he mumbled something she couldn't hear, so she repeated the question.

"There's something else back here." He sprang up. "Something pink. Do you want me to get it?"

It occurred to her then that there could be something dangerous behind that old moldy sofa and if Bruce Brewer came to any harm, she would be liable, she and the entire school. So she hesitated, but Bruce didn't. He bent way over, headfirst, then his chest, then part of his legs. And then he squealed.

"Bruce, are you all right?" she asked rather hesitantly.

The only response was another squeal.

Mrs. Hopwood advanced towards the couch. It was as if Bruce was standing on his head. All she could see were two rather heavy legs sticking straight up in the air. The top part of his body was sandwiched between the wall and the couch.

"Help me, Mrs. Hopwood," he begged in a high pitched voice. "I'm trapped."

Mrs. Hopwood, who had never been good at crisis management, was not sure what to do. If she moved the couch, there was a very good possibility that Bruce would fall entirely behind the heavy piece of furniture, headfirst. On the other hand, if she attempted to yank his legs and pull on him from that end, she might cause greater harm, maybe even break his neck.

Meanwhile Bruce was still crying out for help.

"Please, Mrs. Hopwood. I'm bleeding now. I think I might have broken something."

This isn't good at all, Mrs. Hopwood thought as she dashed into the hall. She looked up and down at the still corridor and the door to the girls' room flew open and out walked those very same first grade girls who had been roaming the halls aimlessly a few minutes ago. Mrs. Hopwood thought that they were definitely up to no good, but she was hardly in a position to talk about being up to no good, so she quickly called to them.

The girls came quickly and one of them, a skinny redhead with two socks that didn't match, peeked into the teachers' lounge and gave a small gasp of surprise.

"Who is that?" she asked.

"Help!" Bruce cried.

"Girls—" Mrs. Hopwood almost shoved them out of the teachers' room (when she remembered that under no circumstances were teachers to put their hands on their students, although it was a little late for that now) "—go and get Nurse Abby and be very fast."

The girls zoomed to the staircase and she could hear their little feet pounding. (Running on the staircase was another infraction and Mrs. Hopwood could only hope that one of the girls wouldn't fall and add to the confusion.) Mrs. Hopwood wasn't sure what Nurse Abby could do, but she figured that Nurse Abby was in a better position to rearrange Bruce without breaking any body parts.

Suddenly a murmur broke forth and out stepped Amelia Johnston with her group of sullen eighth graders. She was obviously taking them to art, which meant Mrs. Hopwood's prep was over.

But she could hardly leave Bruce.

"You better get yourself down to the art room, girl," Mrs. Johnston said. "It's my time now."

Mrs. Johnston advanced into the teachers' lounge and her eyes widened.

"Help me!" Bruce cried out in a rather loud voice. Evidently he had heard Mrs. Johnston's voice and he believed that she was more likely to be of aid (which was certainly true).

Mrs. Johnston did not hesitate, even when the entire eighth grade class (consisting of twenty-seven students) followed her into the lounge (which clearly wasn't allowed) and most of them screamed louder than Bruce, although they had no idea who he was.

Mrs. Johnston did not even ask what happened.

"Whose legs are those?"

"How did he get behind the couch?"

"Boy, is he going to be in trouble!"

And while Mrs. Hopwood was wondering whether Mrs.

Johnston was going to pull on Bruce's legs or move the sofa, Mrs. Johnston marched towards the couch and did both. With one sweeping motion, she yanked the couch backwards and pulled on Bruce's stout legs. Bruce toppled over and fell head-first on the couch. When he finally rolled right side up, he was holding his head on the left side, looking at the crowd of students who surrounded him. His dazed expression scared Mrs. Hopwood, who hoped that he didn't have a concussion.

"Get out of the way!" Father Felix had no qualms pushing through the gaggle of gawkers. He was followed by Nurse Abby, who was holding an ice pack and three Band-Aids, "What happened?" he bellowed and turned to Bruce. "You better have a good explanation for this!"

Bruce merely scratched his head and continued to look confused.

"For one thing, I'd like to know what you were doing in the teachers' room."

Bruce closed his eyes and the left side of his head tilted towards his shoulder.

"You don't know the rules?" Father Felix continued and then turned toward the students, who had quieted considerably. "Does everyone know the rules?"

"Yes, Father," they answered in unison.

"Repeat them for Bruce, because he obviously has lost his voice."

"Students are never to be in the faculty room."

"Mrs. Johnston, take these students down to art immediately. And if I hear a word on the stairs from any one of you, you're all standing on the wall during recess."

The students made a great pretense of grumbling and left the room. The threat from Father Felix was an empty one and they knew it. It was another rainy October day and the children wouldn't be allowed to go to the yard, anyway.

But Amelia Johnston was not so quick to leave and Julia Hopwood knew why. Mrs. Johnston loved to be the hero of every situation, but what was far more important—she wanted everyone to know that she was the hero of every situation. There was no way she was about to vacate the premises until she received her just due.

"I think I better explain, Father." Mrs. Hopwood looked from Father Felix's furious face, to Mrs. Johnston's glaring one, to Nurse Abby, who was still clutching the ice pack and the Band-Aids, to the bewildered Bruce Brewer, who was still holding his head and finally to the two first graders who were promptly escorted out of the room by Father Felix, but not before one of them asked quite boldly, "What happened to that boy?"

Which, Mrs. Hopwood thought, everyone was no doubt wondering.

"It's like this, Father," Mrs. Hopwood started once Father Felix came back into the teachers' lounge and promptly closed the door on all possible onlookers (which meant that the eighth graders were now alone in the hall, and not being terribly quiet either). "I was working on the Educational Evaluation" (which was indeed the truth, even if it made her sound industrious) "and by some force, I tell you, Father, it was almost super-natural, the way the papers just flew right out of my hands and landed behind the couch all by themselves and I tried to move the sofa" (which wasn't quite true) "but it was so heavy I needed help and Bruce just happened to be walking by and I asked him to help me and he did, but he got stuck in the process." She took a deep breath.

Father Felix immediately turned his fury to Bruce, who was still looking rather befuddled. "What is wrong with you!" he yelled. "How clumsy can you be? You were asked to move the couch, not wedge your body behind it! No wonder you got hurt! That happens when you don't know how to obey orders!"

Bruce began to sob softly.

Father Felix shook his head as though he were thoroughly exhausted, as though it had been he who had been moving the couch, and that's when Mrs. Hopwood noticed that Bruce's nose was bleeding and Nurse Abby slapped an ice pack on his head.

Mrs. Hopwood figured that it would be best to continue her tale. "Mrs. Johnston came in and she moved the couch and helped get Bruce free but then I guess he fell..." Mrs. Johnston shot a dark look at Mrs. Hopwood, who was no doubt quite upset that she was now being blamed for a circumstance where she should have come out as the heroine.

Father Felix threw open the door and started to shout. "There will be no fun day for Halloween! There will be no class trip! There will be no graduation ceremony! There will be no eighth grade yearbook! If you can't behave yourselves, you will not graduate!"

Mrs. Hopwood doubted that Father Felix would be able to execute such dire punishments, even if he intended to, and, by the middle of next week, he would have no doubt forgotten all his threats. But, for the moment, he was pulsing with such rage that the eighth graders were reduced to silence.

He turned around and returned to the teachers' lounge. "I will see you both at lunch," he said to Mrs. Hopwood and Mrs. Johnston in an icy tone. "I believe that we have an Educational Evaluation financial meeting."

"Here." For the first time, since he emerged from behind the sofa, Bruce spoke. He stuck a pink vial in Mrs. Hopwood's startled face.

She took it, slightly puzzled, before she remembered that's what Bruce was reaching for when he fell. Mrs. Hopwood opened the pink bottle and poured out several capsules. "Digitoxin," Nurse Abby commented dryly. "Someone lost their heart medicine. Come along, Bruce." She prodded him gently and left the room.

"Don't be late," Father Felix warned Mrs. Hopwood and Mrs. Johnston before he joined Nurse Abby and Bruce.

Mrs. Hopwood turned towards Mrs. Johnston. "I think we're in trouble," she said.

EIGHT

"WHAT WERE YOU THINKING?" were Father Felix's first words to Mrs. Hopwood and Mrs. Johnston when they walked into his office.

"I was just trying to help." Mrs. Johnston took her usual confrontational pose, her hand on her rather ample hip.

And, as usual, Mrs. Hopwood acted flustered. "I just wanted to move the couch to get my papers and Bruce was walking by—"

"You should have found Mr. Ironweed. We pay him to move furniture. You should not have recruited a sixth grader—"

"But Bruce Brewer is a big strong boy," Mrs. Hopwood argued.

"Not anymore!" Father Felix snapped. "He's in Nurse Abby's office bawling his head off. He has a bump the size of a math manipulative. His mother has been called and she's coming to get him. And, just for the record, she's a known troublemaker. Not that she isn't entitled to make trouble, at least in this instance."

"It's all very unfortunate," Mrs. Hopwood said in a rather breezy tone.

"I was just trying to help," Mrs. Johnston repeated, folding her arms.

Father Felix felt a migraine coming on. This job was getting to him. It wasn't meant for a fifty-seven-year-old priest, not one who was so looking forward to retirement.

"All right, what's done is done." He knew a losing battle when he saw one. "Both of you, throw all those papers on the floor and take two seats. We only have thirty minutes, so let's do this quickly."

"Well, do we get to eat?" Mrs. Johnston asked.

"I ordered pizza. Ms. Morningstar will bring it in when it arrives. Okay…" He looked at the mountain of paperwork at his desk and wished he was somewhere else. Anyplace else. "We're working on the financials, right?"

"Father, may I ask a question?" Mrs. Hopwood raised her hand.

He let out an exasperated sigh. Just looking at her striped stockings, in shades of orange and blue, was making him dizzy. "Does your question have to do with the Educational Evaluation?" he asked.

"Is there a teacher on staff who has heart problems?"

He was trying to be patient. "Why do you ask that, Mrs. Hopwood?"

"Yes, why are you asking that?" Mrs. Johnston echoed.

"Well…" She hesitated a bit.

"You want to know the truth." Father Felix could not keep the sarcasm out of his voice. "I'm going to tell you the truth. I have heart problems. From the students, from the parents, and from the teachers."

Mrs. Hopwood leaned forward. "Do you take medication?"

"Not yet. Look, there is no question about it. You two—" he shook his head "—you're a bad combination."

"So you don't know anyone who is on heart medication?" Mrs. Hopwood asked again.

Before Father Felix could tell her to stop asking ridiculous questions, Ms. Morningstar knocked on the door and said the pizza had arrived and he owed $12.98 plus a tip.

He reached into his pocket and took out fourteen dollars and stuffed it into Ms. Morningstar's hand. She looked at the money as though he had handed her scrap paper.

"It's not enough of a tip," she murmured. "The delivery boy won't be happy."

"I'm not happy," Father Felix said. "Why should he be happy?" He sat back down.

"Did you order me a cherry coke?" Mrs. Johnson asked.

Father Felix put his head into his hands and closed his eyes. "I'd like to talk about the financials now."

"Okay," Mrs. Johnston said. "Since you raised that point, let's talk about the missing cookie money. I know you're not concerned that the eighth graders have neither cookies to sell nor money to take their trip—"

"How much is missing?" he asked.

"I'm not sure," she said, "I mean, not the exact amount. But it's hundreds of dollars."

"Well, why don't you get those exact figures," Father Felix suggested. "And then we can go from there. Did anyone call the accountant to get the financial report for last year?"

"I think Miss Pinkerton did that," Mrs. Hopwood said, "before she died."

"Well, where is it?"

Mrs. Hopwood and Mrs. Johnston looked at each other as Ms. Morningstar delivered the pizza.

"Look in her closet," he ordered. "We need a breakdown of the expenditures, instructions, transportation, operation, maintenance, faculty salaries—"

"Speaking of faculty," Mrs. Johnston said as she grabbed a rather large slice of pizza, "I don't think that Mr. Alabaster is working out at all."

Father Felix bit into a piece of pizza. The cheese burnt his mouth.

"For one thing—" Mrs. Johnston was obviously not bothered in the least by the bubbling cheese "—he's teaching those children up there to gamble. I saw it myself."

"I wish someone would teach me how to gamble." Father Felix gulped down his ginger ale. "I'd like to win some money and pay off the debts of the school, maybe have a little left over for myself so I could take a trip to Ouray, Arizona. And maybe I'd never come back."

Mrs. Hopwood took the smallest piece of pizza and began to break it into little strips.

"You don't understand," Mrs. Johnston said thickly, her mouth full of crust. "The students are wild in his classroom. He's allowing them to chew gum and wear sweatshirts and do magic card tricks."

"What kind of tricks?" Mrs. Hopwood said. "Maybe they can entertain my second graders."

Mrs. Johnston hissed at her. "That's hardly the point."

"We have to get these financials done," Father Felix said firmly. "Unless you want to be taking this stuff home and doing it yourselves over the weekend."

The threat muted them.

"Okay." He looked down at what was the jumble of his papers. "One of you will have to go to Ms. Morningstar and get all the enrollment data, not only for this year but for the past two years. We also need to know the parish expenses. Someone should contact Father Archibald—"

There was a brief knock on the door and Ms. Morningstar, who was also chewing pizza, stuck her face in the door. "Mrs. Lovesay is here to see you."

"Who is Mrs. Lovesay?" The pounding in his head was like a jackhammer.

"She's Bruce Brewer's mother."

Father Felix longed for the days when the students had the same names as their parents. He took another gulp of his ginger ale, and wished with all of his heart that it was Jack Daniel's.

"I'll be right back," he told the two teachers, whom he was betting wouldn't miss him at all.

A large intimidating woman holding a cane stood in the hall. "I want to talk to you," she said, pointing the cane in his face. "I want to know why that second grade teacher tried to punish my child by squashing him with a sofa. I need an explanation. And it better be good!"

NINE

WHEN IT BECAME APPARENT to Mrs. Johnston that Father Felix wasn't coming back anytime soon, she and Mrs. Hopwood decided to take the rest of the pizza and retreat to their classrooms.

"Maybe this would be a good time for me to try and get into Miss Pinkerton's closet," Mrs. Johnston said. "I'm really curious about what papers she stashed in there. You want to come?"

Mrs. Hopwood shook her head. "I can't. We only have five minutes left and I have to go to the bathroom and repair my makeup."

Mrs. Johnston nodded and decided that Mrs. Hopwood could indeed use some makeup repairing. Her lipstick had come off, she had tomato sauce on her cheek and her liner was running. Mrs. Johnston didn't wear makeup, so she didn't have such problems.

After trying to balance three pieces of pizza on one paper plate, Mrs. Johnston made it up to the seventh grade classroom. She found Mr. Alabaster in his room on the computer. He barely looked up when she entered.

"I have to get into the closet," she said.

"Be my guest." He was typing madly. "The one in the corner is full of textbooks and bulletin board stuff. The one on the right is locked with a padlock."

That Mrs. Johnston could plainly see and, naturally, that was the closet which interested her. "I'm going for the janitor," she said as she laid down her pizza on a student's desk. She also looked over her shoulder and managed to see that Mr.

Alabaster was on some sort of website, a website that looked like a casino.

He quickly hit the escape button.

"I'll be back," she said.

But finding Mr. Ironweed was no easy matter. He could be anywhere, in the boiler room, in the church, in the library, even outside raking leaves. The easiest thing was to have Ms. Morningstar page him. So Mrs. Johnston trudged downstairs again.

Ms. Morningstar was on the phone. "I don't understand how this could have happened," she said. "I don't remember charging a designer handbag—" She looked up at Mrs. Johnston. Mrs. Johnston could plainly see that she was chewing something.

And it looked like a big, fat chocolate chip cookie.

"It's very clear what happened." Mrs. Johnston could hear Mrs. Lovesay's voice coming from Father Felix's closed office. "That language arts teacher, Mrs. Johnston, doesn't like Bruce. She gave him a D on his English essay just because he had the courage to write about racial profiling."

"Mrs. Johnston is of African-American descent herself," Father Felix argued.

"That's hardly the matter," Mrs. Lovesay said crisply.

"Your son was not writing on topic!" Father Felix said.

Mrs. Johnston wasn't touching this with a yardstick and just when she thought all was lost because her lunch hour was expiring and Ms. Morningstar was not even bothering to get off the phone with Sears or MasterCard or whoever was chasing her, Mrs. Johnston saw Mr. Ironweed coming down the hall, carrying a saw.

"I need the keys," she said to him.

He looked at her as though she had made a perfectly unreasonable request.

"I need to get into Miss Pinkerton's closet."

Mr. Ironweed shook his head. "I cannot do that without permission from Father."

"I have his permission," Mrs. Johnston insisted. "It has to do with the Educational Evaluation."

With the mention of Educational Evaluation, Mr. Ironweed looked as if he was going to vomit. "I'll have to get the master keys," he grunted.

Mrs. Johnston sat on the bench and waited for a few agonizing minutes. She could hear her children downstairs in the cafeteria screaming and yelling and she knew that it was time to pick them up and it was unfair to keep them down there with Bonnie Crossover, but since Miss Crossover was often out for no reason whatsoever, she could hardly complain about keeping the eighth graders a few minutes longer.

But it took Mr. Ironweed more than a few moments to come back with a large key ring, and when he did, he grumbled all the way up the stairs.

"She's not a nice person," he said. "She's been sharp with me several times and in the end people get what they deserve. I believe that, I believe that firmly."

Mrs. Johnston felt obligated to ask whom Mr. Ironweed was referring to, although she really had no interest whatsoever.

"My sister—Harriet. Do you know what she did to me last night?"

Mrs. Johnston half listened because everyone knew that Mr. Ironweed's sister Harriet had died three years ago. They had a service for her at St. Polycarp, even though she lived in Minnesota. But Mr. Ironweed kept talking about her because he felt guilty, leaving her to die in the nursing home alone, at least that was the theory. Mrs. Johnston wondered how prudent it was to keep a janitor at the school who did not know the difference between past and present, but Mr. Ironweed was pretty good at fixing things and at St. Polycarp broken things were more of a priority than a sound mind.

"She's on heart medication, too," Mr. Ironweed said. "I saw her pass it out."

"That's terrible," Mrs. Johnston said. She was relieved when they finally reached the classroom that Mr. Alabaster was gone, probably to fetch his seventh graders, who, no doubt, would come bursting through the door at any given moment.

It took another five minutes and a half dozen tries with the keys before Mr. Ironweed managed to open the locked cupboard. The inside of the closet was a tribute to Miss Pinkerton's life, organized and tidy, and Mrs. Johnston found what she was looking for right away.

A huge wad of papers held together by three rubber bands, neatly labeled Educational Evaluation Self-Study.

"Shall I lock it again?" Mr. Ironweed asked.

Mrs. Johnston nodded, because she did not want Mr. Alabaster in that closet, although he had a perfect right to be. And it was not a moment too soon, for a flood of seventh graders came tumbling in the room with a deafening roar. Then Mr. Alabaster let out a shrill, earsplitting whistle, and they all screeched to a halt, taking their seats meekly.

Mrs. Johnston tried not to be impressed.

"Oh, Mrs. Johnston," Mr. Alabaster said, "I brought the eighth grade upstairs for you. They're waiting outside of your classroom."

If he expected to be thanked, he had another think coming. Mrs. Johnston liked getting her own class and walking them up the stairs herself. It meant less time that she actually had to teach.

"Miss Crossover asked me to do it," Mr. Alabaster said. "She has a prep now and you were late..."

Mrs. Johnston's only response was to grab the folders and storm out of the room, where she screamed at her own class. Two boys actually had the audacity to throw a hat back and forth between them.

She waited until they were seated and quiet and then announced that it was time for DEAR, which stood for Drop Everything And Read. The students begrudgingly took out their worn paperbacks (although she couldn't imagine what else they would rather be doing. It wasn't as though reading was hard for most of them). But instead of reaching for the JC Penney or Newport News catalog, Mrs. Johnston snapped the rubber bands off the Educational Evaluation folders and began to sort them.

They were labeled quite nicely in black ink and, while Mrs. Johnston was searching for the personnel folder, her eyes settled on the financial report. She spotted a white sheet of paper and in the middle a red notation.

MISSING: COOKIE MONEY—FOUR HUNDRED AND SEVENTY-FIVE DOLLARS AND THIRTEEN CENTS.

TEN

HILDA DANVERS, the fifth grade teacher, was enjoying her lunch in the park.

Father Felix frowned on such behavior. He encouraged camaraderie among the teachers and he believed that if they all ate together in the teachers' lounge, they would grow to like one another. This made no sense to Miss Danvers, who was of the opinion that familiarity breeds contempt. The more she saw of certain teachers, the less she liked them. This did not include Tina Belgrave, the kindergarten teacher who was her pal. But Mrs. Belgrave had taken her children to visit the firehouse today and they were all eating lunch there. Miss Danvers also got along well with Bonnie Crossover, the fourth grade teacher, but Miss Crossover had lunch duty today. So Miss Danvers would rather eat alone.

Miss Danvers especially didn't like Mildred Pinkerton and had been quite vocal about her feelings (which, in view of what had happened to Miss Pinkerton, wasn't such a good thing). But the truth of the matter was that Miss Pinkerton's death was a great relief to Miss Danvers. Because it was only a matter of time before Miss Pinkerton learned that Miss Danvers had lied on her job application.

At the bottom of the application, there was a single question. *Have you ever been convicted of a crime?* And, of course, Miss Danvers had written no.

Evidently Father Felix had never checked. Probably because it never occurred to him that Miss Danvers had anything to hide.

Miss Danvers had been at St. Polycarp for three years.

And then the process for certification had begun.

With another teacher as chair, any other teacher as chair, it wouldn't have mattered. But Miss Pinkerton was a stickler for detail (as far as Miss Danvers was concerned that was probably what led to her death. All that nitpicking strained her heart), and she intended to do a thorough check on each faculty member.

The day before she died Miss Pinkerton had left a note in Miss Danvers's mailbox.

She said that she had discovered something upsetting and she wanted to talk to Miss Danvers as soon as possible. Could Miss Danvers please get back to her?

And while Miss Danvers was deciding what to do, Miss Pinkerton conveniently dropped dead.

Miss Danvers seemed to be in the clear except…except she knew from experience that Miss Pinkerton took very detailed notes. And, somewhere in that batch of Educational Evaluation papers, well, there was no telling what was in those folders.

If she was only dealing with Julia Hopwood, her anxiety might have been lessened. And Miss Danvers, clever as she was, had offered to head the faculty committee. But Mrs. Hopwood had already assigned that to Mrs. Johnston.

And it was a well-known fact that Mrs. Johnston loved trouble. Although right now she was on the hunt of some missing cookie money.

Miss Danvers had to find a way to get those Educational Evaluation papers.

ELEVEN

JULIA HOPWOOD WAS having a horrid night. After she finished her day of teaching needy second graders, she had an appointment with her son's guidance counselor at the private school he was attending. The guidance counselor was no cheerier than Nurse Abby.

He told her that they had discovered bottles of NyQuil in her son's locker and it was their belief (the Headmaster and the Dean of Discipline were also present, which in Julia's mind made it three against one) that Alexander was a drug abuser. Mrs. Hopwood was perfectly shocked by the accusation and argued that Alexander suffered from cold symptoms (which wasn't true).

The Dean of Discipline took charge of the conversation and retorted, even if Alexander had a raging cold, it didn't explain what he was doing with a dozen bottles—except, perhaps, making himself high. The dean also accused Alexander of selling the NyQuil at reduced rates to students, who were eager to follow in his path.

And then the Headmaster whipped out Alexander's latest academic report and said that they were gravely concerned about his dipping marks. They suggested a therapist as soon as possible, especially if there was added stress in the home. They also threatened that if Alexander did not bring up his marks and cease taking NyQuil, they would have to dismiss him.

It was Mrs. Hopwood's intention to defend her son but she could not speak, she was too close to crying and she did not want to appear like a weak parent (which would only further their contention that Alexander's home life was to blame). She stood up, thanked them and sobbed all the way home.

She had to wait until Mr. Hopwood went out for an evening stroll. She could not tell her husband. He would yank Alexander out of the school faster than a first grader gobbled up animal crackers, because he considered the school an absolute waste of money, especially when his business was so shaky.

As soon as Mr. Hopwood left, Mrs. Hopwood had a raging argument with her son. Alexander, at first, denied it and then became quite testy that they had actually opened his locker without his knowledge.

Mrs. Hopwood's tears seem to affect Alexander and he quietly retreated to his room. Mrs. Hopwood knew her son felt guilty, but was his remorse enough to stop his erratic behavior? And then she wondered if he were capable of stopping all by himself, if he wanted to.

Mrs. Hopwood took a book from the shelf, entitled *Medications and Their Effects*. She wanted to learn all about NyQuil and what it was doing to her son. She was looking through the index when the phone rang.

Mrs. Hopwood did not want to answer the phone. She did not want to talk to anyone and when the caller ID flashed with Mrs. Johnston's number, she was even less inclined to pick up the receiver.

Mrs. Johnston did not care to hear about Mrs. Hopwood's family problems—she could not empathize, since she was at a different point in her life entirely. She thought she was having problems with her twin toddlers and all Mrs. Hopwood could tell her was "just wait," which wasn't what Mrs. Johnston wanted to hear at all.

"Julia, I know you're there." Mrs. Johnston's voice had a tinge of panic to it. "Please pick up. It's an emergency."

Everything was an emergency to Mrs. Johnston. She had no ability to discern that which was important.

But then Mrs. Johnston said something which really piqued

Mrs. Hopwood's interest and made her momentarily forget about the NyQuil crisis.

"I think she did it."

Mrs. Hopwood lunged for the phone. "Who are you talking about? And what did she do?"

Mrs. Johnston went into a convoluted story about getting keys from Mr. Ironweed to open poor Mildred Pinkerton's closet and how Mr. Alabaster wasn't helpful. This tale was several times interrupted by Mrs. Johnston screaming at her twin boys to stop climbing on the refrigerator.

"Anyway, what you have to understand," Mrs. Johnston continued with much vigor, "is that I had to wait on the bench for Mr. Ironweed and do you know what I saw?"

Before Mrs. Hopwood could utter "what," Mrs. Johnston burst, "Get down right this minute, Jeffery James! So help me God, if you don't, I'm coming up there and I'm going to crack you one! Anyway," she continued in a softer tone, "Ms. Morningstar was on the phone with a bill collector."

"Well," Mrs. Hopwood started, who herself hadn't paid her Lord & Taylor bill yet this month, "maybe—"

"All right, that's it! Justin Joseph, you're going right to bed! How many times have I told you not to crawl into the dryer! Your brother could close it! I could close it!

"Do you want to spin around! Do you want to get a concussion! And you know what else?" She continued her conversation in a normal tone of voice. "Ms. Morningstar was chewing on a chocolate chip cookie. A large chocolate chip cookie."

"Just like the ones we used to sell," Mrs. Hopwood said thoughtfully.

"Then I went and got her folders, poor Miss Pinkerton's I mean, and there it was in big red print." Mrs. Johnston's voice bellowed again. "I'm counting to three. If you are not down from that refrigerator in that time, I'm going to slap you. You have been warned, Jeffery James."

Mrs. Hopwood was thumbing through the medical book and had found the section on NyQuil. Evidently taking too much of the drug, instead of making you sleepy, would arouse you. It was a cheap way of getting high.

"Well, don't you want to know what it said in big red print?" Mrs. Johnston demanded.

"What did it say?"

"It said that four hundred and seventy-five dollars and thirteen cents is missing from the cookie money. Now, you and I both know if Miss Pinkerton had investigated the matter, she investigated it thoroughly and there is no doubt that someone had her hand in the till."

"And you think—" Mrs. Hopwood closed the medical book "—that it's Ms. Morningstar?"

"I do. And let me tell you why—I've had it. Hold on for a minute."

It was a long minute and Mrs. Hopwood was tempted to hang up. Especially when she heard a sharp slap followed by a loud wail. Then some footsteps running. And then Mrs. Johnston screaming, "I'm going to get you too, Jeffery James. Look what you've done to my dryer!"

Mrs. Hopwood opened the medical book again. Her hand landed to the page which contained information on Digitoxin.

"Anyway, I'm back. It makes perfect sense, doesn't it? I mean, the woman is in debt. We know that. She has credit card companies calling her all day long. She's the one who actually receives the cookies and she's supposed to be the one who pays the man. According to the cookie man, he has never received the money and we have never received the cookies. She's the missing link." Mrs. Johnston shouted suddenly, "I'm warning you!"

"I don't know." Mrs. Hopwood was in a most mellow mood. "I feel sorry for Ms. Morningstar."

"I feel sorry for her, also. I can only imagine what it must be like to be a single mother with three children. I'm having a hard enough time with two."

One is a nightmare, Mrs. Hopwood thought, but she didn't say this aloud because it was much too complicated and she knew that Mrs. Johnston didn't want to hear it.

"But we can't allow this to continue," Mrs. Johnston said firmly. "After all, my eighth graders are entitled to go on their class trip, aren't they? And Ms. Morningstar has to own up to what she did. Don't you agree?"

Mrs. Hopwood was reading about the effects of Digitoxin and she wasn't liking any of it.

"Don't you agree?" Mrs. Johnston repeated.

"What should we do?"

"Tomorrow we have that faculty meeting. Sister Scholastica is coming to look over our Educational Evaluation progress—"

"Don't remind me." Mrs. Hopwood was feeling ill enough.

"You and I are going to demand to see Father Felix alone. We're going to tell him our suspicions. Just one minute—"

"I've got to go," Mrs. Hopwood said. "I have another call."

"Come in early tomorrow," Mrs. Johnston ordered. "We can discuss this in the teachers' room."

Before Mrs. Hopwood hung the phone up, she heard more wailing and Mrs. Johnston screaming.

Mrs. Hopwood scanned the information about Digitoxin, which was a medication used for congestive heart failure. The problem was that if you didn't have heart failure, it could *cause* heart failure, especially if it were somehow mixed into food, and the recipient ingested an overdose.

Like in a cup of coffee.

Digitoxin slowed the pulse, retarded heart contractions and increased the amount of blood flowing to the heart.

Giving the person a heart attack.

Then Mrs. Hopwood began to wonder if poor Mildred

Pinkerton had not died a natural death at all, but had been the victim of poison. And the motive for her murder was the missing cookie money.

TWELVE

FATHER FELIX WAS LATE for the faculty meeting, which was something that unnerved him. He often lectured his staff on the importance of being punctual, stressing that there was no excuse for tardiness. It was up to him as the principal to set the example.

But he had gone for a walk around the park to clear his head and it had started to rain. Then when he got back to the rectory to take a quick shower, there was no hot water and the housekeeper wasn't coming in (something about her husband's phlebitis), so by the time he actually arrived at the school, the faculty meeting was just about to start. He didn't even have time to go to the teachers' lounge and grab a cup of coffee, which really didn't matter because since poor Mildred Pinkerton's death the quality of coffee had gone steadily downhill.

Much to his dismay Amelia Johnston and Julia Hopwood were waiting for him outside his door.

"Father," Mrs. Johnston said with a determined look on her face, "Mrs. Hopwood and I must speak to you."

"This isn't a good time." He fiddled with his keys. "Sister Scholastica, no doubt, is in the art room waiting to begin the meeting and it would be rude to keep her and the rest of the faculty waiting."

"It's very important," Mrs. Johnston insisted. And then she gazed in a rather uneasy fashion at Ms. Morningstar, who was on the phone.

Father Felix intended to be firm. Mrs. Johnston had a habit of pushing people around, which made her a fine teacher, but still he was the one in charge. And besides, Mrs. Hopwood did not have an urgent look on her face at all. Rather, she seemed embarrassed and confused. There wasn't a doubt in Father Felix's mind that Mrs. Johnston had incited her unnecessarily.

"I'll meet with you during lunch," he said as he yanked his office door open and proceeded straight past them. "Now, both of you please go into the art room and tell Sister Scholastica to start the meeting. I'll join you in a few minutes. And ladies—" he stopped them as they were walking down the hall "—don't sit near one another."

The few minutes grew to be a half an hour because Father Felix was not eager to sit through a lecture on the importance of certification and then hear the teachers report, one by one, in a monotone drawl, their progress on course studies, personnel, finances, resources and student body.

Nevertheless, he knew his duty. Because he was a man who took his responsibilities very seriously, he entered the art room and took a seat in the back. Sister Scholastica was rambling on about how unfair it was that the Iowa Test of Basic Skills assumed such importance when creativity counted for nothing, but nevertheless it was a game and they all had to learn how to play it.

Most of the teachers were staring at her with blank expressions on their faces, except for Mrs. Hopwood, who seemed to be taking furious notes, and Mrs. Belgrave, who was eating Doritos from a bag and crunching with considerable noise.

"What I'm interested in," Sister Scholastica said, and from the feedback of the teachers, Father Felix guessed that none of them cared, "is how this is handled at other schools. How much preparation is actually given to the preparing of these standardized tests?"

No one offered any opinions.

Mrs. Hopwood continued to write.

Sister Scholastica noticed it also. "Mrs. Hopwood," she said in a testy voice, "why don't you tell us about your last school? How much weight did they give to standardized testing?"

Mrs. Hopwood looked bewildered for a moment. "I didn't have a last school." She shrugged. "I mean, this is my first teaching job."

"I see," Sister Scholastica said and from her expression, Father Felix guessed that she wanted to add that she was hardly surprised. She looked down at a sheet of paper in front of her.

"Miss Crossover."

Bonnie Crossover looked up and began to play with her gold bracelet.

"I see from the faculty report that you spent some time teaching at another elementary school. How did they deal with testing?"

"They didn't like it," Miss Crossover whispered.

"The teachers didn't like it?" Sister Scholastica raised her eyebrows.

"No one liked it."

And Mrs. Hopwood continued to write.

Father Felix was not pleased at all. Sister Scholastica was an educational consultant and she didn't come cheap. He wanted the teachers to get their money's worth from her but as usual his staff was ill prepared and disinterested. And to make matters worse, while Sister Scholastica was calling on Miss Danvers, Mrs. Hopwood passed the piece of paper to Mrs. Johnston (via Mrs. Greber and Mr. Alabaster).

Somehow Father Felix knew that the note had nothing to do with the Educational Evaluation.

He watched as Mr. Alabaster, who had been leaning back on his chair, pushed forward, allowing the chair to crash down on all four legs, creating a loud bang. Mr. Alabaster apologized immediately to a rather irritated Sister Scholastica and then passed the note to Mrs. Johnston.

Father Felix watched as Mrs. Johnston bent down and wrote quite a lengthy reply.

When the question and answer period was over (which

was really quite brief since it consisted mostly of questions), Sister Scholastica resumed her lecture on cafeteria services.

And Mrs. Johnston tapped Mr. Alabaster and handed him a piece of paper.

Father Felix jumped up from his seat and in front of Mrs. Johnston's shocked face and Mrs. Hopwood's humiliated one, grabbed the note and exited the room. He was quite furious with both teachers. Didn't he have enough problems with the students? Here they were, two perfectly grown women, passing notes during a faculty meeting, when they should have been paying attention, especially Mrs. Hopwood, who was chairing the Educational Evaluation committee and was supposed to be learning how to do it from Sister Scholastica.

And he blamed Mrs. Johnston, too, who was always so bossy but seldom, if ever, had any facts to confirm her adamant opinions.

On the way to his office, he passed Ms. Morningstar in the hall. In a rare moment she was off the phone and he asked her if she would mind going to the store and getting him a cup of regular coffee. He even gave her a dollar extra so she could buy a cup for herself, for he suspected that she was having money problems.

And then he closed the door to his office and began to read the notes.

Amelia—
After we hung up the phone, I thought about what you said. I think you're right.

She is definitely involved in the missing cookie money. But then I began to look through this book I have that tells all about different medicines and their effects, and I learnt something that is quite alarming. Digitoxin is a drug used for people who are prone to heart attacks. But if you give an overdose of this drug to someone who doesn't have heart problems, it could cause a heart attack. This information got me thinking.

I don't know if you remember but I found that bottle of Digitoxin, or rather Bruce Brewster found that bottle of Digitoxin under the sofa.

    What if—what if—poor Miss Pinkerton was murdered? What if she knew who we suspected is the thief and the thief knew she knew and killed her by putting some pills into her morning coffee? Wouldn't that be just too horrible! Because now we're not dealing with a robbery at all, but something far more sinister. And we, you and I, with our curious natures, could be in danger. My only question is—who gets murdered over missing cookie money?

And then it was Mrs. Johnston's turn to reply.

Julia—
I have an answer for you. Catholic schoolteachers get killed over cookie money. It's just the sort of petty behavior that might result in one's murder. You still have the vial of pills, don't you? I think we might need it for material evidence when the police come calling, and make no mistake about it, they will come calling. You and I will meet with Father Felix and break the news to him gently (you know how he hates bad news and tends to blame the messengers). One thing is for certain—we owe it to poor Mildred Pinkerton to bring her killer to justice.

Father Felix sank his head down to his desk and told himself that this could not be happening. He had to put an end to these nasty rumors right now, before they could travel any further. If he didn't like Mrs. Johnston and Mrs. Hopwood so much, he would fire them both immediately for starting up such trouble.

    But where could he possibly find two teachers at this late date? And besides, letting them go would hardly stifle the story. On the contrary, Mrs. Johnston would probably march straight to the local television station and demand coverage. She might even attempt to contact Miss Pinkerton's sister in Maine and try to enlist her help.

He would have to speak to them immediately. But before that—it wouldn't hurt to pray.

THIRTEEN

FINALLY IT WAS TIME to break for lunch and, as far as Amelia Johnston was concerned, not a moment too soon. If she had to listen to Sister Scholastica one more second, she was going to scream and scream and scream and carry on like her twin boys.

She grabbed Mrs. Hopwood and pushed her in the direction of Father Felix's office. "Let me do the talking," she said. "I know what to say, and how to work around him."

"I'm not so sure of that." Mrs. Hopwood looked dubious. "Besides, I'm the one who discovered the connection between Digitoxin and poor Mildred Pinkerton."

"That is true," Mrs. Johnston conceded, "but you tend to be dramatic and you know how Father Felix hates flamboyance."

She gave a firm knock on his door and he invited them in. She took the seat with the nice soft cushion because she suspected that they would be there a little while. Maybe a long while, especially if Father Felix decided to call the police. With a little luck, they would all miss the afternoon session or maybe the Educational Evaluation meeting would be canceled altogether.

Maybe the entire certification plan would be aborted.

Father Felix was silent for a few moments, leaving Mrs. Johnston to surmise that he was trying to gather his thoughts. She looked at Mrs. Hopwood, who was at the edge of her seat, and who was probably dying to launch into a complicated explanation, so before anyone else could speak and steal her well deserved thunder, Mrs. Johnston asked, "Don't you wonder whom we suspect?"

Much to her astonishment, Father Felix shook his head.

"I know we shouldn't have been passing notes," Mrs. Hopwood interjected, "and we do apologize for that." To her credit, she looked at Mrs. Johnston, but before Mrs. Johnston could say a single word, Mrs. Hopwood hurried on. "But this is a matter of great importance and—"

Father Felix raised his hand. "Don't say another word."

"But—" Mrs. Johnston started.

"Either one of you!" he snapped.

Mrs. Johnston, defeated, sank back into her chair.

"Now, I want you both to listen to me very carefully. Are you listening?"

Mrs. Hopwood nodded, Mrs. Johnston did not. She was feeling rather surly, being deprived of a voice.

"I don't want this Educational Evaluation thing. That's the truth. And I'm telling you this as friends. But the parish is insisting, the diocese is insisting, the PTA is insisting, at least those parents who give a damn. I know this is a tiresome process and if you're not committed to the school on a long-term basis, your interest in having it accredited, the long drawn-out process of actually obtaining certification, can be grueling."

"I'm sorry—" Mrs. Johnston could not hold her tongue "—but what does this have to do with poor Mildred Pinkerton's murder?"

At the word *murder,* Father Felix cringed.

"I think what he means," Mrs. Hopwood attempted to translate, "is that we should have been paying attention and not passing notes during the meeting."

"That's not what I mean!" Father Felix slapped his hand down on the desk and both Mrs. Johnston and Mrs. Hopwood jumped. He drew a long breath. "What I mean is that your attempt—" it seemed to Mrs. Johnston that he was staring straight at her, and didn't even look in Mrs. Hopwood's direction, which was most unfair, since by her own admission, Mrs. Hopwood was the one who came up with the murder theory "—to make trouble, to start rumors that might seriously hamper our efforts to obtain accreditation—"

"So let me understand this." Mrs. Johnston was having a hard time keeping her temper in check. "What you're trying to say is that it's more important that we get certified than the murder of Miss Pinkerton be solved and her killer be brought to justice."

"That is not what I'm trying to say at all." Father Felix was speaking in a very measured voice. "I have absolutely no reason to believe that Miss Pinkerton was murdered. An autopsy was performed—"

"But that's the thing about Digitoxin!" Mrs. Hopwood practically leaped out of her seat. "It won't show up in an autopsy, I mean, maybe it might, if you're actually looking for it—"

"You have no proof to substantiate this ridiculous theory!" Father Felix bellowed.

Mrs. Johnston decided it was up to her to be the voice of reason. "Okay." She decided to calm Father Felix by pretending to agree. "I wasn't the one—" she turned towards Mrs. Hopwood, who was at glaring at her "—who thought of the murder theory. But I am certain of one thing. Someone has stolen my cookie money. And that is a fact. Miss Pinkerton wrote it down in her notes, which I took from her closet. If you don't believe that I actually went into her closet, I suppose you could ask Mr. Ironweed." Mrs. Johnston considered this for a moment. "Well, maybe not. Nevertheless, we cannot ignore this cookie issue."

She had scored a point. She could tell by Father Felix's silence. "I'm afraid to ask whom you suspect," he finally said.

Mrs. Johnston leaned forward and whispered, "Lily Morningstar. Think about it. She handles the delivery. She pays the man. And yesterday I saw her eating a cookie. It's probably the only cookie on the premises. Now, I ask you, where did she get that cookie?"

A loud rap interrupted Mrs. Johnston's dramatic delivery. In walked Ms. Morningstar, who announced that the accountant was on the phone with the figures that Father Felix had requested.

"Could you put him on hold for a few minutes and come in here?" Father Felix requested. "And close the door."

"You mean you're just going to ask her?" Mrs. Johnston shook her head.

"What would you suggest?"

"We could set a trap," Mrs. Hopwood said.

Father Felix frowned and was still scowling when Ms. Morningstar entered. He didn't waste a minute. "For the last two months—" he started.

"Actually it was last year also." Mrs. Johnston could not help but interrupt.

"Please!" he said, quite exasperated.

"I have been giving you two hundred dollars a month to give to the cookie man."

"You have?" Ms. Morningstar looked completely bewildered.

Father Felix continued. "But we haven't been receiving any cookies. Do you know what's been happening?"

"To what?" Ms. Morningstar asked.

"To the money!" Mrs. Johnston said.

"To the cookies!" Mrs. Hopwood added.

"Ladies, please!" Father Felix said.

"I don't know anything about two hundred dollars a month," Ms. Morningstar claimed and Mrs. Johnston wondered if sometime in her youth she had taken acting lessons.

"I put an envelope on your desk on the eighth of each month with cash in it," Father Felix said. "And labeled it neatly, cookie money."

Ms. Morningstar shrugged. "I never saw any envelope with cookie money."

"I saw you eating a cookie." Mrs. Johnston sprang up. "With my very own eyes."

"I brought it from the store."

"They don't sell those kinds of cookies at the store across the street!" Mrs. Johnston insisted.

"I bought it at the deli by my house!" Ms. Morningstar fired back as though she suddenly realized that she was a suspect and was enraged by the thought.

"Didn't you wonder—" Mrs. Hopwood got into the act "—why we weren't selling cookies anymore?"

"No, quite frankly I did not," Ms. Morningstar said in a testy voice. "I have other things on my mind besides cookies."

"That we don't doubt," Mrs. Johnston said.

"What do you mean by that?" Ms. Morningstar challenged her. When Mrs. Johnston failed to answer, she turned her attention to Father Felix. "I thought perhaps you were going to sell something else, like Christmas wrapping paper, or Valentine candies, or Easter jelly beans. Or maybe—" she shot a dark look in Mrs. Johnston's direction "—someone had an argument with the cookie man, because let's face it, the eighth grade teacher is rather hard to get along with."

Mrs. Johnston almost lunged at her.

"That's enough!" Father Felix shouted. "Ms. Morningstar, go back to your desk and put the accountant through."

"I don't like being accused of stealing!"

"We're sorry," he said.

"You're not the person I want an apology from!" Ms. Morningstar gave Mrs. Johnston a nasty look and then slammed the door on her way out.

Father Felix pushed the speaker button on his phone. "Sorry to keep you waiting, George. What's the total on the cafeteria cost?"

"That would be about fifteen thousand dollars," a loud

baritone voice broke through. "And on grants you're looking at another twenty. You could put down twelve for mandated services."

Father Felix scribbled the figures on a piece of an envelope and then thanked George and pressed several buttons on his phone.

"Now listen, ladies, and please don't interrupt me. I don't want to hear anything more about poor Mildred Pinkerton being murdered by an overdose of Digitoxin. I don't want you to go around accusing anyone of stealing cookie money. I don't want you to start any rumors. If I could possibly execute it, I wouldn't want you two to even speak to one another."

"What about the cookie money?" Mrs. Johnston insisted.

"I will handle the cookie money."

"What if I could bring you proof that Miss Pinkerton was murdered?" Mrs. Hopwood asked.

"You will not be able to bring me any proof because such proof does not exist. And in the meantime, Mrs. Hopwood, you are wasting valuable time. You should be working on the Educational Evaluation, your crooked bulletin boards and your lopsided blinds. In the interim you should try to hand in some legible lesson plans. Now, please go back to the art room. The Educational Evaluation meeting is about to begin."

"But we didn't get to eat lunch," Mrs. Johnston complained because her stomach was growling.

"That's not my fault!" Father Felix barked. He stood up and opened the door for them.

"Bet he gets to eat," Mrs. Johnston muttered.

"He certainly was nasty," Mrs. Hopwood said.

Ms. Morningstar gave Mrs. Johnston a death stare as she walked by the secretary's desk.

It wasn't until they returned to the art room that Mrs.

Johnston was told by practically every one of the teachers, after speaking to the accountant, instead of turning off the speakerphone, Father Felix had inadvertently turned on the intercom.

FOURTEEN

JULIA HOPWOOD WAS gathering her belongings when Albert Alabaster whizzed over to her. "Would you like a ride home?" he asked.

She was rather surprised by his question. Since he had been hired, she had very little to do with him. For one thing, they didn't even work on the same floor. Because she taught primary grades, her classroom was situated on the second level next to the office. Mr. Alabaster was located across the hall from Mrs. Johnston.

"I saw you the other day waiting for the uptown bus. So I asked Ms. Morningstar where you lived."

Mrs. Hopwood thought that this was a rather odd thing to do. She looked at Mrs. Johnston, hoping she would notice, hoping that she would come barreling over, but Mrs. Johnston was in deep discussion with Sister Scholastica.

"I don't live too far from you and I go by your street on the way home. Not on the way to school, I have to drop my sister off. But I could give you a ride. No problem at all."

Now getting a ride home was rather appealing to Mrs. Hopwood, since it was getting crisp out and waiting in the chilly October wind and then stepping onto a crowded bus and fighting for a seat was most exhausting, especially after a rigorous day.

Yet Mrs. Hopwood didn't know Mr. Alabaster at all and she thought something about him was rather peculiar.

The next moment she told herself that she was being ridiculous. He was a teacher at St. Polycarp, entrusted with children. And even if there was a murderer at large (in spite of

Father Felix's refusal to believe it, Mrs. Hopwood still thought there was a distinct possibility that poor Mildred Pinkerton had been killed), the murderer could hardly be Mr. Alabaster since he had been hired after the incident.

"I guess it would be all right," she agreed rather reluctantly, but not before missing the astonished expression on Mr. Alabaster's face, who probably believed from the bottom of his heart that he was doing her a favor. "You could take me home today and we'll see how it works out."

He glared at her (which was quite all right, since recently Mrs. Hopwood was growing quite used to being glared at). "Well, let me get my things, and I'll meet you down here in about ten minutes."

The moment he was out the door, Mrs. Johnston scooted over and asked what was going on.

"Mr. Alabaster is giving me a ride."

"No!"

"He says he lives in my area."

"Call me the moment you get home and tell me all about it."

"I think it will be uneventful. I really do."

But Mrs. Hopwood could not have been more wrong.

MRS. HOPWOOD hadn't stepped two feet into his low to the ground, banged up Firebird when Mr. Alabaster leaned over her (in a most invasive way).

"So you think she was done in?"

For a moment Mrs. Hopwood didn't know who he was talking about. She was too busy trying to find somewhere to sit in the rather confined space. "What?"

"Do you think the old bat was murdered?"

"You mean Miss Pinkerton?"

He nodded and thankfully sank back into the driver's seat. He turned on the engine and without glancing at any mirrors (Mrs. Hopwood did not have her license—if the truth be told she had flunked the driving test three times—but she knew enough to know that you didn't pull out of a parking space without checking the road), he merged with the oncoming traffic.

"I mean Miss Pinkerton. You know what my students told me? They said she was a real witch. So now I'm thinking that maybe one of them did her in. Stole their grandmothers' medications. I've seen their grandmothers and, from the looks of them, a lot could be or should be on heart medication. So one of the bolder pupils sneaks into the teachers' lounge and wacks her. Ever think of that?"

Mrs. Hopwood had to admit that it was a theory she hadn't considered.

"I got an uncle who is a private investigator. You know what I'm thinking?"

Mrs. Hopwood couldn't even begin to guess. She was too busy monitoring her own pumping heart. Mr. Alabaster was going sixty miles an hour in a thirty mile an hour zone.

"I'm thinking he might be interested in investigating the case."

Mr. Alabaster passed a school bus and narrowly missed hitting a rather hefty boy, who was carrying a yellow school-bag. The irate bus driver honked her horn several times. It did nothing to deter Mr. Alabaster, who managed to be several miles away from the scene in several minutes.

"The only thing is that he's a cheap SOB. He's probably going to demand some money up front. Maybe you teachers could all chip in. You couldn't really count on me because, after all, I didn't know Miss Pinkerton. From what I heard on the intercom, I don't think that Father Felix would be too willing, though. What do you think?"

Mrs. Hopwood was too busy trying to find the seat belt to do much thinking.

"I don't know how long I'm going to be able to stay at St. Polycarp, just between you and me. I love the kids and some of the teachers are okay, but what's the story on Mrs. Belgrave? She's really a stuck-up snob. And Miss Danvers hasn't been too friendly either. And when I had a splinter in my finger, Nurse Abby threw the tweezers at me and then threw me out of her office. I don't consider that very nurselike."

Mr. Alabaster was trying to get by a garbage truck. There wasn't enough space. That did not deter him in the least. Quite unabashed, he managed to squeeze through, denting his car several times in the process.

It occurred to Mrs. Hopwood that he might be on drugs.

"I'm starting my own business, you know, so I need some capital, which is why I took the teaching job. Once I can get enough money together, I'm off and running. Do you know anyone who might want to lend me a couple of thousand?"

Mrs. Hopwood had finally found the seat belt, but when Mr. Alabaster stopped for a red light, he jerked the car and the belt slid out of her hands.

"I got a business plan and everything."

He started up again, throwing her forward.

"Good thing I don't have air bags." He chuckled. "In the meantime I'm going to have a good time with the kids, you know. Teach them how to have fun. I think education should be fun, don't you?"

Mrs. Hopwood thought it best not to answer.

"So think about it, hiring my uncle. If one of the students is a killer, don't you think we should know that? The kids seem to like me, but you never know. I could be next. Someone could put an overdose in my Perrier water or sprinkle arsenic on my blueberry muffin. Not to speak of you." He turned his head towards Julia, narrowly missing a crippled woman limping in the road.

"Me?" she squeaked.

"The murderer knows that you're onto him. I suppose it could be a she. We all heard your voice as clear as a bell this afternoon. He or she might decide to put matters to rest by putting you to rest. Sorry—didn't mean to scare you."

Mrs. Hopwood was plenty scared and plenty relieved when he stopped the car on her block.

She gathered her Lillian Vernon tote bag and opened the door. "Thanks for…" She never got to complete the sentence. Mr. Alabaster was gone in a flash, giving Mrs. Hopwood barely enough time to get her left leg out of the car.

By the time she got home, Mrs. Hopwood needed a glass of chardonnay, an indulgence she usually only allowed herself on the weekends.

SHE HAD JUST POURED the white wine when the phone rang.

"What happened?" Mrs. Johnston screeched.

"I think he's was trying to kill me."

"No!"

"You have no idea how fast he drove. Words cannot describe my terror."

"Will you be going home with him tomorrow?"

"Only if it rains." Mrs. Hopwood took a sip of her wine. "His uncle is a private detective. He thinks we should hire him to find out who killed Miss Pinkerton. He went as far as to suggest it could be a student."

"Oh my God! That is such a good idea! Jeffery James, don't even think about pouring that cranberry juice in the washing machine."

It was a mistake telling Mrs. Johnston that. Even with her head clouded by the wine, Mrs. Hopwood realized that.

"We should do it," Mrs. Johnston said.

"He would charge us."

There was silence.

"Not to speak of the fact that if Father Felix found out what we're up to, we'd all lose our jobs."

"I am warning you, Jefferey James, don't do it!"

"I have to go." Mrs. Hopwood heard the front door slam. It was either her son or her husband. She wondered what it would be like to be alone—just for an hour.

"I never considered a student, but I suppose he has a point. I mean, why couldn't it be a student? A student could very easily steal that cookie money and maybe Miss Pinkerton had already spoken to someone in her class—what did you do?" Mrs. Johnston screamed. "So help me God!"

"I'll talk to you later." Mrs. Hopwood hung up the phone. She was feeling rather ill. The ride had left her nauseous and the wine on an empty stomach made her head ache.

And the mere suggestion that she was in danger gave her a rather unsettling feeling.

Of course, she didn't believe it. Not for one moment. But what if…

Alexander stuck his face in the door. He looked rather sheepish. "I've been suspended. You have to go in tomorrow and talk to them."

Mrs. Hopwood sprang up. "I work. Ask your father to go!"

"You know how he is. He'll end up punching someone in the face."

Mrs. Hopwood felt like punching someone in the face too. Instead she went into the bathroom and hid in the tub for a good long time.

FIFTEEN

"Excuse me, Mr. Ironweed."

She was standing in the door to the boiler room, like a vision in blue, smelling like honeysuckle. Even though he had expected her, her presence jolted him and he found it hard to catch his breath.

"I'm so sorry to bother you."

"You're not bothering me." He cleared his throat. He was hoping that she couldn't detect his nervousness.

"But the lock on my classroom door is stuck again and my key doesn't work—"

"Don't you worry. I'll get you in there in a jiffy."

"Okay. I've got to stop by the office and run off some worksheets. I'll meet you upstairs then."

This wasn't the way he had planned it. It was important that they be there together, to talk, to form a bond. He knew he was old enough to be her father, but stranger things had happened. Look at all those movie stars.

And besides, love knew no age.

He gathered his tools and then he waited for fifteen minutes.

When he finally made it up to the third floor, she was waiting for him and ever so grateful to see him approach.

"I'm sorry," he said. "I got a phone call."

"That's okay." She smiled. She had one single dimple on the right side. Same as Millie.

He pretended to be working hard, jiggling the lock and all. But the truth was that he knew exactly how to undo what he had done less than a half an hour ago.

"You feeling okay?" he asked.

"Why?" Her hand went immediately to her face, touching the small scar above her left eyebrow. "I don't look so good?"

"Oh no, you look mighty fine. It's only that you were out sick on Monday."

"Yes. I had some sort of stomach flu on Sunday. When you teach, you know, it's difficult to leave the classroom. Not unless you can get an adult to watch the children, and the other teachers, well, they're all busy with their own classes."

"I could do it."

She looked startled by the remark.

"I could watch your class anytime you wanted me to. I'd stand there and write the names of all the bad children on the board for you."

"Well, that's very kind of you." She had a sweet, soft voice.

"Okay, I think this will be all right." He made a great pretense of rattling the door.

"Maybe I shouldn't lock it anymore. I mean, this is the third time this month that it's got stuck."

"Oh no, you keep locking it. With everything that's going on around here, it wouldn't be a good idea to keep your classroom wide open. You can always call on me."

"I appreciate that. Thank you so much, Mr. Ironweed."

"Call me Ian."

She nodded and went into her classroom. He had to stop himself from following her.

He practically bounced down the stairs, arthritic knees and all.

He was making progress.

SIXTEEN

HILDA DANVERS TIPTOED through the corridors of the second floor. There was something eerie about an empty school. Especially St. Polycarp. Especially since the death of Miss Pinkerton. Especially since all those rumors were circulating around like the pigeons that had found their way into Miss Danvers's fifth grade class last year.

Mrs. Johnston was in. At least the light in her classroom was on. Miss Danvers had spent some time rehearsing what to say. It was important that she not draw suspicion to herself, important that she act nonchalant. She liked Mrs. Johnston, she really did.

But Mrs. Johnston was rather moody and unpredictable, which made her difficult to approach.

"Good morning," Miss Danvers greeted Mrs. Johnson, who was sitting at her desk, copying something busily from a textbook.

Mrs. Johnston looked up and flashed a quick smile.

Good sign, Miss Danvers thought. "I was reading in the teachers' room about these subcommittees for the Educational Evaluation and I saw that you're the head of the personnel section."

Mrs. Johnston merely nodded and kept scribbling.

"I was wondering if you needed any help because I know we're all supposed to do something—"

"Yes, as a matter of fact, I do."

Miss Danvers breathed a quiet sigh of relief.

"Maybe you could watch my class next week while I use the phone to do some background checks."

Miss Danvers felt as though she couldn't breathe. This wasn't what she had in mind at all. For one thing, the thought of watching Mrs. Johnston's seventh grade class filled her with a cold terror. She did not like seventh graders (even if they had once been her fifth grade class). Seventh graders were at the mercy of raging hormones, they didn't get along with their teachers, with their parents, or with one another. As far as Miss Danvers was concerned the only way to keep a seventh grade class under control was to drug them, which clearly wasn't allowed.

Miss Danvers merely nodded and then added hastily, "I thought if you needed help in the actual work—"

"No, I've got that pretty much under control. But if you'd like to participate on the building section, I'm sure that Mrs. Hopwood would be glad to have you join the committee." She snapped the textbook shut. Miss Danvers jumped.

"Okay," she said and gave a feeble smile as she exited the room. Next week, she thought, a background check. When next week, she wondered, and who was going to be checked on? How thoroughly?

There was no doubt in Miss Danvers's mind that Mrs. Johnston had to be stopped.

If she wasn't, well, it was only a matter of time before she discovered that Miss Danvers was a compulsive shoplifter.

SEVENTEEN

MRS. HOPWOOD WAS GOING to be in late, so said the morning messages. Something about her son. Mrs. Johnston found it difficult to believe that, even as teenagers, children could be so problematic. No one told her that when she announced that she wanted to get pregnant. Everyone lied and said how wonderful it was.

Today was dress-down day, which meant for a dollar the students got to wear their own clothes, what the school referred to as "street clothes." Mrs. Johnston was against the idea. When the children were out of uniform, they behaved badly and were much more difficult to control. And she was exhausted from being up with the twins all night.

"Today we're going to have a grammar test."

The entire class groaned.

Mrs. Johnston rang the silver bell on her desk and said, "Not another word!"

Marlene Rodriquez's arm shot up in the air.

Mrs. Johnston acknowledged her with a nod.

"How come you didn't tell us so we could study?"

"Did you ever hear of a pop quiz?"

The class was quiet for several minutes. Until Matthew Lupus mumbled, "It's not fair."

"Even if I had given you notice, I doubt very much if you would pass," Mrs. Johnston said viciously. She took some satisfaction in his humiliated expression. She reached inside her schoolbag and gave the test papers to Lori Landon to pass out.

A few minutes later Lori announced rather gleefully that they were two papers short.

"Do you want me to go down to Ms. Morningstar and tell her to make some more copies?" Lori offered.

Mrs. Johnston did not want Lori to go anywhere. She tended to get lost around the boy's bathroom, lurking there, waiting for someone to come by and notice her. Instead Mrs. Johnston sent Herbert Pace, a reliable boy, who had never been in a stick of trouble.

"The rest of you can start," she instructed.

"Is it true," Ethan Rosario questioned, "that Miss Pinkerton was actually murdered?"

The class let out a collective gasp and then the babble of voices erupted.

"There is no proof," Mrs. Johnston said, and at least that much was the truth. "Now be quiet!"

"But what am I supposed to do? I don't even have a copy of the test," Ethan complained.

"Pray," she replied.

Mrs. Johnston reached into her desk to look for her gossip magazine. It was not in her top drawer where she was certain she had left it. She opened two other drawers and found it in the bottom, which puzzled her. Because she knew that she had not put it there. Someone had moved it.

She eyed the class but no one was eyeing her. It could be anyone.

Mrs. Johnston leaned back and began to browse through the pages, debating on whether or not she should start the crossword puzzle. She was not supposed to be sitting down and certainly not supposed to be reading, but she was pretty good at deciphering footsteps. If Father Felix decided to pay her a visit, she'd rise up pretty quickly.

Herbert returned a few minutes later, carrying one sheet of paper. "Ms. Morningstar says that she's very sorry but she's too busy right now to make any copies for you."

Amelia Johnston felt her insides burning. She immediately

gave the original to Ethan Rosario, who was gazing around, probably hoping to start a bit of trouble.

She rose from her seat and saw Mr. Alabaster walking down the hall.

"Are you on a break?" she snapped at him.

"My kids are in music. I have to pick them up."

"Could you do me a great favor?"

"I guess," he said, wary because, after all, as Mrs. Johnston herself knew, she had not been too welcoming to him.

"Just make me a couple of copies of this test paper." She grabbed Ethan's away from him, which was quite all right, since he was still trying to figure out the date.

After Mr. Alabaster had left, Mrs. Johnston went immediately to her desk and took out a Post-it. She began to scribble frantically. In a note to Mrs. Hopwood she explained exactly what had happened, how Ms. Morningstar absolutely refused to make copies for her and after all wasn't that Ms. Morningstar's job? This was hardly fair and Mrs. Johnston intended to take it up with Father Felix during lunchtime.

Mrs. Johnston stapled the note shut and then sent Herbert down to the second grade classroom. "But before you go," she instructed him, "make sure that Mrs. Hopwood is in her room. If Father Felix is in there, you are to return immediately upstairs, note in hand. Do you understand?"

He understood and scooted off. Mrs. Johnston was still fuming and barely said thank you to Mr. Alabaster when he gave her the copies he had made.

Herbert was back in a flash, announcing that Mrs. Hopwood was there, collecting homework, and she had written Mrs. Johnston a note in return. Except Mrs. Hopwood hadn't bothered to staple it. Perhaps she wasn't used to doing such things, because her own classroom children could barely read.

At any rate, her note was simple and to the point.

Maybe you should apologize to her.

The message infuriated Mrs. Johnson (who was already

quite bitter). She believed that friends should be firmly on your side, whether or not you were right, especially if you weren't right, and the thought that Mrs. Hopwood was siding with that cookie thief (and maybe teacher murderer) was something Mrs. Johnston couldn't abide.

One thing that Mrs. Johnston was good at, actually there were a lot of things that Mrs. Johnston was good at, but one thing she excelled at was making trouble.

She intended to make a lot of trouble for Lily Morningstar, with or without Julia Hopwood's help.

EIGHTEEN

FATHER FELIX WAS BUSY on his computer when he heard a rap on the door. And he knew, somehow he just knew, that there was a problem. Since Miss Pinkerton's death, he had been besieged with nothing but problems. She had been the senior teacher, the others (even if they didn't like her) looked up to her and, in her own way, she managed to keep them in line by acting in a professional manner.

But now everything was spiraling downhill.

The knocking grew more frantic.

"Come in," he said in a weak voice because he was feeling rather weak.

In stepped Mrs. Johnston with murder in her eyes. "Can I speak to you for a moment?" Before he had a chance to answer, she knocked over the books on the seat across from his, and sat her large frame down. "I have a problem."

That didn't surprise Father Felix in the least.

"I had to have some copies made. I sent Herbert down to Ms. Morningstar. She refused to do it."

Father Felix thought it best to nip this right in the bud. "No, that's not true. Ms. Morningstar was running off the monthly calendar. It has to go home with the students today. She couldn't stop the machine just to make two copies for you. Besides, teachers really should make their own copies. I thought we went over that at the September faculty meeting."

Mrs. Johnston pinched her lips together in a scary fashion. "Is that so?"

"Is that all?"

"Well, it may interest you to know that I sent Mr. Alabaster down to ask her to make copies. And he was successful."

"That's because he made those copies himself and because Ms. Morningstar had finished running off the monthly calendar by the time he arrived."

By the furious expression on her face, it was clear to Father Felix that Mrs. Johnston did not believe him. Wasn't it enough that he was a priest, a man of the cloth? Evidently not.

"I was right here," he insisted. "Really."

"I'm a teacher." Mrs. Johnston folded her hands across her chest. "Ms. Morningstar is a secretary. It seems clear to me where your loyalties should lie."

"Your professions have nothing to do with the matter. My loyalty lies with the truth."

"Father Felix." The door opened and Ms. Morningstar stared darkly at Mrs. Johnston. "Father Lawrence is on the phone. He says it's important."

"You'll excuse me, Mrs. Johnston."

But Mrs. Johnston was not about to go quietly into the night. "You haven't heard the last of this!" She stormed out of the office.

Ms. Morningstar shook her head in sympathy as Father Felix picked up the phone.

"Larry, what's doing?"

"Listen, I just came from a diocese meeting and…"

Father Felix did not like the silence that followed.

"Well." Father Lawrence hesitated. "They're going to be closing some of the schools in September. They can't afford to keep them open and that's the plain truth of the matter."

Father Felix's stomach fluttered. "So what are you trying to say?"

"I'm calling to give you a heads-up. You'll be getting a letter. St. Polycarp is on that list. The diocese is going to be closing your school unless you step up the enrollment. And you have to get that Educational Evaluation certificate. It's imperative."

"So." Father Felix took a deep breath. "It is possible that I can turn the situation around?"

"I suppose so." But Father Lawrence sounded rather dubious. "But, well, you do have that cloud hanging over your head."

As far as Father Felix was concerned there were several clouds, all about to burst. "To what are you referring?"

"You know...that teacher's death."

"She had a heart attack!"

"Well, the rumor is that she was murdered."

Father Felix clutched his hands together. "I have two very imaginative teachers working here. Unfortunately, they egg each other on. Don't you think that if there was one shred of evidence the police would be investigating?"

The moment that Father Felix said that, he realized that he had made a mistake. Father Lawrence was an old friend. They had attended seminary school together but that didn't mean that he wouldn't instigate a police investigation on his own.

"Everything is great here," Father Felix lied (and to another priest), "and I'm going to work very hard to keep this school open."

"Well, I hope so."

"And I appreciate your telling me this."

Father Felix hung up the phone, aware that he had just uttered another lie. He did not appreciate Father Lawrence telling him this. Not at all. He wondered why he should care whether or not St. Polycarp closed. It wasn't as though he loved his job as a principal. Most of the time, he hated it. It was one aggravating scenario after another. If the teachers weren't angry with him, the parents were. If the parents weren't, the diocese was. And the students were always angry. It was a no-win situation.

But St. Polycarp had been in existence for over a hundred years. It had educated Italian students, Irish students, Polish students and now Spanish and African-American students. It was a neighborhood school and the parish had stood strong, a beacon, even if the area wasn't what it used to be.

It was not going to close on his watch. It was a matter of pride.

Somehow he was going to find a way to keep the doors open. And then afterwards, if he decided to apply for a transfer, do something else with his life, so be it. On his resume, it would go down that he saved a crumbling school.

One thing was for certain. He couldn't let anyone know that St. Polycarp was in trouble. That might work in his favor, but, on the other hand, it might just be the final nail in the coffin. People were terrified of sinking ships. They wanted to abandon them. If they didn't anticipate a job in the fall, teachers started to look around at other schools. And in the meantime they didn't teach as well. Parents scrambled to find placement for their children and there was no question about their renewing their contracts. Some of them might even yank their children out mid-year, especially in the light of Miss Pinkerton's death.

Father Felix had to quench any questionable rumors about her demise, which meant he had to find a way to silence Mrs. Hopwood and Mrs. Johnston. He couldn't fire them, even if he wanted to. For one thing, Mrs. Johnston would have the union down his throat faster than the potato crisps served once a year in the cafeteria disappeared. She also belonged to a score of other hostile organizations that seemed to do nothing but picket and stir up rabble-rousers. And then there was the real possibility that if the two teachers were let go suddenly, it might only lend validity that the stories they were spreading were true.

He was going to have to find a way to distract them. Mrs. Hopwood was easily distracted. All you had to do was throw a shoe catalog her way. But Mrs. Johnston was like steel, completely unbendable and quite good at persuading other teachers.

He was getting another migraine. He opened his drawer

and looked around for his Advil, but he couldn't find his pill bottle. He wondered for a moment if someone had stolen it.

He wasn't even going to go there.

NINETEEN

THE SCHOOL WAS DESERTED. At least that's what Mr. Ironweed believed. It was nearing six o'clock, the after-school kids had been picked up, the teachers had all driven away in their fancy cars, the cafeteria was closed, scrubbed clean, waiting for morning breakfast.

He loved the school during this period, twilight time he called it. And as he walked around from classroom to classroom, sweeping the floors and emptying the trash, he could swear he could see the wispy forms of all of the students who had ever walked down the halls, he could smell the Avon perfume worn by all of the former teachers. If he listened real hard, he could even hear their voices whispering the multiplication tables, especially the ones who had passed on. Especially the ones that had died right here in this school. Like Miss Pinkerton.

But today Mr. Ironweed was not his usual chipper self. He was not enjoying the quiet time because this morning something had happened. Something that had angered him.

He had caught Mr. Alabaster flirting with Miss Crossover. He hadn't liked Mr. Alabaster from day one. A young, flashy whippersnapper. He couldn't imagine what possessed Father Felix to hire him in the first place but, after all, Mr. Ironweed was just a simple janitor, not a priest with all those fancy degrees, so what did he know?

One thing Mr. Ironweed *did* know was that Mr. Alabaster was far too young for Miss Crossover. Although Mr. Ironweed didn't know how old she was, he was betting that Bonnie Crossover was in her middle thirties. She had those cute little wrinkles around her eyes. And Mr. Alabaster? He couldn't be a day older than twenty-five.

Miss Crossover needed a more mature man, a man who might protect her, a man with a steady job to help her pay bills, a man who owned a nice little home of his own, where she could move right in. (Although Millie probably wouldn't want her to do any major redecorating.) But women were fools. And sometimes boys with a lot of hair and brightly colored shirts and fast cars could put a spell on the innocent.

Well, Mr. Ironweed was about to nip that in the bud.

First he went up to her classroom on the pretext of emptying her trash. But then he did what he did every night. He looked through her desk drawer. Usually he didn't find anything interesting but this afternoon his search was rewarded. He found something of an extremely personal nature. He folded the piece of paper and stuck it in his pocket.

When he finished, he tiptoed (although why he did this when the school was clearly empty was a mystery even to himself) out of her room, went down a flight of stairs and entered the main office. He reached for the master key and approached Father Felix's door. Although Mr. Ironweed had full rein to clean the school, he was not permitted into Father Felix's office. Father Felix preferred to clean his own area, which really was quite comical because anyone could see that it hadn't been dusted or vacuumed in years.

Within minutes Mr. Ironweed opened the door, snapped on the light, and stepped on something which had fallen to the floor. He bent down and picked up a manila envelope. Someone had written *Cookie Money* on it and then *I'm sorry* underneath. Mr. Ironweed opened the envelope (which wasn't sealed) and saw four crisp hundred dollar bills, seven tens, and five ones and assorted change. If Mr. Ironweed were a thief he might have taken the money. But Mr. Ironweed was a man of principle, a man of honor. He put the envelope on top of the pile of papers on the chair in front of the desk.

And then quietly he approached the file cabinet.

At first he was afraid that it would be locked, but it wasn't. He had to open several drawers; some of them were filled with cash, bills and coins, confirming Mr. Ironweed's opinion that Father Felix was a very careless man, in spite of his degrees and his profession. But at least he knew how to keep folders nice and neat. And in alphabetical order.

He grabbed the one which read *Bonnie Crossover* and, carefully using a pen and a small scrap of paper from Father Felix's desk, copied down her home phone number as well as her address. He was almost finished when the answering machine snapped on.

He jumped up and upset the papers (which had been swaying vicariously) on the chair. They fell to the floor with a soft thud.

"Father Felix," a woman's voice (whom he did not recognize) spoke into the answering machine, "this is Sister Santina from St. Jude School. Again I have to tell you how sorry we are about Miss Pinkerton's heart attack. We would like to reschedule your visit for the first week of January, if you can find someone to send in her place. Also, I want to alert you that we will be mailing out our Educational Evaluation book, which Miss Pinkerton, for some strange reason, never received. If you have any questions, you can call me back at…"

Mr. Ironweed wasn't listening. He heard a car pull up in front of the building. He didn't think for one moment that the person was about to ring the bell. Nevertheless, a light could be seen from the outside and if the person had any connection to the school, he'd be in trouble.

Quickly he picked up all the papers from the floor and piled them again on the chair in no particular order, since he very much doubted that they had had an order to begin with.

Then he replaced the files back into the cabinet, switched off the lights and shut the door, locking it behind him.

TWENTY

HILDA DANVERS WAS going down to breakfast to grab a couple of blueberry muffins when she stumbled upon Myrtle Miller, a cafeteria lady, sobbing in the kitchen. Miss Danvers knew that some of the other teachers did not treat the kitchen staff well. They acted as though the servers were their own private chefs, but Miss Danvers went out of her way to be nice to everyone. She especially liked Myrtle, who always treated her well, gave her double portions of potato crisps and saved the extra oatmeal cookies for her.

"What happened, Myrtle?" Miss Danvers asked, chewing her blueberry muffin.

"Something terrible!"

Miss Danvers took a large gulp of coffee and said the first thing that came to her mind. "Someone you know is being deported?"

Myrtle looked at her as though she were mad.

Miss Danvers guessed again. "Are you sick?"

Myrtle nodded and put the crumpled handkerchief to her swollen eyes.

"Is it—" Miss Danvers swallowed "—is it terminal?"

Myrtle thought for a moment and then said, between tears, "It could be. It's my heart."

Miss Danvers took another bite of her muffin. She did not think that this was such bad news. Her uncle had lived forty years with a heart condition and when he finally died, he was run over by a pickup truck.

"There are medicines…" Miss Danvers said in an attempt to be comforting.

"I had my medicines and they're gone."

"You can't get them anymore?"

"I lost them."

"Well, that's simple enough," Miss Danvers said. "Just explain to the pharmacist—"

"You don't understand!" Myrtle snapped at her, which Miss Danvers thought was rather rude. She was just trying to be helpful and besides, she had to go upstairs and run off some math sheets before Mrs. Hopwood monopolized the copying machine with coloring papers. "This isn't the first time I lost my heart medication. I lost it when we were in Jamaica. And last month, I misplaced the pills at my sister's house. Thank goodness, we all prayed to St. Anthony and we found them. Then a few weeks ago, I lost the bottle in school. I thought I had taken it out of my bag, put it by the water cooler and when I turned around to get it, the bottle was gone. Gone too was the pretty pink vial my daughter had brought back from a trip to Greece. My husband was very mad. The insurance doesn't cover replacements. And then today, I went to take my pills and they're not in my handbag. I could have sworn I put them in my makeup bag this morning. But the makeup pouch is gone also, my new Amber Rose lipstick and my mirror with my initials on it, MMM—"

"Well, maybe you just *thought* you put it into your handbag." Having finished her blueberry muffin, Miss Danvers was heading for the door. "Lots of times I do that. I swear that I brought something to school but I really left it on the counter at home—"

"No, no, no!" Myrtle's sorrow had changed to hostility. "I called my son and asked him to look around and he told me, no, Mommy, you didn't leave it at home. I am either going cuckoo, or someone is stealing my medicine!"

Miss Danvers did not say what she thought. That Myrtle, who seemed to be in her mid-sixties, perhaps was getting a little forgetful, because why would someone want to steal her medicine? Perhaps if it were a narcotic…

"I don't know how to tell my husband. We have no money for more pills and he has such a temper! If I don't get my pills, I will die!"

Miss Danvers didn't know what to say. She could hardly offer to pay for the prescription herself. Although the cafeteria ladies might not believe it, her financial position was just as precarious as theirs, maybe more so. At least they had husbands.

So she said the only thing she could think of, the thing that Catholics seem to take great comfort in. "I'll say a prayer."

Myrtle nodded and Miss Danvers left, happy to escape, hoping that the copy machine was not in use. And as she climbed the stairs to the first floor, she remembered vaguely that someone had found a bottle of pills in a pink bottle. But she could not remember who had said such a thing, and she wasn't even sure if it was someone in school or maybe just someone in a television program.

Well, no harm done, she thought, it would come to her soon enough.

TWENTY-ONE

JULIA HOPWOOD WAS IN the process of explaining the difference between a noun and a verb when her door flew open.

"You have a phone call," Ms. Morningstar announced. "I told him you were in class but he said it was important."

Mrs. Hopwood did not like important calls. They made her anxious. "Who is it?" she asked.

"Your son," Ms. Morningstar said in a clipped voice. (She had been treating Mrs. Hopwood differently since Mrs. Johnston had accused her of stealing the cookie money but as far as Mrs. Hopwood was concerned, this was guilt by association. She didn't agree with Mrs. Johnston. Maybe she should tell Ms. Morningstar that, although it was probably too late.)

"Well, I guess I should talk to him."

Ms. Morningstar shrugged.

"Do you think you could watch my class?"

"I'm sorry, but I'm right in the middle of typing up the agenda for the next faculty meeting and Father Felix wants to look at it by the end of the day."

Mrs. Hopwood didn't know what to do. She could leave her door open. The secretary's desk was just across the hall. Maybe she could reach the phone several feet and actually peek into the classroom.

She had to find out what Alexander wanted.

"Class, I have to leave for a moment."

"Is your son in trouble?"

"Did he get thrown out of school?"

"What does he want?"

Mrs. Hopwood was going to ignore such questions.

"I want everyone to list all of the nouns you can think of in your notebooks. When I come back, I will give a prize to the one who has written the most nouns."

"What's the prize?"

Mrs. Hopwood opened her drawer and took out a large Hershey's Kiss.

"Wow!"

"Linda Lou, I'd like you to come up here and write the names of the students on the blackboard who dare to speak after I leave the room."

"I don't want to."

Mrs. Hopwood was rather surprised by her frankness.

"I'll do it." Mary Elizabeth stood up.

"If I do it, I won't be able to be in the noun contest," Linda Lou explained, "and I won't have a chance to win the candy."

"I don't want to write down nouns anyway," Mary Elizabeth said. "I'm not sure what they are."

Mrs. Hopwood handed Mary Elizabeth the chalk. She could see she'd probably have to review the definition of nouns when she returned.

Her heart thumping hard and heavy, she approached Ms. Morningstar's desk. She was browsing through a Lerners catalog as she handed the phone to Mrs. Hopwood.

"What is it, Alexander?" Mrs. Hopwood asked her son in wavering voice.

"Well, it's like this, Mom. I just thought you'd like to know that I don't have any school today."

"What?"

"I forgot to tell you. It's teacher conference or something. I'm hanging out with Jason."

"Who's Jason?"

"A senior."

"But you're only a sophomore."

"So? He's cool."

"Is he one of your customers for NyQuil?"

"Mom, let it go."

"Was this why you called me out of class?"

"I won't be home until late tonight. Jason's going to take me to one of these clubs—"

"You can't go."

"You're kidding. Right?"

"You're underage. Alexander—"

"I'll be home by midnight. Promise."

Mrs. Hopwood hung up the phone and decided to take a quick trip to the bathroom. She hadn't gone since early morning and her bladder was bursting.

She was only gone a few minutes and was almost at her classroom door when she heard Father Felix's voice booming. "What's going on here?"

She sped inside. The children were mute, their heads hung low. Mary Elizabeth had returned to her seat, still holding the chalk.

Mrs. Hopwood noticed that her desk drawers were wide open.

"Mrs. Hopwood, you might be interested in knowing that while you were out of the room, several of the students, including Victor, stand up, Victor—" Victor, a rather rotund boy with black curly hair and black framed glasses sprang to his feet "—were actually going through your desk drawer. And Mary Elizabeth was just standing there, peering over him. The entire class was talking, several of your students were running around—"

Mrs. Hopwood was wondering why she hadn't heard the commotion when she was mere feet away.

"And the classroom door was closed," Father Felix added.

"I left it open."

"Well, someone closed it."

"Who closed the classroom door?" she asked.

There was no answer.

"Who closed the classroom door?" Father Felix shouted.

The class was silent.

"I want an answer."

Still no one spoke.

Father Felix looked at the clock. "I see we have a few minutes until dismissal time. Well, it may interest you all to know that no one, and I mean no one, is going home until we find out what happened here."

Several of the girls started to weep.

Mrs. Hopwood figured that it was up to her to provide, at the very least, a partial explanation. "I'm afraid that I received an emergency call from my son. I asked Ms. Morningstar if she could watch the class for a few seconds but she was too busy typing the agenda for the faculty meeting." Mrs. Hopwood searched Father Felix's face, hoping that his expression would betray him, but it was blank. "I gave the class an assignment and asked Mary Elizabeth to write down the names of the students who talked while I was out of the room."

"Mary Elizabeth, stand up."

Mary Elizabeth sprang out of her seat. Victor sank in his chair.

"Who told you to sit down?" Father Felix bellowed.

Victor rose, more slowly this time.

"Go stand in the corner by the crucifix."

Victor shuffled toward the cross.

"Now, Mary Elizabeth," Father Felix started, "maybe you can explain why there are no names on the board."

"Well," she gulped, "I was going to write the names but then—"

"Then what?" Mrs. Hopwood asked softly.

"The students all started to get out of their seats and I wasn't sure what to do because you didn't say anything at all about writing the names of people who were walking around and, at first, no one was actually talking. And then the chalk broke and I needed another piece and I didn't know what to do, so I opened your drawer—"

"You are never, never to touch private property. Do you understand?" Father Felix screamed at her.

"I understand," Mary Elizabeth said in a meek voice.

"Go on with your story," Mrs. Hopwood said.

"And I moved a few things…"

Father Felix frowned at her.

"And then I found this little car and I picked it up—"

"It's my car," Victor said.

"I took it away from him—" Mrs. Hopwood turned towards Father Felix "—because he was playing with it during religion."

"Then it's not his car anymore. It belongs to the school."

"And then everyone started to talk," Mary Elizabeth said, "and before I could write down any names Father Felix came in and—"

"Sit down," Father Felix said. "Don't ask her to do any more favors, Mrs. Hopwood. She's useless. And I still don't know who closed the door."

Ms. Morningstar stuck her head in. "Father, Miss Crossover would like to meet with you. Do you know when you'll be free?"

"Not today. I'm staying right here until the dismissal bell and maybe after that. Maybe until midnight or until tomorrow morning."

Arianna Gonzalez let out a wail.

"But you could do something for me, Ms. Morningstar," Father Felix said. "You could bring me a glass of ice cold water."

"Certainly, Father."

"Would anyone else like a glass of ice-cold water?" he asked.

Several brave students raised their hands.

"Well, you're not getting any!" Father Felix lunged forward. "Not until I know who closed that door!"

Ms. Morningstar left the room and Father Felix sat down

in Mrs. Hopwood's chair, which meant that Mrs. Hopwood had to stand.

"We're going to stay here all day and all night until someone confesses. And you can forget about fun day on Halloween. No one in this class is going."

Arianna Gonzalez's hand went up in the air.

"And I mean no one!" Father Felix snapped.

Arianna did not put down her hand.

"What is it, Arianna?" Mrs. Hopwood asked.

"Victor did it," she sniffled.

"He did." A few more students confirmed her accusation.

"Victor!" Father Felix yelled. "Come to the front of the class immediately!"

Victor, looking not in the least bit intimidated, trudged over to Mrs. Hopwood's desk.

Father Felix put his face very close to Victor. "Did you close the door?"

"Yeah." Victor shrugged. "I did it."

"WHY?"

"'Cause I wanted to play with my car and I was afraid that Mrs. Hopwood would come back and she would see me. This way I figured I'd have a little warning."

"Take your backpack. You're going home."

Mrs. Hopwood looked at the clock, noticing that it was almost time to go home anyway.

"I'm calling your mother."

"She's in Puerto Rico."

"Your father."

"No one knows where he is."

"I'm calling your guardian."

"What does that mean?"

Father Felix ignored the question. "Not because you were playing with your car. Not because you were in the teacher's desk without permission. But because when you were asked to tell the truth, you didn't. You took the coward's way out. Do you understand?"

Victor scratched his head.

"When I ask you a question, I want an answer. Do you understand?"

"Yes."

"Yes, Father."

"Yes, Father," Victor repeated in a lackluster voice.

The door flung open and Ms. Morningstar came in with a small glass of water.

"Give that to Mrs. Hopwood," Father Felix instructed. "She looks as if she could use a glass of water."

Mrs. Hopwood did indeed need a glass of water. And after Father Felix left with Victor, after she finished packing up the children and making sure they had what they needed to go home, after they were dismissed, she returned to the classroom.

It was then that she realized that more than a glass of water, she needed a good stiff drink.

Her Educational Evaluation file was gone.

TWENTY-TWO

MRS. JOHNSTON WAS IN the middle of bathing her twins when the phone rang. She was tempted not to answer it, because everyone knew that to leave two two-year-old boys in the bathtub alone could easily lead to an attempted murder charge. But when the answering machine clicked on and she heard Mrs. Hopwood's voice, she promptly lifted out one boy after another, threw them towels, instructed them to dry off, and raced into the living room.

She picked up the phone, just as Mrs. Hopwood was explaining that something peculiar had happened.

"What?" she said breathlessly.

"Oh, I wasn't sure—"

"I'm here. Jeffery James, didn't I tell you to dry off? Get your wet butt off the couch! I was just giving the kids a bath."

"I had to leave my classroom today, unattended. Just for a few minutes because Alex called and said it was an emergency, which it really wasn't. Anyway—"

"I am warning you!"

"Someone closed the door—"

"Did you get caught?" Mrs. Johnston asked.

"As a matter of fact, I did. Father Felix came barreling in."

"You could get written up for that. Where's your towel?"

"I know, but that might be the least of it."

"Really? You both have ten seconds to dry yourselves off and get into your pajamas or no ice cream!"

"When I got back into my classroom, my drawer was open.

One of the students was looking for a toy. After everything settled, I noticed—"

"That's it. No ice cream!"

Justin Joseph began to wail so loudly that Mrs. Johnston could not hear Mrs. Hopwood, which really would be a shame because she suspected that something really interesting was about to go down.

"All right, all right," she conceded. "I'll give you both another chance. Go get into your pajamas."

"I noticed that my Educational Evaluation folder was missing," Mrs. Hopwood said hurriedly.

Mrs. Johnston slumped down onto the wet sofa.

"Did you hear me?" Mrs. Hopwood asked.

"Yes, I heard you. Maybe you just misplaced it."

"I don't think so."

"You know, that's really strange." Mrs. Johnston was keeping her eyes on the twins as they dumped the bureau drawer open and began to rummage through underwear in order to find their pajamas, which were under their pillows. "Because yesterday I had the distinct impression that someone had been in *my* desk drawer. My magazine had been moved."

"I really believe," Mrs. Hopwood said, "that someone stole that folder."

"Did you tell Father Felix?"

"No, by the time I realized it was gone, he had already left the building. He had an appointment with the podiatrist or something. Besides, I'm sure to get blamed because I left the class unattended."

"Well, that's not when it happened," Mrs. Johnston said. "No one could have come in and stolen that information in full view of the students. That's just when you noticed that it was missing."

"Are these my pajamas?" Jeffery James was wearing his snow suit.

"You have to tell Father Felix, because if someone broke into your classroom—"

"I never lock it."

"Oh, you might get in trouble for that."

"Zip me up, Mommy."

"I was never given a key." Mrs. Hopwood seemed quite exasperated, which only irritated Mrs. Johnston. After all, she wasn't the one who had two toddlers running around naked ruining her furniture and her life. "Look, I didn't have all the papers. I gave you some—"

"Yes, and I have a few folders right here," Mrs. Johnston said. "Well, somewhere in my house. But Father Felix should know that a couple of folders are missing, that someone took the papers. Because as far as I'm concerned that cookie money and the death of Miss Pinkerton are far from settled."

"Zip me up, Mommy."

"Those aren't your pajamas!"

"I guess I'll talk to you tomorrow before school starts. We're going to have to get together and figure out what's missing."

"I'd be happy to go into Father Felix's office with you." Mrs. Johnston heard water splashing. Justin Joseph had probably climbed back into the tub. "I've got to go." She hung up the phone and raced into the bathroom.

Justin Joseph had thrown six towels and one mat into the tub.

Mrs. Johnston wondered when her husband was coming home from the university where he taught and how much it would cost to hire a live-in nanny.

TWENTY-THREE

FATHER FELIX WAS WAITING for Mrs. Hopwood when she arrived the following morning. He had invited her into his office. He noticed that she was looking rather nervous and rushed, but he had come to believe that was just her normal expression.

"I'm glad that we have a few moments alone," Mrs. Hopwood said, which to Father Felix's mind meant that the conversation wasn't going to go quite as he anticipated and that Mrs. Hopwood had a problem. He had not called her into his office to listen to her problems. He had enough of his own.

"I'm sorry about what happened yesterday..."

Slightly relieved, he waved her inside.

"After you left, well, actually, after I dismissed the students I noticed that something was missing from my drawer."

"If you're talking about money, Mrs. Hopwood, I have to tell you that I've cautioned everyone not to keep valuables in their desks. Not that our students can't be trusted, but temptation—"

"It wasn't money," she interrupted, "or valuables. It was a couple of the Educational Evaluation folders."

He stared at her for a few long moments. "Those are valuables," he finally said firmly.

"I know. But it wasn't *all* the folders. Mrs. Johnston has some of the paperwork because she's leading the committees on faculty and finance—"

"Maybe you put it somewhere else and you just thought..." He knew that Mrs. Hopwood tended to be rather scattered and disorganized.

She shook her head. "I don't think so."

"Well, what do *you* think happened to it?" he snapped. The moment the question tumbled out of his mouth, he realized that he had made a grave error. He was now giving her an opportunity to embellish on one of her theories, no doubt already thoroughly discussed with Mrs. Johnston.

"I think it was stolen. Someone wanted that folder and it has to do with the missing cookie money and, quite frankly, poor Mildred Pinkerton's death."

"I would suggest," he said, "that you go back to your classroom and take another stab at finding it. Perhaps you left it at home, or in the faculty lounge." Mrs. Hopwood was shaking her head, which he found rather annoying, so he decided to annoy her. "If you like, I could help you look. Perhaps in your back closet."

Mrs. Hopwood looked horrified by the offer. Father Felix knew that to open the door of one of Mrs. Hopwood's closets was to risk a swift and sudden death, while textbooks and statues and math manipulatives and bulletin board paper and markers and easels came crashing down. But he was about to ask Mrs. Hopwood a favor and this wasn't a good time to bask in what others perceived to be his authority.

"I'm sure it will turn up. Now, the reason I asked you in here—I don't know if you're aware of it, but Miss Pinkerton was supposed to observe a school in Washington, D.C., as part of her duties as chair of the Educational Evaluation. She was put on a team to grade a school on their own certification process. The visit was scheduled for last week. After her…" Father Felix paused and then said rather quickly "…her unfortunate heart attack, the visit had to be canceled. But it has since been rescheduled. I was hoping that you would like to take her place."

Mrs. Hopwood stared at Father Felix as though he were speaking Latin.

"In other words," he continued, "you would leave on a Sunday. You would take the train to Washington. You would stay in a hotel with four other teachers from the diocese and you would visit the school on Monday, Tuesday and Wednesday. There is an entire evaluation process, and you would be trained. Of course, the diocese would pay all your expenses and I would get a substitute for your classroom."

"Well, I don't know. My husband, my son—"

"I'm sure they could manage." From what Father Felix knew of Mrs. Hopwood's son, he wasn't sure of that at all. "Maybe it would be good for them. And it would give you some time away, time to stay in a nice hotel, to eat dinner every night in a nice restaurant, to meet nice, new people..."

He could tell she was wavering.

"And from what I understand the hotel is right across the street from a major shopping mall."

Mrs. Hopwood perked up right away. "What kind of shopping mall? What sort of stores?"

"Well, I imagine—" Father Felix was not going to outright lie "—there will be clothing stores and shoe stores and makeup stores." He didn't tell her that the street was a major highway and she would hardly have time to sleep, let alone shop. "And this wouldn't happen until the first week of January, after the Christmas vacation. In the meantime, you'll receive the information from the school to look over in preparation for your visit."

"I guess it would be all right," she said rather reluctantly.

"Splendid. You'll find it a great help for your own work here as chair of our committee." He stood up. "I guess it's time for Morning Prayer."

After she left his office, it occurred to Father Felix that if some of the folders for the Educational Evaluation were indeed lost, that might have serious repercussions. All the work that Miss Pinkerton had already done would have to be repeated all over again, and this was not an ambitious group.

He'd have to be sure Mrs. Hopwood found that folder.

TWENTY-FOUR

"So HE ASKED ME TO go on this observation," Mrs. Hopwood said to Mrs. Johnston as she unwrapped her tuna Subway sandwich in the teachers' room.

Mrs. Johnston had a nasty look on her face. "Why didn't he ask me?"

"I am the Chair—"

"Don't even go there!"

"Well," Mrs. Hopwood said as she tore open her bag of Cheez Doodles, "how could you even manage to get away? It's not as though you could leave the twins. And Father Felix needed someone who could get out of town for a couple of days."

"He could have asked." Mrs. Johnston opened her own roast beef sandwich and bit into it angrily. "But he hates me."

"He does not. And you wouldn't want to go," Mrs. Hopwood said. "*I* don't want to go."

"Then why are you going?" Mrs. Johnston asked in an accusatory tone.

"I have to. I've been in so much trouble lately." Mrs. Hopwood scooted her Cheez Doodles across to Mrs. Johnston, hoping to appease her. "Getting poor Bruce stuck behind the couch and then leaving my class unattended and losing some of the Educational Evaluation folders—"

"That wasn't your fault." Mrs. Johnston grabbed a rather large serving of the Cheese Doodles. "You can't be responsible for a thief."

"Who's a thief?" Mr. Alabaster came floating into the

teachers' room, carrying a paper plate from the cafeteria. He had a large serving of beans and rice and two rolls.

Miss Crossover, Miss Danvers and Mrs. Belgrave came in shortly afterward and took their places at the table. And then Nurse Abby arrived with her one sour apple and one small orange.

"Did you notice that Leonard was out today?" Mrs. Belgrave asked Nurse Abby.

Nurse Abby shook her head. "He's going through such an emotional time lately. His father tried to kill his mother in a drunken rage."

"What these children have to endure." Mrs. Belgrave shook her head sadly.

"I met that mother," Nurse Abby said. "She's quite obese and the truth is I would have liked to have killed her myself. When Leonard got hurt last year in the playground and I bandaged him up, she practically accused me of malpractice. She was extremely hostile."

"Why does everything have to do with being obese?" Mrs. Johnston put down her roast beef hero in a huff.

"I didn't mean anything by it." Nurse Abby took a rather large chunk out of her apple.

"It's obvious that you hate fat people," Mrs. Johnston said.

"I didn't say that," Nurse Abby muttered.

"You inferred it." Mrs. Johnston turned towards Mrs. Hopwood. "Didn't she?"

Mrs. Hopwood knew that to go against Mrs. Johnston in front of a group of teachers was suicide. "Well…"

"I don't think she meant that at all," Miss Danvers, who was slightly overweight herself, said.

Mrs. Johnston glared at her.

"That brings up a rather interesting point." Mr. Alabaster drove his plastic fork into the beans and grimaced. Mrs. Hopwood guessed that he was about to learn why none of the teachers ate cafeteria food. "When is murder justified?"

"Murder is never justified," Miss Danvers said. "Not according to the law."

"Forget the law," Mr. Alabaster said thickly because he was in the middle of chewing.

"It's justified in self-defense." Miss Crossover, looking extremely frustrated, was trying to microwave a bag of popcorn but the microwave kept stopping every few seconds.

"Aside from that," Mr. Alabaster said. "I mean, if someone really gets on your nerves—"

"A lot of people get on my nerves. I'd like to kill them myself," Nurse Abby said as she started to rip open her orange. "And not just fat people."

"Do you remember a couple of years ago," Miss Danvers said suddenly as she popped open her Tupperware container, "there was a case about a woman. I saw it on *Unsolved Mysteries*. She poisoned her husband because he cut up her credit cards. And she escaped too, before they could arrest her."

"Sounds justifiable to me." Mrs. Hopwood wanted her Cheez Doodles back.

"What is with this microwave?" Miss Crossover asked.

"I love your pocketbook." Miss Danvers rubbed the leather on Miss Crossover's tan hobo bag.

Mrs. Hopwood felt a stab of jealousy. No one had said a word about her pink and orange pocketbook.

"It's Prada," Miss Crossover said in a hushed tone.

"Amelia, when you have a moment do you think you can replace the water bottle?" Mrs. Belgrave asked.

"I don't know why that should be my responsibility," Mrs. Johnston said.

"Because you're the strongest?" Mrs. Hopwood guessed.

Mrs. Johnston looked straight at Mr. Alabaster. He shrugged and said that he had a bad shoulder. Mrs. Hopwood guessed he probably got it in a car accident.

"What about Nurse Abby?" Mrs. Johnston asked. "She looks mighty strong."

"I'll do it after I finish my fruit," Nurse Abby said. "Getting back to justified murder, no one has the right to tell you what to do."

"If they're paying the bills, they do." Mr. Alabaster pushed the rice and beans aside and started on his roll. "That woman was what I call a smart murderer. Do you ever think about how many murderers go uncaught because the death doesn't even go down as murder?"

Mrs. Hopwood and Mrs. Johnston stared at one another.

"You mean like Miss Pinkerton?" Mrs. Belgrave whispered.

The door flew open and Father Felix swept in, carrying several slices of pizza. The room grew still. He sat down at the head of the table and eyed the teachers one by one, stopping at Mrs. Johnston, and then at Mrs. Hopwood.

"We don't talk about murder in this school." He stared directly at her, as though she initiated the conversation. Then he turned his glare to Mr. Alabaster. "This is an elementary school, Mr. Alabaster. And it is important that we keep the atmosphere pleasant for all of our students. Trying to scare one another by spreading ridiculous rumors is counterproductive and may eventually filter back to the parents. Now, who saw the rerun of *7th Heaven* last night?"

Mrs. Hopwood thought it most unfair that they couldn't even discuss what they wanted in the teachers' room, on their own time, with one another. And as far as she knew, Father Felix had done nothing about finding the missing cookie money. And her Educational Evaluation report was still missing.

Mrs. Hopwood knew that Mrs. Johnston would be phoning her from home that night.

TWENTY-FIVE

MISS DANVERS WAS walking to her car when she ran into the cookie man. She didn't know his name but she had liked his face. He always seemed as though he was in a good mood, with a bright smile and twinkling eyes. He probably didn't know her name either but he greeted her warmly and said how nice it was to see her.

"Oh, I miss those chocolate chip cookies," she said. Miss Danvers binged frequently on sweets and especially those big fat cookies.

"I miss bringing them in," he said, "and I was hoping that maybe the school had changed its mind. I'd be happy to deliver them again."

Miss Danvers, who was really out of the loop, because she was so worried about her own criminal record, knew nothing of why the cookies had suddenly stopped coming.

"Doesn't Father Felix want them anymore?" she asked rather innocently.

"Guess not." He shrugged. "I got a call from Ms. Morningstar saying that the school decided against them. Do you know why?"

She shook her head. "But I could find out," she said quickly. "Father Felix is not here. He had to leave early. He had a doctor's appointment for his allergies. But I could talk to him tomorrow and tell him to give you a call."

"I'd appreciate that, ma'am, I really would. It would be worth a dozen cookies to you."

He handed Miss Danvers his card and drove away in a van labeled "Curtis Cookies." Miss Danvers stood for several moments in the street, looking at his card, decorated with a large cookie, when the front door of the school slammed shut.

It was Mrs. Johnston and she was marching towards her car, carrying quite a lot of books.

Miss Danvers stopped her and asked, "Do you know why the cookies stopped coming?"

TWENTY-SIX

MRS. JOHNSTON WAS IN Father Felix's office at seven-thirty the following morning, dragging Mrs. Hopwood, who was walking several paces behind her.

Father Felix had barely gotten in himself. He had just snapped open his coffee cup and was removing the top from the aluminum pan, so he could bite into his cheese omelet and enjoy his home fries, when the ladies came marching into his office without so much as a good morning, or is this a good time, or even a simple knock.

"We have proof." Mrs. Johnston always began her conversations somewhere in the middle, as though she expected people to be on the same wavelength. He hoped that it wasn't proof that someone had offended her. The medicine from his allergies was kicking in and he was feeling drowsy and much too old for all this nonsense.

He took a rather large gulp of his coffee to fortify him for what was ahead.

"Miss Danvers ran into the cookie man after school," Mrs. Johnston said. "And do you know what he told her?"

Father Felix shook his head. In the meantime, Mrs. Hopwood was looking very uncomfortable, as though she would have loved to sit down. Her eyes were scanning the room for empty chairs, but all of the seats were covered with useless papers. It was one of the ways Father Felix kept people out of his office, although it didn't work very well.

"He said that Ms. Morningstar called him and canceled the contract for our school. She told him that his cookies were no longer necessary."

Father Felix was too stunned by this news to answer.

"If you don't believe me, call in Miss Danvers. She's in her classroom right now."

"That won't be necessary." The omelet tasted like rubber and he distinctly told them cheddar and they had given him Swiss and why was everything such a battle? "I will speak to Ms. Morningstar this morning. I will get this straightened out. I promise."

"You said that days ago!" Mrs. Johnston protested. "I know you think that I'm taking too much of an interest in this cookie matter, but they are my eighth graders and I'm the one who will have to organize the class trip and how will I do that without money, I'd like to know." She folded her arms across her chest.

"I will handle it," he shouted and almost caught a soggy home fry in his throat.

Mrs. Johnston scowled and then walked out of the office, pushing Mrs. Hopwood ahead.

Father Felix heard her mutter to Mrs. Hopwood, "You were a lot of help."

He was going to have to deal with this, no doubt about it. If Ms. Morningstar had been caught stealing, he'd have to get rid of her, replace her with another secretary, which wouldn't be easy to find. Ms. Morningstar had been the school secretary for ten years. She'd won the respect of the parents and guardians (not an easy thing to do—Father Felix himself hadn't managed it). She could put her finger on a missing document faster than a pre-K student could scoot down the hall in a game of tag. She knew the history of St. Polycarp and former pupils often came back to the building just to visit her.

In all the time that Ms. Morningstar had been school secretary, there wasn't a blemish on her record. He couldn't have written something negative in her file, even if he wanted to. For her to start stealing didn't make sense.

But he had overheard her on the phone. Evidently, she was having trouble with credit card companies. Maybe taking the few dollars the school had allotted for cookie money seemed like a temporary solution to her.

Father Felix rose and started down for Morning Prayer. He would deal with it later in the day. And in the meantime, he would pray to St. Anthony that somehow, somewhere, the money would be found.

"I DIDN'T DO IT," Ms. Morningstar, mortified, was close to tears as she sat in the chair across from him. He had cleared the papers and debris because he wasn't about to accuse her of being a thief while she was standing up.

She might faint.

"It's only that—"

"I didn't do it!" she protested louder, and Father Felix was afraid that someone would overhear their conversation. Someone like Mrs. Johnston, who was in the office, running off copies, and Father Felix was guessing that she had one ear towards the door. "The next thing you know," Ms. Morningstar continued frantically, "you'll accuse me of murdering Miss Pinkerton!"

"No one said anything about murder." Father Felix played with a paper clip, glancing quickly at Ms. Morningstar's tearing eyes. "One of the teachers ran into the cookie man—"

"You don't think I know who that teacher was!" Ms. Morningstar jumped up.

"It wasn't me!" Amelia Johnston yelled from the other side of the door.

Father Felix leaped out of his chair, threw open the door and confronted Mrs. Johnston, who was standing there with a cup of coffee in one hand, and assorted papers in the other. "This is a private conversation," he said quietly. "I am trying to solve this problem. I will have better luck—"

Mrs. Johnston walked away but not before staring darkly at Ms. Morningstar, who stuck her tongue out at Mrs. Johnston.

"Father, I'm going to the store." Nurse Abby came out of her cubicle. "Would you like a banana?"

"No and I would prefer that you didn't leave the school right now. I'm having a meeting with Ms. Morningstar and I need you to listen for the phones, just for a few moments. Do you mind?"

Nurse Abby nodded. "Oh, I see you've picked up your office. All those papers…"

Father Felix quietly closed the door on her dumbstruck face, sank down in his chair, and began again.

"The teacher in question is not Mrs. Johnston. The cookie man told this teacher that you called and canceled the cookie contract. I have to admit I don't know what to think. I can't imagine you doing something like that, but the cookie man has no reason to lie. Does he?"

"Did it occur to you—" Ms. Morningstar, in spite of her sniffling, leaned forward in a most aggressive manner "—that maybe someone *did* call the cookie man, and maybe someone *did* cancel the contract, but maybe that someone wasn't me? The cookie man doesn't know my voice."

Father Felix was ashamed that he had not considered that possibility. But he was fast to think of a rebuttal. "I guess the question is why would anyone steal the cookie money? And that, of course, points to motive. Now—" he had completely undone the paper clip, it was straight as an arrow "—some of us have overheard you talking on the phone—"

"To credit card companies." Ms. Morningstar collapsed into her seat once again. "Do you know why?"

"Well." It was considerably harder to bend the paper clip to its original shape than it had been to straighten it in the first place. "I just assumed—"

"You just assumed?" she mocked him. "A man of the cloth and you just assumed?"

Before Father Felix had a chance to defend himself, Ms. Morningstar continued with her tirade. "I don't know how it happened but someone got hold of my credit card numbers.

They didn't take the actual cards. I would have missed them, if they had. But they got the information and they have been charging up a storm. Buying things I never would have bought for myself, shoes, coats, handbags, and having the merchandise sent to a PO Box. It has been a nightmare. Look at me, Father Felix." Father Felix looked up from the paper clip. "Do I look like someone who has a lot of nice clothes? Do I even look like someone who *wants* a lot of nice clothes?"

Father Felix thought it best not to comment, but since he had known Ms. Morningstar, he had never seen her in anything but neutral colored slacks, turtlenecks in the winter and T-shirts in the spring.

"I'm not like Mrs. Hopwood, who goes around bragging that in 180 days she hasn't repeated an outfit twice, or Miss Crossover with her designer handbags, although I think they're probably knockoffs, or Mrs. Johnston who refuses to put anything but Lands End clothing on the back of her twins."

"Well." Father Felix had given up on the paper clip.

"Now I am not saying that the person who has helped themselves to my credit cards is the same person who stole the cookie money and murdered poor Mildred Pinkerton—"

"Miss Pinkerton was not murdered!" Father Felix said louder than he had intended. "Listen." He assumed a softer tone. "You yourself know how vicious rumors can spread. So I think you can sympathize—"

"My uncle Roy is a policeman," Ms. Morningstar interrupted. "I think that we should have him come to the school and investigate the matter. He could call all the staff into a room, the way they do on those late night television movies, and ask questions—"

"I don't think that will be necessary, Ms. Morningstar."

"Well, it's fine for you to say." Ms. Morningstar sniffled. "It's not your reputation that's being clouded."

Father Felix thought it rather fruitless to say that his reputation was already quite muddied. "I promise you, I will get to the heart of this matter. In the meantime, I'd like to ask you not to repeat any of this conversation."

Ms. Morningstar stood, clutching her tissues. She opened the door and encountered Mrs. Hopwood and Miss Danvers and Nurse Abby and Miss Crossover and Mrs. Belgrave.

"Like everyone doesn't already know," Ms. Morningstar muttered.

Father Felix rose, went over to the door and slammed it on their startled faces.

One thing was for certain. This was not the end of the matter, not by a long shot.

TWENTY-SEVEN

"HE DOESN'T THINK THAT Ms. Morningstar did it." Mrs. Hopwood was seated in Mrs. Johnston's class for lunchtime period. The only reason they were allowed to eat by themselves was because they were supposed to be working on the Educational Evaluation. "I guess she cried a lot."

"That would get to him." Mrs. Johnston had an enormous piece of devil's food cake and a cup of coffee. It was her entire lunch and she was hoping that Mrs. Hopwood didn't think she was going to get a taste. Mrs. Johnston would sooner buy another slice of cake for someone than share her own.

"Well, she did make the point—" Mrs. Hopwood was chewing her peanut butter and jelly sandwich with distaste "—that she's not the sort of person who likes to buy a lot of fancy clothes."

"So?" Mrs. Johnston said with great hostility, because she did not want to rush eating her cake. "Just because someone doesn't look like they have money doesn't mean that they're not in debt. They could live in a palace—"

"I think she lives in a walk-up."

"They could be driving a fancy car."

"I think she takes the bus."

"She could be a compulsive gambler and owe money to the Mafia or she could be supporting a sick father—"

"I think he died."

"Or—" Mrs. Johnston ate the frosting first, spreading it on her tongue "—she could have a boyfriend in trouble with the law and she needs bail money."

"I think she and Jonathan broke up."

"Probably because he was in so much debt and she was tired of covering for him! And why—" Mrs. Johnston took a big hunk of cake "—do you insist on defending her?"

"I feel sorry for her. And I just don't know if she did it." Mrs. Hopwood shrugged.

"Well, someone stole that cookie money."

Mrs. Hopwood nodded in agreement and then took out four marshmallow cookies, much to the relief of Mrs. Johnston. "You better show me the papers you took from Miss Pinkerton's closet. That way we can figure out what's missing and go from there."

Mrs. Johnston rose, and, keeping her eye on her chocolate cake, went over to her schoolbag and pulled out a folder. "I'd be lying to you—" she handed them to Mrs. Hopwood "—if I told you that I actually looked through them. I've been dragging them back and forth for the last couple of nights, thinking I'd read them at home but by the time I get the twins settled, I can barely find the way to my own bed. And—" she resumed eating her cake "—I'm not about to leave them in my classroom, not after what happened to your papers."

Mrs. Hopwood held her cookies in one hand and the papers in another. "All right," she said as she chewed. "I know I had the financial records, which are going to be a pain in the neck to replace. Although, Father Felix has some of those figures. I guess I'm going to have to call the accountant to get the others."

"I can see why she might want those papers." Mrs. Johnston didn't bother to say which *she* she was referring to.

"You have the sections on the curriculum…"

"Which I'm sure are fascinating," Mrs. Johnston said sarcastically.

"I had the part on the building and some of the faculty stuff, although you have…" Suddenly Mrs. Hopwood stopped talking and stared down at the piece of paper in front of her, a puzzled expression on her face.

Mrs. Johnston abandoned the last of her cake and peered

over Mrs. Hopwood's shoulder. On a piece of paper, there was a list of the faculty at St. Polycarp, their names and their addresses. And then on the top of the paper, someone, probably Miss Pinkerton, Mrs. Johnston surmised, had written in red pen: *Someone is not who they appear to be.*

Mrs. Johnston and Mrs. Hopwood stared at each other for several seconds before Mrs. Hopwood spoke. "There's a grammar error here."

"You're kidding. Right?"

Mrs. Hopwood shook her head. "*Someone* is singular, meaning one person. *They* is plural. It doesn't match."

"Who cares?" Mrs. Johnston had finished her cake and could now turn all of her attention to the strange matter in front of her.

"Don't you see? If Miss Pinkerton had followed the rules of grammar—"

"She was a math teacher!"

"She would have written either *he* or *she*," Mrs. Hopwood explained. "And then we would know if this someone was male or female."

Mrs. Johnston looked down at the list. "There are only two men. Father Felix and Mr. Ironweed."

"And it could very well be one of those two."

"Or anybody at all," Mrs. Johnston said thoughtfully. She grabbed a piece of paper and began to make a list.

Miss Pinkerton has a heart attack.
A bottle of lethal pills are hidden and then found.

"What are you doing?" Mrs. Hopwood stretched her neck.

Miss Pinkerton suspects that the cookie money has been stolen.
Educational Evaluation papers are missing.
Miss Pinkerton suspects someone is not who they

(Mrs. Johnston crossed out *they* and substituted *he/she*) *appear to be.*

"I hope you don't teach handwriting," Mrs. Hopwood said.

Mrs. Johnston hissed. "I'm making a list of reasons why Miss Pinkerton might have been murdered."

"And we're going to give this list to Father Felix?" Mrs. Hopwood said in a shaky voice, but Mrs. Johnston could not tell if Mrs. Hopwood's voice was shaky because she had stuffed an entire cookie in her mouth or because she was fearful of involving the principal.

"Certainly not," Mrs. Johnston said. "He's incompetent. At least as a detective. He's taking the attitude that he doesn't want to know, which is very unfair to poor Mildred Pinkerton. This is between you and I."

"You and me," Mrs. Hopwood corrected.

Mrs. Johnston stood up. "We're going to solve this on our own."

"Can we do that?" Mrs. Hopwood was looking at the clock, something she did quite often, because for some strange reason Mrs. Hopwood always seemed to be in a rush, even when she had noplace in particular to go. "And besides, won't it be kind of dangerous? I mean, if there is a killer and he thinks that we think—"

"What are you trying to say?" Mrs. Johnston asked before Mrs. Hopwood could escape into the corridor. "That you're going to let a murderer go unpunished because you're fearful?"

"Well...yes," Mrs. Hopwood said in a feeble mutter.

"Then consider this," Mrs. Johnston, who liked to think of herself as strong, powerful, and resolute, continued, "you are taking Miss Pinkerton's place as chair of the Educational Evaluation. That's a well-known fact. And if Miss Pinkerton did stumble upon something because of her position, the murderer may believe that you might stumble upon the same thing. So you're not as safe as you think you are."

Mrs. Johnston watched as the blood drained from Mrs. Hopwood's face. "I don't think that's very nice," she said.

"I am not interested in being very nice," Mrs. Johnston said. "I'm interested in saving your life."

"Yeah, right." Mrs. Hopwood was gone in a flash, probably back to the safety of her second grade class.

Mrs. Johnston would have to call her tonight and remind her not to eat or drink anything in the teachers' room.

TWENTY-EIGHT

MRS. HOPWOOD RETURNED to her classroom, quite shaken. She sank down on her desk chair and drew a deep breath. She knew her friend Amelia Johnston and she knew that Mrs. Johnston tended to exaggerate situations. But if there was any chance…

She opened the bottom desk drawer and underneath the progress reports and the thematic units she reached for the pink vial of pills. She examined it carefully and thought about what she should do with it. Maybe give it to Amelia Johnston. Let her be the one in danger.

"Julia." Miss Danvers entered the room. "I was wondering if you could do me a favor."

Mrs. Hopwood didn't feel like doing anyone a favor right now.

"Could you switch recess duty with me tomorrow? I have a doctor's appointment—" Miss Danvers stopped midsentence. "Where did you get that bottle?" she asked.

From her tone of voice, Mrs. Hopwood suspected something was very wrong. "I found it behind the couch in the teachers' room."

"Those are heart pills."

"Are they yours?" Mrs. Hopwood asked.

"No, they belong to Myrtle. She's been looking all over for them. They're the second vial—"

"Who's Myrtle?"

Miss Danvers seemed irritated, as though Mrs. Hopwood had asked a stupid question. "She's one of the cafeteria ladies and we all know that they aren't really paid well and medication is expensive."

"Oh." Mrs. Hopwood could think of nothing else to say.

"Are you going to return them?" Miss Danvers asked.

"Well, of course I'm going to return them."

"It's just that she lost them a while ago…" It seemed to Mrs. Hopwood that Miss Danvers was going on in a rather accusatory manner, which she didn't appreciate. "And without her medication…"

"I know."

"I could give them to her now," Miss Danvers offered.

Mrs. Hopwood glanced at the clock. It was time to pick up her class from lunch and she had to go to the cafeteria anyway. "I'll hand them to Myrtle myself and apologize for keeping them."

Miss Danvers stared at Mrs. Hopwood as though she expected more of an explanation but none would be forthcoming. Mrs. Hopwood had already decided that she had to be very careful in whom she confided. She didn't know Miss Danvers that well and, after reading the statement Miss Pinkerton wrote, Mrs. Hopwood was beginning to wonder if she knew anyone at all.

"So can you do it?" Miss Danvers asked. "Switch lunch duties with me?"

Mrs. Hopwood hated lunch duty, pure and simple. It consisted of standing in the yard, freezing to death, while children ran around knocking you down or hitting you on the head with a basketball. Then when you were finally permitted to go inside, it was up to the teacher on duty to keep order in the cafeteria or at the very least to prevent the children from injuring one another with plastic forks. Or hurting you.

But it really didn't matter to Mrs. Hopwood if she did it on Wednesday or Thursday so she agreed to switch.

When Mrs. Hopwood went down to the cafeteria to the group of screaming children, she realized that she didn't even know who Myrtle was. She peeked into the kitchen where several women were scrubbing pots and pans in a rather lack-luster manner. "Do you need anything, Mrs. Hopwood?" a rather obese lady with a pretty apron asked.

"Yes, I need to speak with Myrtle."

"I'm Myrtle." The woman frowned.

Mrs. Hopwood took out the bottle of pills which she had placed into her neon yellow jumper and Myrtle's scowl faded and changed to a bright smile. "Oh, thank you, thank you! Thank you, St. Anthony." She grabbed the pills away from Mrs. Hopwood. "Where did you find them?"

"They were behind the couch in the teachers' room."

"You mean in the office?"

"No, the teachers' room." The woman wasn't understanding, so Mrs. Hopwood repeated "the teachers' room" in a louder tone of voice.

"Please." Myrtle put her hands over her ears. "I'm not deaf."

"Do you know the teachers' room on the third floor?"

Myrtle shook her head.

"Were you ever there?"

Myrtle ignored the question. "Did you find my other bottle of pills?"

The way Mrs. Hopwood's heart was thumping, she thought that she might need those pills herself. "You're missing another bottle of pills?"

"They were stolen, just like these. Only my other pills, they were in my makeup bag with my Amber Rose lipstick and my Estée Lauder compact, which had my initials engraved on it, MMM, Myrtle Maria Miller. I put my makeup bag down for two minutes in the ladies' room, I go into the cubicle, I come out and it's gone."

"Are you sure?"

The frown was back. "I am sure. I told Miss Danvers last week." Myrtle opened the bottle. "Why, there are only two pills left," she said. "When I lost them I had just gotten the prescription filled. There should be at least a dozen pills in here. What happened to the rest of them?"

Mrs. Hopwood didn't dare say what she suspected. They went into Miss Pinkerton's coffee.

"Oh, Mrs. Hopwood," Miss Crossover's high pitched voice beckoned, "do you want to take your class up now? Because I have a prep and I can't keep them—"

"I'm coming."

"Mrs. Hopwood, are we going to work on our Halloween projects today?"

"Mrs. Hopwood, how many days till fun day?"

"Mrs. Hopwood, can we have a spelling bee?"

"Mrs. Hopwood, Linda Lou said my mother eats corn-flakes for dinner!"

"Mrs. Hopwood, Damien just pulled my braids, and he did it real hard."

"Because you stepped on my foot."

"Mrs. Hopwood, you look like you're going to throw up."

Mrs. Hopwood felt as if she was going to throw up. Another bottle of pills was missing, which just might mean that the murderer planned to strike again.

And this time she might be the victim.

TWENTY-NINE

FATHER FELIX WAS TALKING to his brother on the phone in his office about the possibility of finding a parish in Arizona when Ms. Morningstar knocked on the door.

"Sister Augusta is on line one," she whispered ominously.

"I've got to call you back." He hung up on his brother before his brother could utter a word of protest.

Sister Augusta was the superintendent. She was the most powerful woman in the diocese, the most powerful person in the state when it came to Catholic education. If she was calling him personally, that was not a good sign.

"Did she say what she wants?"

Ms. Morningstar shook her head. "Should I ask?"

"I think not."

It could be anything, Father Felix told himself, but one thing was for certain. It was something important.

"Good morning, Sister," Father Felix said with an exuberance he didn't feel.

"Good morning to you, Father. How are things at St. Polycarp?"

"Oh, they're coming along."

"Yes, well, I'm hearing some very unsettling rumors."

"People like to talk," was the only sensible thing Father Felix could utter.

"I suppose that's true. But you are applying for Educational Evaluation so we want to make sure that everything is on the up and up."

Father Felix didn't know what she meant by that statement. So he said nothing.

"I'll be coming to see for myself."

Father Felix felt as though he was trapped in a rather bad dream.

"Today is Thursday. How about Monday? Would that be a good day?"

Father Felix knew that there would never be a good day. Not Monday or Tuesday or the rest of the week or the rest of his term at St. Polycarp. But he could hardly say that to the superintendent. She had the right to visit the school. She had the right to yank the school out from under him.

"Monday would be fine." His voice came out rather raspy and thick.

"I'll see you then." The connection was broken before he had the chance to say goodbye.

What did she want? Would she look around? Would she want to talk to some of the teachers? Some of the students? Some of the parents? Sit in on the classes?

He reached for the phone and pressed the speaker button. "This is an announcement for all teachers. There will be an emergency meeting after school today at three o'clock."

A collective groan erupted.

"It won't last more than fifteen minutes but it is imperative that every faculty member attend."

He had to stress at the meeting how important it was that the entire staff be upbeat and optimistic. That they gave the impression that everything was under control at St. Polycarp, from class management, to enforcing the standards, to increasing enrollment.

And he had to clean out his office.

MISS CROSSOVER WALKED IN late, which he found very annoying. He didn't want to start the meeting without her. She gave a quick little smile as she slid into a seat.

"All right, I promised you that the meeting would be brief, and I will keep it short. I just received a call from the superintendent's office." All of the teachers leaned forward. "Sister Augusta has decided to pay us a visit."

"What for?" Mrs. Belgrave had her hand in a bag of taco chips.

"She just wants to make sure that everything here is—" he paused and then added, because he could think of no other way to put it "—everything is going well."

By the expression on Mrs. Johnston's face, it was obvious that she didn't think that everything was going well. "When is Sister Augusta coming?" she asked.

"Monday."

"Monday?" Mrs. Hopwood gasped.

"Monday?" Miss Danvers repeated.

"That's right, Monday. Everyone listen carefully." He stared at Mrs. Belgrave, who was crunching the bag. "I want you all to plan a very special lesson for Monday, in case Sister should drop in on your classrooms, lessons that involve active learning. Any tests you might have planned cannot take place when Sister is present. Also, I want you to look over your classroom and make sure that your bulletin boards are up to date and the students' works are prominently displayed. Now, Sister may want to speak to you individually, and if she does, you are to keep the conversation on neutral grounds. Any complaints or concerns you might have are to be addressed to me personally. The repercussions may be great to St. Polycarp if we lead Sister Augusta to believe that the school is not catering to the best interest of our pupils." Father Felix paused. He was rather pleased with his speech and thought it got right to the heart of the matter.

"Does this have anything to do with the murder of poor Mildred Pinkerton?" Mrs. Hopwood asked.

"Does this have anything to do with the missing cookie money?" Mrs. Johnston questioned.

"Or Bruce Brewer almost being decapitated by the sofa in the teachers' room?" Mrs. Belgrave was back to eating her taco chips but not before her face flushed when Mrs. Hopwood glared at her.

"Will she be looking at our work for the Educational Evaluation?" Miss Danvers asked stiffly.

"I have no reason to believe that this is anything but a routine visit," Father Felix snapped. "But it's just that kind of loose talk that can stir up all sorts of trouble and cause Sister Augusta to think badly of this school!"

The teachers were quiet.

"Are there any intelligent questions?" he asked. He waited for a half a second. "All right, then. I'm counting on all of you."

He left the room first and didn't miss the muttering behind him. He could plainly hear Mrs. Johnston complaining about something. And, as usual, stirring up the rest of the teachers.

Maybe he could have a talk with her, try to get her to realize how important it was that the school stay free of any scandal. But right now, he had to clean his office.

Ms. Morningstar had already left for the evening. She usually stayed a little later but since the cookie incident, she did exactly what she was supposed to do and not one bit more. Well, he could hardly blame her for not wanting to stick around in a place where everyone thought she was a thief.

He looked at the mountain of papers littering his desk, his chairs, his floor. *This is going to take hours,* he thought. He pulled the wastepaper basket towards him and got started.

Fifteen minutes later, he found the cookie money.

THIRTY

THEY WERE ALL BUSY at a meeting downstairs when Mr. Ironweed was busy on the third floor.

He stopped first in Bonnie Crossover's classroom and went into her desk. There was nothing of any interest there. Father Felix was still speaking when Mr. Ironweed stood on one of the student's chairs, hoping it didn't cave in. He reached for the ceiling, creating a small hole in the already decrepit tile. Then he went about his business, from classroom to classroom, emptying the trash.

He was wondering how soon it would be before it started to rain, when he found something interesting in one of the wastepaper baskets. A big, fat folder labeled Educational Evaluation. Maybe someone threw it away by accident. Maybe he could pretend to find it and be a hero in Miss Crossover's eyes.

He took the folder downstairs to the boiler room and stuffed it into his desk drawer.

Then he forgot all about it.

THIRTY-ONE

"I THINK HE DID IT."

Mrs. Hopwood had just walked in the door. She had a slight headache and the only reason she had answered the phone in the first place was because she thought it might be Alex, explaining why he wasn't home from school yet.

"Who did what?" she asked in a weary voice as she reached for the bottle of Chablis.

"You know how Miss Pinkerton wrote that someone was not who they appear to be?"

Mrs. Hopwood poured herself a half a glass and took a rather large sip, which prevented her from answering.

"Do you remember?"

"Of course I remember," Mrs. Hopwood answered irritably. "I could hardly forget. Especially since you convinced me that I was the killer's next target."

"Well, I figured who Miss Pinkerton was referring to."

Mrs. Hopwood decided that she best sit down for this news.

"It's Father Felix."

"What?" Mrs. Hopwood hopped up again, almost spilling her wine in the process.

"I am telling you it's Father Felix, and I'm surprised that we didn't come to that conclusion some time ago. It is so obvious."

"It is?"

"Of course. All the clues point his way. For one thing, how do we even know that he's a priest?"

"Well, he does say Mass—"

"Any fool with a Missal can recite words. It's not hard. And he's always talking about moving to Arizona. Did you ever know a priest who wanted to move to Arizona?"

"I never knew anyone who wanted to move to Arizona." Mrs. Hopwood gulped her wine.

"Well, there you are. You know the kind of people who want to move to Arizona? People who are running away from something."

"I just don't think—" the front door slammed and Alex came barreling in. Mrs. Hopwood would ask him later where he had been "—that the diocese would have sent us a serial killer disguised as a priest."

"The diocese doesn't know!" Mrs. Johnston insisted. "Because Father Felix has fooled them also."

"It sounds rather far-fetched." Alex had gone into his room and was now blasting the stereo.

"Oh, does it? Then consider this. Miss Pinkerton had some very tangible concerns. She was worried about the cookie money and from the note we found she suspected that someone in the school had lied about his identity."

"Or credentials."

Mrs. Johnston was quiet. For a moment. "Don't you think that the normal thing for Miss Pinkerton to do would be to go to Father Felix and tell him what was bothering her?"

"Well, maybe she did and…" Mrs. Hopwood was finding it hard to concentrate with that monotonous beat in the background. "Well, maybe she did."

"She did not. And do you know why she did not? Because she couldn't confide in Father Felix. He was the main suspect. Doesn't it sound suspicious that he expects us all to cover this up? Any other principal would be afraid for the staff, afraid for the students, if they thought a killer was roaming the halls. Not Father Felix. He's in complete denial. Someone in the school is a thief. He is making no effort to find out who that person is. Because he already knows. And he wants no talk of poor Mildred Pinkerton's passing because he's afraid that if you and I dig deep enough, we're going to uncover the truth. And…" Thankfully, Mrs. Johnston finally paused for breath, "I think he stole your Educational Evaluation. He could have done it when you were out of the class, and he was pretending to yell at the students. And I believe that he also took Myrtle's pills. He always gets in early. He could have easily…" Mrs. Johnston paused again. "What is that awful racket in the background?"

"My son is playing his stereo."

"Oh, it's really hard to talk with all that noise."

"Speaking of noise, where are the twins?" The half a glass of wine had definitely mellowed her.

"The housekeeper took them to the park. I wish she'd keep them out until bedtime, but I suppose the woman has to go home sooner or later. I'm telling you, I'm right about Father Felix. And I intend to have a discussion with Sister Augusta on Monday."

Mrs. Hopwood did not think that was a wise decision and she told Mrs. Johnston so. "If you're wrong about Father Felix and you go and blab to Sister Augusta, he's going to be very angry and is sure to fire you. And if you're right and blab to Sister Augusta, he's going to be very angry and is sure to kill you. It's a lose-lose situation."

"Well, I'm not going to go into great detail with Sister Augusta. I just want some information on his background. Oh God, here they come. I can hear them screeching. In the meantime, if I were you, I would not eat or drink anything that Father Felix gives you. You know how now and then he hands out those horrid cookies and candies he claims come from benefactors? Politely refuse. Don't drink coffee or bottled water around him or leave your beverages unattended. Not even to go to the bathroom. And don't stay in a deserted building with him. I gotta go."

Mrs. Johnston promptly hung up the phone. Mrs. Hopwood knew that her friend tended to exaggerate but still quite a bit had happened at St. Polycarp this year and it was barely the end of October.

Miss Pinkerton had definitely stumbled upon some damaging information as the head of the Educational Evaluation Committee. And now Miss Pinkerton was dead. Who knew who was next?

Mrs. Hopwood decided from now on she was going to keep a very low profile. She went into her closet and reached for her navy suit.

THIRTY-TWO

MRS. JOHNSTON WAS IN the middle of explaining the difference between plot and theme when two third graders came prancing into her classroom and handed her a note. "This is from Father Felix," the girl with two missing teeth and three pigtails announced.

Mrs. Johnston opened the note. *I would like to see you during your music prep.*

"Tell him all right," she said hastily.

"What does he want?" Adam asked.

"Are you in trouble?" Lori wondered.

"Are we in trouble?" Matthew raised his hand.

"I don't have to answer these questions," Mrs. Johnston said. "Everyone start reading the next short story and then tell me what the theme is."

The class released a giant grunt which Mrs. Johnston chose to ignore. Instead, she sat down (although Father Felix did not encourage his teachers to sit, he also wasn't planning to come to the third floor or he wouldn't have sent the girls up with the note). Ordinarily, Mrs. Johnston would be spitting mad. Preps were meant for preparation, grading papers, running off tests, filling out student charts, not sitting in the principal's office, listening to a lecture.

But today she was very curious as to what Father Felix had to say for himself. Was it possible he would slip and give her more ammunition? The timing was perfect because of Sister Augusta's visit.

And Sister Augusta must have her own suspicions or why would she be coming to St. Polycarp? Unfortunately, Mrs.

Hopwood was not interested in helping Mrs. Johnston but then again...

When all was said and done, how well did Mrs. Johnston really know Mrs. Hopwood? She claimed that her husband's business was about to go bust. But that didn't prevent her from dressing to the nines every day.

Mrs. Johnston couldn't help but wonder where Mrs. Hopwood was getting the extra money for her shoes and handbags.

"PLEASE HAVE A SEAT," Father Felix said when Mrs. Johnston entered his office.

The first thing that Mrs. Johnston noticed was how clean and organized everything was, as though Father Felix had finally put away all of his papers.

As though he had something to hide.

The second thing she noticed was that he had closed the door behind them. She reminded herself that they were not alone. Ms. Morningstar was on the other side of that door, although just last week she had accused Ms. Morningstar of being a thief.

Well, being a thief was better than being a murderer.

Mrs. Johnston perched at the edge of her chair.

"Would you like a Snapple?" Father Felix brought out a glass bottle of peach iced tea, Mrs. Johnston's favorite. She could not decide whether or not it had been opened.

"No, thank you," she said politely.

"How about some candy corn?"

The candy was in a Halloween bowl shaped like a ghost. Anything could have been sprinkled on it.

"No, thank you."

"I have a favor to ask you."

Mrs. Johnston didn't reply.

"Miss Pinkerton, as we both know, was the senior teacher because she had been here for so long. But she kept to herself quite a bit and I have a feeling that, although the staff respected her, they didn't particularly like her."

Mrs. Johnston didn't think it would be a good idea to speak ill of the dead.

"On the other hand you have many friends among the faculty. For instance, Mrs. Hopwood admires and looks up to you. As does Miss Danvers, and Miss Crossover, and Mrs. Belgrave."

He was flattering her. But why?

"I'm going to take you into my confidence."

Mrs. Johnston immediately sat up tall. This was exactly what she was waiting for.

He reached into his drawer. For one silly second Mrs. Johnston thought he might be taking out a gun. She clutched the arms of her chair, preparing to duck. But instead Father Felix held a manila envelope.

"I found this among my papers when I was cleaning my office." He handed it to her.

She took it from him gingerly. On the front someone had printed *I'm sorry* and then *Cookie Money*. She opened the envelope and saw four one hundred dollar bills, and seven tens, five ones and assorted change. "I don't understand," she said, thoroughly confused. "How long was this in your office?"

Father Felix shrugged. "I really couldn't say. Obviously, someone took the money and then gave it back. Weeks could have passed and I just didn't notice it."

Mrs. Johnston had never heard of such a flimsy story in her entire life. She was sure that Father Felix had fabricated the note just so she would stop asking questions. But she was far from finished. She wasn't about to tell him that. She merely nodded.

"So you see," he smiled and said in a rather cagey voice, "the entire matter has been cleared up."

Except who took the money and gave it back? And who

was the woman who called and canceled the contract? And why did she do such a thing?

Mrs. Johnston stood up and handed the envelope back. "I'm glad," she said.

"I'm not finished," Father Felix said.

She slumped back down.

"I want this insanity to end. This talk of missing cookie money and the passing of poor Mildred Pinkerton, the attempt to make something out of nothing. What we need to do as a school is to come together, to get our Educational Evaluation, to plump up the enrollment, to raise our scores in the state tests, to really make a difference."

Mrs. Johnston wondered why she was hearing a speech from Father Felix which was really meant for the multitudes.

"I know, even though you haven't come to me directly, you have not given up on solving this supposed mystery. I am begging you to let it rest, to be the voice of reason for the other teachers, the teachers who aren't as bright, who are easily influenced by such a powerful person as yourself. You are a natural born leader, Mrs. Johnston. You have more influence over the staff than I do. You can use your position to stir up trouble and do irreparable damage to the school or you can lead St. Polycarp to new heights. That's your decision."

As Mrs. Johnston sat there and listened to the shameless flattery, it occurred to her that a weaker person might succumb. Actually, she herself might have easily been taken in. If she hadn't suspected that Father Felix was a cold-blooded murderer. A killer who realized how close he was to being caught and wanted to keep her off track.

"I hear what you're saying, Father." She stood up, hoping that he wouldn't pull her down again. "You make quite a bit of sense. And let me tell you—" and this part was the truth "—I am utterly devoted to St. Polycarp. I would never do anything to hurt the school."

He nodded at her, obviously satisfied with the outcome.

But Mrs. Johnston wasn't the least bit satisfied with the

outcome. And, as she left his office, she even managed to flash a brief smile at Ms. Morningstar, who did not return her grin. (After all Mrs. Johnston had accused Ms. Morningstar unfairly.)

From the tone of Father Felix's conversation, it was very clear to Mrs. Johnston that someone had gone to him and told him that she intended to look into the matter. Someone had confided that, as far as Mrs. Johnston was concerned, he was a suspect.

Mrs. Johnston picked her children up from the music room and they hummed a tune all the way up the stairs (which drove her crazy). She gave them a writing assignment in retaliation and then she wrote a brief note to Mrs. Hopwood. She asked Thalia to bring it down to the second grade.

The note was chilling and straight to the point. It read, *You told.*

THIRTY-THREE

MISS DANVERS WAS SEETHING. Nurse Abby had offered to come into her class to talk to her children about health and Miss Danvers readily agreed because, after all, a break was a break.

When Nurse Abby arrived first thing after lunch, carrying a shopping bag with posters and hand-outs, Miss Danvers made a beeline for the store for a cup of coffee. (She didn't really feel good about drinking coffee in the teachers' room, after what happened to poor Mildred Pinkerton.) Fifteen minutes later, she came back with a cup of coffee and a rather large chocolate chip muffin (which she hadn't paid for). She really didn't know if leaving Nurse Abby alone with her children was allowed because, after all, Nurse Abby was a nurse, not a teacher.

So Miss Danvers came back to the classroom, sat in the back, unwrapped her muffin, undid the top of her French vanilla coffee, and proceeded to listen.

The lecture was on fat people.

Now since Miss Danvers was hardly model thin, and since Miss Danvers was stuffing herself with a calorie laden muffin, she took great offense at the presentation.

"The fact of the matter is," Nurse Abby said in a monotone voice, "that overweight children become overweight adults. Children who are obese tend to have a higher risk of heart problems, joint problems, breathing problems and social problems."

Nurse Abby seemed to be staring straight at Dior Dunking,

a rather rotund girl who sat in the first row. Dior looked as though she was about to burst into tears at any moment.

"Do you want to be a fat adult?" Nurse Abby asked the class and the class answered in unison, "No, Nurse Abby."

"Then regardless of what your parents might give you to eat or the cafeteria might serve, you have to take some responsibility. I've seen the snacks that the fifth graders bring in. Fruit Roll-Ups, which are full of carbohydrates, taco chips, which are full of fat, drinks which are nothing more than sugared water, on occasion, cookies and even candy bars. Are these foods giving you energy? They are not. They are merely making you fat. It is sad but true. Society does not like fat people. They discriminate against fat people. That's the bad news. The good news is that you can do something about it."

Because of her anger, Miss Danvers was chewing louder than she intended. The noise came to Nurse Abby's attention and when she saw what Miss Danvers was eating, she scowled at her.

Several of the students turned around and stared at their teacher.

"Is it all right to eat muffins?" Lenora asked.

"How about cake?" George questioned.

"What's the difference between a chocolate chip muffin and a chocolate chip cookie?" Damien raised his hand.

"There is no difference," Nurse Abby said. "Those foods are your enemy."

She reached inside her shopping bag and produced a rather large poster of the food groups. "You can see—" she propped the poster up against the chalkboard "—the sort of foods that will work in your favor."

Miss Danvers had finished her muffin and she had had enough. This was still her classroom. These were still her children, even if they were her *fat* children. She would not be bullied by Nurse Abby.

She stood up and proceeded to the front of the classroom.

"Thank you so much, Nurse Abby," she said. "That was a lovely presentation. Perhaps you can come back another day, but right now, class, we have to start the Halloween project that we talked about last week."

"What Halloween project was that?" Christian, who was as skinny as a bean sprout, asked.

Miss Danvers helped Nurse Abby pack up her belongings and she actually escorted the nurse to the door. Nurse Abby looked a little insulted, but Miss Danvers figured that Nurse Abby had insulted plenty of people in her day, including her. Miss Danvers practically slammed the door in Nurse Abby's face.

Then she had to think of a Halloween project.

WHILE THE CHILDREN were busily writing their essays on their favorite Halloween characters, Nora and Louise from the third grade knocked politely and came into the classroom, carrying a note.

Miss Danvers opened it cautiously.

I am sorry about the lecture but I do think your children are unhealthy. And it was signed Nurse Abby.

Miss Danvers resisted the temptation to scribble *That's just your opinion* on the bottom of the note and return it. Instead, she thanked Nora and Louise and then told her students that once they finished their essay they could turn their papers over and draw a picture to match their stories.

Drawing always resulted in a great deal of confusion because, although everyone had crayons and markers, no one liked their own art supplies. Students were inevitably getting out of their seats to borrow someone's orange or black or complaining because someone had stolen their pink marker.

And in the midst of this bedlam, Father Felix walked in. The students scurried to their seats as he eyed them malevolently. "I am coming to check the classrooms," he told Miss Danvers as he glanced at her bulletin boards.

Miss Danvers was somewhat artistically inclined so she

wasn't too worried as he examined her All Saints display, where each child had written about a favorite saint. He looked at it for a few moments and then said, "You see this?" He pointed to a paper in the right hand corner. "It should be down about a half a inch to match the other side."

Miss Danvers nodded, that was easy enough to fix. And while she was looking for the staple remover, Father Felix bent down and was reading something on her desk. She tried to remember if she had left anything incriminating out, and then she saw it was only Nurse Abby's note.

"She was here," Miss Danvers began to explain, because surely Father Felix could see what a lunatic she was, "and she—"

But Miss Danvers never got to finish her statement. Father Felix yanked the note off her desk. "I'm taking this with me," he said.

And with a pale face and a trembling hand, he left her classroom.

THIRTY-FOUR

It was three o'clock on a Friday afternoon and the teachers were anxious to leave the building. They actually stood at the front door, waiting for the exact hour when they could flee the premises. All except Nurse Abby and Bonnie Crossover.

"I really have to talk to you, Father," Miss Crossover said. This impending talk brought a feeling of great apprehension to Father Felix. So far Miss Crossover had been absolutely no problem at all (except for the occasional Monday when she didn't show up for school). Other than that, she was somewhat reliable, never drew attention to herself, never sent down unmanageable students, never fought with the other teachers, and was never behind in her paperwork or her bulletin boards.

"I'll be with you in a few minutes, but I have to meet with Nurse Abby first," Father Felix told her.

"I'll wait." Miss Crossover sat down on the bench right in front of his office.

Father Felix closed his door and asked Nurse Abby to have a seat.

She refused.

"Father, I have a date with my trainer at the gym. I have to be there at exactly three-thirty because I pay for the hour and he has another appointment—"

"This won't take long." Father Felix reached for the note Nurse Abby had sent Miss Danvers.

"I'm not surprised she said something," Nurse Abby said in a rather vicious tone. "She told me that I could talk to her class about health issues and I did. Most of her class is extremely overweight. What can you expect when their teacher is hardly the picture of a fit woman? I may have hurt a few feelings, but then again I may have saved a few lives."

"This isn't about your presentation and has nothing whatsoever to do with Miss Danvers."

He had confused her. Father Felix could see that, which meant he could get her off guard. He opened his drawer and took out the envelope from the cookie money and handed it to her.

Nurse Abby paled slightly and said that she didn't understand, but Father Felix, with years of hearing confessions, knew that was a lie.

"Look at the two *I'm sorry*s. They're identical, the print, the pen. You stole the cookie money."

Then Nurse Abby did sit down. But still her posture remained erect and combative. "I didn't steal it," she explained. "I just didn't give it to the cookie man."

"You called him and canceled our contract and pretended to be Ms. Morningstar."

"No, actually I didn't mention any name at all. He just assumed that I was Ms. Morningstar. And I returned the money to you promptly. I put it under your door. It's not my fault that it got buried under an avalanche of papers."

Father Felix was more than a little shocked over Nurse Abby's righteousness. Flustered, for a moment he didn't know what to say.

"Your children are obese," she said. "And quite frankly, so are some of your teachers. And the parents—"

"Those parents pay our salaries!"

"Not mine." Nurse Abby pinched her lips together. "I'm paid by the city. And it is my job to ensure the health of your students."

"No, that's not your job!" Father Felix snapped. "It's your job to administer to the injured, to apply Band-Aids to the kids who trip in the school yard, to check the students' hair for lice, to dole out medication sent from home—"

Nurse Abby looked at her watch and rose. "What harm did it do?" She shrugged.

"What harm did it do?" Father Felix found himself screaming. "The missing cookie money gave rise to the rumor that poor Mildred Pinkerton was murdered. It became a motive."

"It's hardly my fault if you have a histrionic staff who would rather be detectives than teachers."

Father Felix drew a deep breath. "Nurse Abby, this is an elementary school. It is not a Weight Watchers center. If we make the decision that the school is going to sell cookies, it is not up to you to sabotage our efforts. Is that clear?"

Again, she shrugged. "Oh by the way, Father, just so you know, what I told you—consider it a confession. I believe that you're bound by a seal." And then she opened the door and left Father Felix's office without turning back once.

Maybe he shouldn't have screamed at her. Not today, not when Sister Augusta was coming to visit on Monday. Sister Augusta was a thin, birdlike woman, and who knew how she felt about selling cookies at the school? And if Sister Augusta should talk to Nurse Abby...

And, meanwhile, he couldn't say anything. Not if Nurse Abby had actually made a confession, which he doubted. He wasn't in his habit, he hadn't said any prayers and what about her penance? Still, Nurse Abby could make a great deal of trouble and with the superintendent coming...

Of course, Nurse Abby was a nut. But Sister Augusta was a little nutty herself.

"Is it my turn now?" Bonnie Crossover stuck her face into Father Felix's office.

Father Felix had quite forgotten about Miss Crossover and the thought that there was more trouble on the horizon filled him with a cold dread.

"Come in," he said. His first instinct was to apologize for what she might have heard, mainly his yelling at Nurse Abby, but then he decided against it. Miss Crossover might have heard nothing, and even if she had, if Father Felix apologized, it would lead her to believe he was in the wrong.

Miss Crossover closed the door, which only furthered his suspicion that this was not a social call.

She sat down in the same place where just minutes before Nurse Abby had sat.

"Father, I hate to be a problem."

"It's all right. You've been here how long?"

"This will be my second year. And you know I don't come to you with any little thing—"

"I know that." He really didn't have the time or the energy for a lengthy introduction. "Just tell me how I can help you."

"I'm afraid that I'm being bothered, harassed really."

"By a student?"

She shook her head.

"A parent?"

She shook her head again.

His stomach knotted. "Another teacher?" Right away, he suspected Mrs. Johnston.

But Miss Crossover shook her head for a third time.

Father Felix felt as though he were playing charades. "Who then?" He had to fight to keep his voice on an even keel.

"Mr. Ironweed."

"The janitor?"

She nodded. "I know it sounds crazy, but I think he has a thing for me."

Father Felix leaned back in his chair and wished he were at home, in church, in Arizona, anyplace but here at St. Polycarp after three on a Friday afternoon.

"If you don't believe me…"

He believed her. Bonnie Crossover was a pretty woman, with jet-black hair and bright blue eyes. And the scar about her eyebrow only made her look soft and vulnerable. Her clothes were simple and at the same time, they looked very expensive and classy. He could understand how a man could be attracted to her. But Mr. Ironweed had to be going on seventy.

"Sometimes he calls me Millie," Miss Crossover said.

"Millie was his first wife."

"I figured that."

"Look, Mr. Ironweed has been the janitor here for years and years and years. His mind is beginning to wander but basically I think he's probably quite harmless."

Miss Crossover shook her head. "I don't think so. If you ask me, he's kind of creepy. He always seems to be watching me. I think he's done something to my lock, so I can't get into my own classroom and I have to go looking for him every morning. I know he goes into my room when I'm not there, and he makes every excuse to be where I am. And there's a leak in my classroom. I think he punctured the hole in the ceiling himself. He's back and forth with a pail all day long. It's very disruptive, not only to me but the students. Somehow he must have gotten hold of my phone number because I'm getting these calls at night and when I say hello, he hangs up. I'm a little freaked out."

Father Felix was feeling a little freaked out himself. The knot in his stomach was tightening and he found it difficult to breathe, like there wasn't enough air in the room. He wondered if he was having a panic attack. Never in a million years had he expected something like this.

"If you would just talk to him," Miss Crossover suggested.

"I'll talk to him." Father Felix managed to keep his voice level. Although he knew that talking to Mr. Ironweed would do absolutely no good at all. He would have to file a complaint and that involved paperwork and paperwork took time and there was no telling what could occur while they were waiting. "In the meantime, if you could just try to be a little patient with him…"

Miss Crossover stared at Father Felix, as though what he had asked her to do was sheer impossibility.

With great difficulty he managed to stand up. "Thank you for bringing this to my attention."

"Thank you, Father." Miss Crossover left his office, buoyant, almost jubilant, probably believing that Father Felix would solve the problem. But there were too many problems in the school and he was shaken in his confidence to take action.

He thought of a line from an Emily Dickinson poem. "At least to pray is left—is left…"

He would pray even though he was beginning to wonder if St. Polycarp Elementary School was worth saving.

THIRTY-FIVE

HE HAD TO FIND A WAY to make her see how important he was, how he could keep her safe, how no one could care for her the way he could.

He thought and he thought and then he got a splendid idea.

On Sunday night he went hunting down in the ghetto. He brought a black plastic trash bag and nice piece of raw steak. Then he hid in the corner, and he waited.

As he sat there, he thought about all the things he had done in his life, all the bad things. If Father Felix should find out, then he was history. But at seventy-four years old, why should he care?

He'd have a nice retirement, enough to take care of the two of them. She'd never have to teach bratty kids anymore, never have to wake up to an alarm clock, never have to reach her pretty arms up high to hang a bulletin board. She'd be on easy street.

And she'd be convinced real soon. When she knew what he was capable of.

He saw the shadow of the first one approaching. He leaned over, caught it, and kept it prisoner in a cage.

AND THEN there were others.

THIRTY-SIX

ON FRIDAY NIGHT, Julia Hopwood called Amelia Johnston. Mrs. Johnston did not answer the phone, so Mrs. Hopwood left a message on her machine, which was as vague as the note she had received that morning.

"I'm very confused. What did I tell? To whom did I tell? I haven't spoken to anyone except my class. Please explain."

Mrs. Johnston called her back ten minutes later. Mrs. Hopwood picked up the phone and before she even uttered hello, Mrs. Johnston shouted out, "You told Father Felix that I suspected him."

"I did not!"

"You certainly did."

"If he told you such a thing, he's a liar. I don't like calling a priest a liar, but if he is a liar," Mrs. Hopwood continued, "then you may be right and he's a murderer as well. And maybe he's not even a priest."

Mrs. Johnston didn't respond.

"Did he tell you that?"

"Well no," Mrs. Johnston said, "but he called me into his office and it was very obvious that he knew that I wasn't about to give up on my investigation. He practically pleaded—" she hesitated for a brief moment "—and then he told me that he found the cookie money."

"Really?" Mrs. Hopwood sat down on her bed.

"He made it sound very mysterious."

"Doesn't that end the matter?" Mrs. Hopwood was feeling slightly relieved, because she did not like the feeling that she was at great risk.

"It does not," Mrs. Johnston burst out. "We have assumed that the reason poor Mildred Pinkerton was murdered was because the cookie money had been stolen. Now, we find out that the cookie money was never stolen at all, which makes no sense whatsoever. But even if that's true, it wasn't the reason she was killed. We saw it—in her own handwriting. Someone is not who he appears to be."

"They."

"Pardon?"

"She wrote they," Mrs. Hopwood corrected Mrs. Johnston and then thought better of it.

"Whatever," Mrs. Johnston said in an abrupt tone of voice. "I intend to get to the heart of the matter."

"Yes, that would be a good idea," Mrs. Hopwood said, trying to sound enthusiastic. As far as she was concerned, Mrs. Johnston could investigate until June graduation and she would just humor her. Unlike Mrs. Johnston, Mrs. Hopwood did not care for trouble. There was plenty of trouble right at home.

Mrs. Hopwood was rather looking forward to Monday and Sister Augusta coming, because it meant a break in the routine. She had instructed her class to be on their best behavior and had promised them candy corns if they were quiet and respectful.

She was even more pleased when a schedule circulated and her name was among the few who would actually meet with Sister Augusta.

Bonnie Crossover's name was on the list, but it being Monday, she was out sick. Father Felix called in a substitute, a woman by the name of Miss Frost, who looked quite frightened and, considering the behavior of the fourth grade when their teacher was absent, she had every reason to be scared.

Unfortunately, Mrs. Johnston was not scheduled for a meeting, and she wasn't pleased.

She sent a note down with an eighth grade student and Mrs. Hopwood knew that it wasn't good news for her.

You can see that I'm not on the schedule, she wrote, *and what does that tell you? Father Felix does not want me to talk to Sister Augusta. I am going to try and corner her during lunch, but if I don't have the chance, then it's up to you. You have to pump her for information about Father Felix and, if you have the opportunity, tell her about the strange things that have been happening here. Do you promise?*

Mrs. Hopwood did not make promises lightly. She nodded at Matthew, who was holding a tissue to a bloody nose.

"I'm supposed to wait for a reply," he said in a muffled voice.

Mrs. Hopwood wasn't sure how to answer. Then the door opened and Father Felix, who would be watching her class, barged in. Mrs. Hopwood sent Matthew on his way, and gave her students an arithmetic assignment. Father Felix seemed rather nervous and Mrs. Hopwood wondered if it had anything to do with her meeting with Sister Augusta.

For a second his expression gave validity to Mrs. Johnston's suspicions, but Mrs. Hopwood quickly tossed the thought aside.

She had never met Sister Augusta before and Mrs. Hopwood found her rather formidable. She was tall and thin, dressed in a partial habit. A few curly black locks stuck out of her veil. She had a rather pointy face, bulging eyes, a high forehead, and dark, heavy eyebrows.

Mrs. Hopwood thought, all in all, she looked remarkably like a witch's hat.

"Please sit down," Sister Augusta said, when they met in the teachers' lounge, just inches from where Miss Pinkerton had collapsed in a crumpled heap.

Mrs. Hopwood tried to relax in her chair.

"The reason I wanted to meet with you, Mrs. Hop-scotch—"

"Hopwood."

Sister Augusta frowned. She obviously did not like to be corrected.

"My name is Hopwood."

"Oh, I'm very sorry." Sister Augusta looked down at the purple folder in front of her. "Someone had written Hopscotch. At any rate, I understand you are now the chair of the Educational Evaluation Committee."

"That's true." Mrs. Hopwood was looking at the coffeepot and wondering if it would be rude to pour herself a cup. Maybe not, if she offered Sister a cup as well. But then again, there was no telling how long that coffee had been sitting there and who had been in and out of the teachers' room. But if Sister drank first and, after a few moments, she seemed as right as rain…

"So where do you stand?" Sister Augusta glanced at Mrs. Hopwood's rather low cut parrot green V-neck sweater in distaste.

Mrs. Hopwood had been thinking of the coffee and paying no attention whatsoever, so she was rather puzzled by the question.

"You mean on the upcoming senatorial election?"

"I mean," Sister Augusta said, rather annoyed, "on the Educational Evaluation. What have you done?"

Mrs. Hopwood had done nothing at all, except move around some papers, at least the papers she could find. But she wasn't about to admit any of this to Sister.

"Well," she stuttered, "we have committees."

"And what have your committees done?"

"Well…"

"Mrs. Hopper—"

"Hopwood."

"I don't think you really understand how important this Educational Evaluation is to St. Polycarp, to Father Felix. This certification from the diocese means that St. Polycarp has met all the educational standards from the state. This will result in an increased enrollment, and let me be honest with you, Mrs. Hopper, if you refuse to do the work—"

"I'm not refusing," Mrs. Hopwood said as she studied the corner of the room, startled at the flicker of movement.

"If you are negligent in performing your duties—"

"I'm not negligent." The problem was that it had dashed under the table so quickly that Mrs. Hopwood could not be certain if what she had seen was just a shadow or something far more alarming.

"Father Felix would not have put you in charge if he didn't have full confidence in your ability as a leader."

Mrs. Hopwood felt something brush by her feet.

"Now, I know that this school has suffered a terrible loss with the passing of Miss Pinkerton. At some time in the future, if things go well, you might want to dedicate a library to her. Do you have a library?"

Mrs. Hopwood looked down at the black creature rubbing against her leg.

She sprang up and released a tumultuous scream. Sister Augusta stared in shock and glanced around helplessly.

"My dear woman," Sister Augusta said, "whatever is the matter?"

The rat was in the middle of the floor watching them. Mrs. Hopwood edged out of the door.

Sister Augusta released a small gasp of surprise and tried to manipulate her way around the rat. Her face had drained of color.

Several students came running to Mrs. Hopwood's aid but when they saw the rat, they shrieked also. "Get out of here, all of you!" Mrs. Hopwood pushed the clamorous mob back. "No one is to go into the teachers' room."

"What seems to be the problem?" Mrs. Johnston went to the head of the line.

"There is a rat in the teachers' room!" Mrs. Hopwood said very dramatically.

"Who is it?" Mrs. Johnston took her aside.

"No, I mean a real rat!"

Sister Augusta had left and was standing in the hall, adjusting her veil, which had loosened in the process. Mrs. Hopwood noticed that she had several bald spots.

"Matthew," Mrs. Johnston instructed as she pulled him out of line. Matthew, who was still holding a bloody tissue, stepped forward. "Go and get Mr. Ironweed immediately."

"Do you want me to get Father Felix?" he asked in a raspy voice.

"Do you not understand the English language?" Mrs. Johnston said. "I asked you to get Mr. Ironweed."

Mrs. Hopwood backed up against a bulletin board where the students had written essays about the dangers of Halloween.

Mrs. Johnston took over immediately. "I am so sorry this had to happen, Sister. Let me introduce myself. I am the eighth grade teacher, Mrs. Johnston."

Sister Augusta glared at her in a most unfriendly manner. Mrs. Johnston shot a surprised look at Mrs. Hopwood, who merely shrugged her shoulders. While Mrs. Hopwood was relieved that the rat had interrupted the interrogation by Sister Augusta, she wanted now to go back to the second floor, to her own classroom, as far away from the rodent as her legs, clad in gold tights, would take her.

But she didn't know if Sister Augusta had to excuse her first.

"Do you have rats in this school?" Sister Augusta asked no one in particular.

"No, Sister," an eighth grader answered.

"I have one at home," another responded, "but he's in a cage."

"I don't understand it at all." Sister Augusta shook her head and her curls bounced up and down.

"What's going on here?" Mr. Ironweed appeared on the scene with a fly swatter. "Someone said there are gnats in the teachers' lounge."

"Rats!" Mrs. Hopwood said. "There are rats!"

"Well, actually I only saw the one," Sister Augusta said dryly.

"Sister, if I could speak to you for a moment," Mrs. Johnston whispered to the nun, "I'd like to tell you that I have a concern—"

"What's going on here?" Father Felix raced up the stairs.

"I had no idea that your school had a rodent problem," Sister Augusta said in an icy tone. "You do understand, Father Felix, that this matter has to be settled before we can even consider the process of Educational Evaluation. Rodents carry diseases and this is a place for children—"

Father Felix clapped his hands and everyone, including Sister Augusta, jumped.

"Mrs. Johnston, take these students back to the classroom. Now."

"But they're on their way to art."

"Now." He pointed in the direction of the hall.

"Mr. Ironweed, go into the teachers' lounge and see if you can corner the rat. Then go to the hardware store and buy a few rat traps. Mrs. Hopwood." Mrs. Hopwood was wondering when Father Felix was going to get to her. "I left your class in the care of Nurse Abby. Please return immediately."

That was all Mrs. Hopwood had to hear. She bounced down the corridor quickly but stopped when she heard hollering coming from the fourth grade.

Cautiously she opened the door and saw Miss Frost, motionless, standing on Miss Crossover's desk. All of the students were on top of their chairs, most of them screaming bloody murder. Two rats were whizzing around the classroom. One bold boy was trying to hit the rats with a yardstick.

Mrs. Hopwood prepared to flee.

"I am leaving." Miss Frost grabbed her coat and her pocket-book and then jumped off the chair. "And I won't be back!"

And before Mrs. Hopwood could say another word, she

had pushed Mrs. Hopwood aside, which meant that she had pushed Mrs. Hopwood farther into the room, and slammed the door behind her.

Now Mrs. Hopwood was not about to be trapped with twenty-five screaming ten-year-olds and two vicious rats. But she couldn't just leave the children by themselves. She threw open the door and was relieved to see Father Felix coming down the hall. She called quickly to him.

"What now?" he asked, his face pale and his body sweaty and trembling.

"I'm afraid that there are more rats in the fourth grade."

"Father Felix," Sister Augusta said, "we're going to have to reschedule this visit. Obviously, we can't have a conversation when all of this is going on."

"Help me! Someone help!"

"I have to go to the bathroom and I'm afraid to get down from my chair!"

"Don't move, Katlin! He could bite!"

"Help!"

"I'm going to go downstairs now." Mrs. Hopwood slid by Father Felix and Sister Augusta and raced to the safety of her own class, where she found Nurse Abby lecturing to a bored classroom on the benefits of eating healthy vegetables.

The door to her own classroom had been closed for mere seconds when the students started to circle her like the rats in the fourth grade.

"Is it true that there are an army of rats in the library?"

"Did one of the rats bite a nun?"

"Did a fourth grader bring them in as a joke?"

"Did someone put a curse on this school?"

And just like that, Mrs. Hopwood remembered that some-one *had* put a curse on the school. Starlight's mother had ranted and raved as she stormed down the hall.

"Children…" Mrs. Hopwood held on to her desk. "Everyone return to their seats and take out their rosaries. We're going to say some prayers."

"For the person who got bit?"

"I heard Mr. Ironweed was sawing those rats up."

"We're going to pray," Mrs. Hopwood said, "for the future of St. Polycarp School."

THIRTY-SEVEN

"WOULD YOU LIKE a ride home?" Mr. Alabaster asked Mrs. Hopwood.

Mrs. Hopwood seemed to be hesitating, but Mrs. Johnston put a stop to that right away. "She would not. Thank you anyway." And then Mrs. Johnston pushed Mrs. Hopwood into a corner.

"It's cold and miserable out and it looks like rain," Mrs. Hopwood said, "and I've had a very hard day. Maybe a ride home—"

"Last time you took a ride from him, he almost killed you. Did you have a chance to talk to Sister Augusta?"

"Right," Mrs. Hopwood said sarcastically. "I voiced all my concerns while the rat listened."

"I must admit that he has quite an imagination," Mrs. Johnston said.

"Who?"

"What do you mean who? Father Felix."

"You think that he brought the rats to school?"

"Certainly."

"I have to tell you, I saw his face. He looked sick."

"It's an act," Mrs. Johnston said firmly. "What better way to distract Sister Augusta than by releasing rodents into the school. Naturally, she's going to flee."

"But this makes St. Polycarp look bad," Mrs. Hopwood argued.

Mrs. Johnston did not like it when Mrs. Hopwood argued. "You don't get it. Father Felix doesn't care if St. Polycarp looks bad. He only cares that the Educational Evaluation is delayed—that we don't find out about his past."

"But he's the one who decided we should have the Educational Evaluation."

"No, he did not." Mrs. Johnston wondered what was making Mrs. Hopwood so combative. "Don't you remember that he told us he didn't even want the certification? He felt pressured."

Mrs. Hopwood nodded. "I guess so," she conceded.

Mrs. Johnston did not doubt it for a moment.

USUALLY MRS. JOHNSTON did not mind staying after school. In fact, she quite enjoyed it. It was better than rushing home to her twins and it gave her a chance to plan the morning's lesson and correct papers.

Because once she got home, she was a virtual prisoner.

But not today. Not when Father Felix was hanging around the building. Not when Mr. Ironweed was roaming the halls with gigantic rat traps. Not when Ms. Morningstar was still at her desk, giving Mrs. Johnston the evil eye.

Maybe Mrs. Hopwood was right and Mrs. Johnston should apologize to Ms. Morningstar. Or maybe she should just do the kind thing and warn Ms. Morningstar that she was working for a murderer.

Instead Mrs. Johnston climbed the stairs to her classroom and stopped in the corridor when she heard giggling coming from the girls' room. She marched in and saw two fifth grade girls putting on lipstick.

One of them, a rather large girl with a freckled face, stopped midair when she spotted Mrs. Johnston.

"What are you girls doing in here?" Mrs. Johnston put her hand on her hip.

"We're in after school," the second girl, with blond hair and blue eyes, and obviously the more audacious of the two, answered.

"And you're supposed to be in the girls' room applying makeup?"

Neither girl responded.

"And bright pink lipstick?" Mrs. Johnston thought the girls looked ridiculous with their very white skin and the gaudy fuchsia, which neither girl had managed to put on straight, staining their lips. "Where did you get that lipstick?" she demanded.

"We found it," the blonde said.

Mrs. Johnston was appalled. "I hope that you didn't find it in the street. People have diseases, all sorts of mouth sores and if you use their lipsticks—"

"We didn't find it in the street, Mrs. Johnston." The first girl put the cap on the container. "We found it in our classroom behind the construction paper."

"Then it's not yours," Mrs. Johnston concluded.

The girls shook their heads.

Mrs. Johnston put her hand out and the first girl dropped the tube of lipstick into it. "Both of you, wipe that lipstick off immediately and go to the after school program. And pray that I don't report you to Father Felix."

Of course, Mrs. Johnston had no intention of reporting the girls to Father Felix. He might kill them, or her, or, at the very least, release an army of rats into their classroom, the way he had in the fourth grade.

Mrs. Johnston looked down at the lipstick. The first thing she noticed was that it was an old-fashioned tube. She checked the brand and discovered that it was from a discontinued line. And the color was obviously out of style.

She tried to think of which teacher would wear such a bright pink. The only person she could come up with was Mrs. Hopwood.

Mrs. Johnston would have to ask her about it. She tossed the lipstick tube in her desk drawer and headed home.

THIRTY-EIGHT

FATHER FELIX SAT BEHIND closed doors. In his wildest imagination, he could have not predicted the outcome of the day. His head ached and his body was stiff and sore from the tension.

Maybe, he thought, maybe Mrs. Johnston and Mrs. Hopwood were not so crazy after all. Maybe someone was purposely trying to sabotage the school, because there was no possible way three rats could suddenly have appeared in the building. Someone had to have brought them in.

But who and for what purpose?

He couldn't imagine one of the teachers doing something like that. The way Mrs. Hopwood had screamed, he thought perhaps that she had discovered another dead body. And for someone who was always afraid of getting her clothes dirty...

The rats had probably come from the fourth grade classroom, which might leave Miss Crossover open to suspicion except Miss Crossover had been absent today so she could hardly have sent the rats in without her.

Mrs. Johnston, as tough as nails and as mean as spit, could have very easily transported rats in her car. But why would she do such a thing? For revenge? Because he didn't take her seriously?

The truth was that he liked Mrs. Johnston, he admired her. And he really thought that the conversation yesterday had gone well. Surely, she could not have turned on him so quickly.

Unless she was psychotic.

Father Felix was convinced that something wasn't right at St. Polycarp. He wasn't about to admit it to anyone because that would only add fuel to the fire and create more bedlam than was already spreading throughout the school.

But something was happening, and it was something evil, and as a priest he knew evil when he saw it.

Then he remembered the strange curse that Miss Mooney had uttered when Father Felix refused to readmit her daughter because of the head lice. As ridiculous as it seemed, shortly after Miss Mooney had damned the school, things started to slide downhill, almost like an avalanche.

It had started with the death of poor Mildred Pinkerton.

If things got any worse, he might even have to call Miss Mooney and beg her to remove the curse, as foolish as that may sound.

Tomorrow was Halloween and it was traditional to have a "fun day" at St. Polycarp. Students got to dress in costumes, decorate the cafeteria and then go downstairs, listen to loud music, eat a lot of junk food, play a lot of useless games and dance in the middle of the room. It was a fundraiser, though, and St. Polycarp needed the money.

Besides, he could think of no good reason to cancel it. Only that he had a real bad feeling in the pit of his stomach. Sometimes things got out of control at the Halloween party, only out of control usually meant that one of the pre-K students tripped and bumped his head, or Father Felix would catch a few eighth graders kissing in the corner, or a fifth grader threw up after eating one too many cupcakes.

Still, with everyone in costumes (even the teachers) and the darkened room and the chaos, it was a perfect breeding place for a catastrophe.

He would forge ahead and pray for the best.

THIRTY-NINE

MISS DANVERS HATED fun day. As far as she was concerned, children shouldn't have fun days in school, and certainly not days when everyone dressed in costumes and ate candy and danced around one another in an obscene manner. Well, at least she could commiserate with the other teachers in the cafeteria.

Although these days she wasn't feeling too friendly with any of the teachers.

Miss Danvers was going over the rules with the students when Mrs. Johnston burst into her classroom. Mrs. Johnston always looked like a lady with a mission, which was precisely why Miss Danvers was slightly afraid of her.

"I just thought you should know, Miss Danvers—" she was speaking in a very loud voice, loudly enough so that all of the students could hear "—that yesterday I caught several of your girls in the bathroom after school applying lipstick."

"Oh my!" Miss Danvers looked her best to seem appalled, but truthfully she didn't care. It was after school, not on her watch. Besides, kids were wearing makeup younger and younger. Look at all those baby beauty contests.

"Evidently they found a lipstick in the trash and were applying it liberally to their mouths."

Miss Danvers shook her head. "Not too sanitary," she mumbled.

"I thought you'd like to talk to your girls about it. I'd rather not mention names."

Miss Danvers was betting that Mrs. Johnston didn't know

any names. "Was it a lip gloss?" she asked, because she was thinking that maybe it was a Chapstick.

"No, it was not a lip gloss," Mrs. Johnston snapped. "It was a real lipstick, a dark lipstick, called Amber Rose."

Amber Rose, Miss Danvers thought, *where have I heard that shade before?*

"Wearing makeup at the age of eleven," Mrs. Johnston hissed, "can only lead a girl into trouble. They'll attract older boys—"

"It's Myrtle's lipstick," Miss Danvers said suddenly. "She lost it."

"Or threw it away," Mrs. Johnston said.

"No, it was in her makeup bag. And her entire makeup bag disappeared. With her heart pills and her Estée Lauder compact with her initials MMM."

If it were possible for an African-American woman to pale, that's exactly what Mrs. Johnston did. Her cocoa-brown skin turned a funny shade of mocha and then she uttered, "What kind of heart pills?"

Miss Danvers struggled to remember. "Digi…"

"Digitoxin?" Mrs. Johnston practically jumped down her throat.

"Sounds right."

"Well," Mrs. Johnston said, "I have a feeling that the makeup was not lost at all, but stolen."

"We did not steal it!" Ashley jumped up. "We found the lipstick in the trash!"

"In whose trash barrel?" Miss Danvers asked.

"Yours. There." Ashley pointed to the wastepaper basket in the corner under the poster with the multiplication tables.

Miss Danvers was trying to figure out how such a thing was possible when Mrs. Johnston asked, "When?"

"Yesterday afternoon."

"You can sit down now, Ashley." Miss Danvers turned towards Mrs. Johnston. "Since the lipstick belongs to Myrtle, if you still have it, maybe I could give it back to her."

"No," Mrs. Johnston said rather quickly. "I'll do that myself. Thank you."

Mrs. Johnston left and the class broke into an uproar. Something about Mary Lou's costume looking too much like Thelma's. Miss Danvers tried to gain control of the class, all the time thinking about the strange behavior of Mrs. Johnston.

She was obviously puzzled by the missing lipstick, which had landed in Miss Danvers's trash bin. But Miss Danvers certainly didn't put it there. Someone else must have taken it from Myrtle (although it was difficult to think of anyone stealing from the cafeteria lady) and then decided that the color was too brassy and just threw it in the first pail she saw.

All Miss Danvers could hope was that no one thought *she* had stolen anything because the teachers in this school were all rather paranoid and crazy and one thing that Miss Danvers didn't want to do was draw attention to herself.

Although she had the distinct feeling that it was already too late for that.

FORTY

MRS. HOPWOOD WAS excusing her children four at a time to change into their costumes in the bathroom. When they were all ready (fifteen minutes after the party started because Emily thought Linda Lou stole her tiara and then found it in her backpack), the class proceeded downstairs in an orderly manner.

Mrs. Hopwood was dressed like a roaring twenties lady. The children didn't know who she was supposed to be but they all agreed that her bright red flapper costume was really pretty as were her yellow spike heels and her sapphire blue mask.

Once they reached the cafeteria, Mrs. Hopwood cautioned her students.

"There is to be no running. There is to be no throwing of food. No one is to leave the premises without checking with me first. Be careful of the younger children and keep your voices low."

The moment she excused them, the pupils raced in all directions.

Mrs. Hopwood entered the room gingerly. The music was so loud she could barely hear herself think. There were children everywhere, dressed as cartoon characters, as action figures, as rap stars, as angels and devils.

The teachers weren't as colorful, although they all wore masks. It was hard for Mrs. Hopwood to distinguish them from the parents since the room was so jam-packed.

She felt someone tug at her shoulder.

Annoyed, she whipped around, ready to reprimand a child.

Instead she found herself facing Amelia Johnston, who was dressed as the grim reaper, wearing all black, a horrific mask and carrying a scythe. The only reason Mrs. Hopwood recognized her was because her hair was sticking up.

"I got you," she said to Mrs. Hopwood.

"What does that mean? I got you." Mrs. Hopwood was rubbing her shoulder, which stung.

"I said I've got news." Mrs. Johnston lifted her mask. "Big news."

"Big news?" Mrs. Hopwood screeched as a ghost inched closer.

Mrs. Johnston gave Mrs. Hopwood a push out of the cafeteria. Mrs. Hopwood didn't think it was such a good idea to leave her children unattended and she thought that if Father Felix saw them they would be reprimanded. She looked around, hoping she could identify Father Felix, but with the jumble of people in her path, she could barely see Mrs. Johnston.

Mrs. Johnston finally stopped in front of the boiler room.

"Yesterday I saw some fifth graders putting on lipstick in the girls' room. I think it's disgusting, really. I mean, they're so young and all."

Mrs. Hopwood could not imagine where this was leading.

"I took the lipstick away from them. Do you want to know the shade?" Before Mrs. Hopwood could respond, Mrs. Johnston answered. "Amber Rose."

"Amber Rose," Mrs. Hopwood said thoughtfully. "Why does that sound familiar?"

"Because Myrtle from the cafeteria lost it."

"That's right."

Mrs. Johnston looked very annoyed. "You already know that?"

"Yes, it was in her makeup bag with her heart pills."

"I don't believe you found that out and you didn't even tell me. You've been withholding information and that is something I would never do to you. What kind of a friend are you, anyway? And what are your real reasons?"

"What is that supposed to mean, my real reasons? I didn't think it was important. Miss Danvers told me that Myrtle had lost her heart medication so I gave her back the pills I found in the teachers' lounge. That's when she said her makeup bag was missing. In the bag was the lipstick and another bottle of pills and a compact."

"And you didn't think that was important?" Mrs. Johnston was now screaming. She was interrupted by a bevy of cheerleaders stampeding down the stairs.

Mrs. Johnston moved Mrs. Hopwood closer to the cafeteria door, where a few older children were hanging out and eating pretzels and chips.

"Do you know what this means?" she whispered as she swooped down to Mrs. Hopwood.

Mrs. Hopwood shook her head, although she had a very good idea of what it meant. She just didn't want to discuss it with Mrs. Johnston, who was certain to panic her.

"It means that there's going to be another filling."

Mrs. Hopwood could barely hear Mrs. Johnston, whose voice had gotten considerably lower. "Filling—like in cupcakes?"

Several of the students stopped chewing and stared at the teachers.

"I said," Mrs. Johnston began to screech again, "that there is going to be another *killing*—like killing as in murder."

Several of the students gasped and stared at Mrs. Johnston.

"Who's going to get murdered?" A girl dressed like Buffy the Vampire Slayer asked.

"None of your business!" Mrs. Johnston snapped and then shoved Mrs. Hopwood into a stairwell.

"Don't you see?" she asked, and what Mrs. Hopwood could see was that Amelia Johnston was thoroughly frustrated.

"The killer wouldn't have even thought about stealing that second vial of pills if he wasn't going to use them on someone else."

Mrs. Hopwood thought it was rather fruitless to comment that maybe Myrtle was just careless and lost her makeup bag, although that still wouldn't explain who had thrown her lipstick away. Besides, Mrs. Hopwood didn't believe that herself.

"I can tell you're not taking this seriously," Mrs. Johnston said. "Well, if I were you, I would, because there is no telling who could be next. Even you. And we both know—"

Heavy footsteps interrupted their conversation. Mrs. Hopwood looked up and saw a man in a priest's clothes, wearing a mask, staring at them.

"I am sorry, Father Felix. I'm going into the cafeteria now." Mrs. Hopwood didn't wait for Mrs. Johnston but instead entered the deafening, hot, claustrophobic space.

"Want to see what I won dunking apples?" Michael held out a small teddy bear.

"Good going!"

"How about a piece of key lime pie?" A woman dressed as a pirate held out a paper plate to Mrs. Hopwood. Mrs. Hopwood loved key lime pie and she was just about to reach her hand out and grab it when she remembered. She looked up to see a woman, who most likely was a parent, but then again she didn't know.

And there was the matter of the missing pills.

She shook her head.

"Are you having fun?"

Mrs. Hopwood turned around and almost fell over Father Felix. He was dressed like a cowboy.

"I'm going up to my office for a few moments. I have some calls to make. Can I trust you to make sure that things don't get out of control down here?"

Mrs. Hopwood thought he must be crazy because as far as she was concerned, things were already out of control.

Children were running everywhere, music was blasting, balloons were bursting, food was smeared on the floor and she couldn't move an inch without stumbling onto another body.

"I'll try," she muttered as Father Felix disappeared.

She wished she could go with him. But she had to watch her class, like she could really keep track of the second graders in this mob. She sank down into an empty chair and spotted Mrs. Johnston in the corner, talking to a parent. Mrs. Johnston seemed to be enjoying a rather large hunk of chocolate cake.

I guess she's not afraid, Mrs. Hopwood thought. Mrs. Hopwood decided to take her chances and reached over and grabbed a large handful of Cheez Doodles.

FORTY-ONE

BUNCH OF STUPID WOMEN! Mr. Ironweed thought angrily as he entered the cafeteria. The nice part about being in costume was that everyone just assumed he was Father Felix and he was getting a whole lot of respect, which he had never had before.

But he had no interest in staying in such an insane atmosphere. That didn't mean he couldn't help himself to some goodies. He grabbed a paper plate and took a slice of pie, a piece of cake, some candy corns and poured himself a nice helping of Pepsi.

As he was walking out of the cafeteria, he bumped into a little kid dressed like a cat. The cake slid off the plate, landed on the floor, the kid slipped and screamed like a banshee.

Some woman came running, maybe it was a teacher, he couldn't tell. The lady was dressed as a leopard in a spandex tiger suit, which wasn't too flattering.

He should make an attempt to clean up. Except no one knew he was the janitor, they just assumed he was the principal. But he did the right thing anyway.

He put down his glass of Pepsi and his pie and his candy and went to the other end of the cafeteria for a napkin. It took him longer than expected because just getting through the muddle of kids was a nightmare. People kept running into him and apologizing profusely (thinking, of course, that he was Father Felix).

By the time he returned to the spilled food, he couldn't find it. Several big girls were dancing. Most likely, they had cake stuck to their shoes and they didn't even know. It wasn't his problem.

He went back for more cake. Then he picked up his chips and soda and glanced at the clock, realizing it was almost dismissal time. Feeling quite hostile, he looked around at the mess. He supposed that it would be up to him to clean it. After all, that was his job, even if it was a thankless one.

Someday soon he'd have someone to share it with. He saw her sitting there and even though she was in a costume, she appeared to be watching him. He wished he could talk to her.

Mr. Ironweed took his cake, his pie, his chips and his Pepsi and went into the boiler room. He slammed the door behind him. He had good mind to lock it, just so he could enjoy his snacks in peace.

He sat down at his desk and leaned back in his chair. First he tasted the cake and thought it much too dry. The key lime pie wasn't much better. Nothing but lime pudding with Cool Whip on top.

No one knew how to bake anymore. Not like Millie, who used to make angel food cake that melted in your mouth and apple pies which she'd top with cheddar cheese. His mouth watered just thinking of it.

He wondered if she could bake.

He opened his drawer and searched around for a napkin. He found a used tissue under that Educational Evaluation folder. Maybe he'd give her the folder later, after the party.

He took a sip of his Pepsi. It had an aftertaste and he wondered if some snot-nosed kid had dropped something in it. He picked up the paper cup and gazed inside. It looked clean enough. He finished his chips that seemed extra salty, washed them down with more Pepsi and closed his eyes.

A five minute cat nap wouldn't hurt, especially since he'd have his work cut out for him once those wild kids left.

He got a bad cramp in his stomach and when he opened his eyes, he was seeing double. A double boiler in the middle of the room, which seemed to be coming towards him, like some kind of giant monster. A double phone, which instantly he went to grab but his hand slipped and the phone tumbled to the cement floor with a thunderous crash.

He was having trouble breathing and he knew instantly that he had been poisoned but how and why escaped him. He had to get help. Hundreds of people were just a few feet away in the other room. If someone could get an ambulance…maybe Nurse Abby… He stood up and then fell down, face forward and with his last breath, screamed out the word, "Help."

But Britney Spears was screaming also and the music was so loud that no one came to Mr. Ironweed's aid as he lay dying a few feet away.

FORTY-TWO

FATHER FELIX COULD hear the beat of the music clear up to his office. The drums were giving him a headache. Well, at least tomorrow was All Saints Day and he wouldn't have to come in to school.

He could use the day off.

He changed out of his cowboy suit and put on his priest's habit. Ms. Morningstar had left early, something about a dentist appointment, but he wasn't quite sure if he believed her. He glanced at the mail she had left on his chair. Heating bill, phone bill, tax bill. He was dizzy just thinking about it. He noticed a large envelope addressed to Mrs. Hopwood. Checking out the return address, he realized that it was from the school she was going to observe in January.

Out of curiosity, he ripped open the envelope and took out their Educational Evaluation book. It was nicely done, with colored type and bright illustrations. Fanning through the text, he saw that St. Jude Elementary School had a basketball court and an auditorium and offered the students a choice between French, Latin and Spanish.

He wished he could have been a principal in an upscale school like that.

He placed the book back on his chair, making a mental note to give it to Mrs. Hopwood when they returned to school on Thursday.

As he walked down the deserted corridor, he remembered that he hadn't spoken to Mr. Ironweed about the situation with Miss Crossover. Not certain of what to say, he had been putting it off. He couldn't come right out and accuse the man, especially since he had been so good to the school.

Catching all those rats.

Thursday. He would do it all on Thursday.

THE UPROAR IN the cafeteria was deafening. The room looked as if it had been hit by a tornado. Children were shrieking and zooming in circles, stepping on deflated balloons and half-finished food. Obviously the teachers had lost control.

He pushed the students aside and made his way to the microphone. He held his fingers up in the traditional peace sign. It took a few moments but one by one the students quieted down and held their fingers up as well.

"This place is a pigsty," he said. "And there is no way that we're going to leave it like this and just go home. The job is too big for Mr. Ironweed. I expect the eighth graders to help him."

A collective groan broke out from the back of the room.

"Call it community service, call it whatever you like. The rest of the classes will go upstairs and prepare to go home. Although tomorrow is a school holiday, it is a holy day of obligation, which means that every student should attend Mass."

Another round of groans.

Father Felix started to dismiss the classes, starting with pre-K, who would take the back staircase, and working his way to the seventh graders, climbing up the front staircase. He saw dwarves leaving, and aliens, and a brave little toaster, and a *Simpsons* character, a rap star and Tinker Bell.

When the room was emptied, he walked up to a frowning Mrs. Johnston. He knew that leaving the eighth graders behind meant that she, too, would have to stay.

"I'm sorry," he said to her, "but the room is a mess and if everyone works together..."

"I understand," she said, but from the expression on her face, it was clear that she did not. Something had happened which turned her against him. It was as if she was walking on eggshells near him, as though she didn't trust him, and he wasn't sure why.

He should help with the cleanup himself, but he had his own cleanup to do. He left the cafeteria and passed by the boiler room. The door was shut. He wondered where Mr. Ironweed was. He wouldn't blame the janitor if he just up and left, walked out the front door of St. Polycarp and never returned.

Sometimes Father Felix felt like doing that himself.

FORTY-THREE

"ALL RIGHT, someone get the broom," Mrs. Johnston ordered.

The twenty-five students, who five minutes ago were bustling around and throwing food at one another, who were dancing and singing, who were taunting younger students, stared at Mrs. Johnston, mouths agape, paralyzed.

"Are you all deaf?" she snapped. "I said someone get the broom."

It was the *someone* that was confusing to them. Mrs. Johnston could see that right away. "Thalia, go get the broom."

"I don't know where it is," Thalia said in a sulky voice.

"I'll get it," George volunteered but it was obvious that he was disgusted by the thought.

"Look upstairs near the trash bin," Mrs. Johnston told him. "The rest of you, start picking up the papers from the floor and throw away the food and the balloons. When that's done, we have to move the chairs and the tables."

"I don't see why it's our responsibility," Adam said, huffy. "Just because we're the oldest."

"Yeah," Marlene chimed in, "it was all those bratty little kids who made the mess. They were throwing pretzels."

The truth was that Mrs. Johnston agreed with her students but, of course, she wasn't about to take their side. "Just get busy. The faster we get this done, the faster we can all go home."

As Mrs. Johnston bent down to help her students, she realized that the floor was going to have to be mopped. But that's where she was drawing the line. That was Mr. Ironweed's job, not hers and not her students'. And where was he anyway?

Weren't they supposed to be helping *him?*

She threw a handful of napkins into the trash bin and then told the students, "Keep working. I'm going to find Mr. Ironweed."

"Yeah, shouldn't he be doing this?"

"Why are we doing his job?"

"My mother is not going to be happy that I'm late."

"I thought your mother was in the Dominican Republic."

"She *is* in the Dominican Republic. But it doesn't matter. She doesn't want me to stay after school, cleaning, like some maid."

The boiler room door was closed and, at first, Mrs. Johnston thought Mr. Ironweed wasn't even in there. But then her shoe caught on something slippery and she noticed that soda was leaking from underneath the door.

Something had spilled inside.

She knocked and called Mr. Ironweed's name. He didn't answer, but then again, she didn't expect that he would.

Slowly she tried to open the door but something hard seemed to block her efforts. It was if something was jammed against the door.

"I got the mop." George shuffled over, holding a rather dirty stringed apparatus.

"Help me push this door open." Even as she said it, Mrs. Johnston knew that she was making a mistake. Something was very wrong in that boiler room and employing a student to help her find out what lay inside was probably not the wisest course of action.

But who else could she get? Father Felix was not an option and she was sure that most of the teachers had already gone home.

George, holding the mop with one hand, helped to push the door with the other.

She glared at him. He put down the mop. It fell on the cement floor with a clang.

"Exert some elbow grease," she said.

"You didn't tell me to get any of that. You just said get a mop."

As Mrs. Johnston threw her body weight towards the door, she heard a loud thump. And she knew.

She just knew.

"Oh my God!" George backed up into the hall.

Mrs. Johnston looked down at the still figure that had fallen on the concrete floor. At first she thought it was Father Felix, because all she could see was the back of a priest's habit. Then she spotted, several inches away, a set of dentures, and she had never known Father Felix to have false teeth.

Her heart thumping, she walked over the body and stooped down. It was Mr. Ironweed, all right. His eyes wide, his white hair spiked up, his tongue hanging out, and he was totally toothless.

"Gross!" George said.

"What's happening?"

Twenty-five students thronged around the door, pushing and shoving one another to peek into the boiler room. Mrs. Johnston was powerless to stop them. She was too busy trying to take in the scene. A cup of soda had fallen on the floor beside the telephone.

It looked as if Mr. Ironweed had tried to get help.

"Oh my God!"

"It's Father Felix!"

"Someone murdered Father Felix!"

"Does that mean we don't have to go to Mass tomorrow?"

Mrs. Johnston noticed that Mr. Ironweed had a stack of papers on his desk and she recognized them as Mrs. Hopwood's missing Educational Evaluation papers. She grabbed them. Then Lori Landon began to scream at the top of her lungs, an earsplitting shriek that sounded like a broken car alarm. Before Mrs. Johnston could to tell her to shut up, she heard someone stomping down the stairs.

"What is going on down there?"

"It's Father Felix!"

"He's still alive!"

"Man oh man!"

"Then who's that!"

"Let me through right now!"

"It's that stupid janitor."

"Who?"

"The old man."

"We got to clean by ourselves?"

Father Felix had made his way into the boiler room. He glared at Mrs. Johnston, who was standing on the other side of the body—as though...as though she had something to do with it.

"I found him like this," she said quickly, setting him straight right off.

"It's obvious what happened," Father Felix said in a most authoritative tone. "The poor old man had a heart attack." He paused for a second and then blared, "And it's no wonder. Working in this insane asylum!"

"How do we even know that he's dead?" Mrs. Johnston recognized Thalia's voice.

Father Felix ignored the question. "Mrs. Johnston, go upstairs to the office and take this mob with you. Call 911."

"Now?" Mrs. Johnston was surprised that her voice had come out all squeaky.

"No, wait a few days," Father Felix said sarcastically. "We'll just let Mr. Ironweed lie here and the rats can feast on him."

"We still have rats in this school?" a student from the back asked.

"Now!" Father Felix screamed.

Mrs. Johnston didn't appreciate being yelled at in front

of her students. She thought it was most unprofessional. She stepped over the body again and almost slipped on the cola.

"All right, everyone, upstairs," she ordered the students.

She didn't have to tell them twice. They charged up the stairs, babbling and chattering about the dead body and what might have happened.

I'll tell you what happened, Mrs. Johnston thought, *there's been another murder.*

It wasn't until she made the phone call and dismissed the students (although they did not go home. Most of them stood outside of the building, waiting for the ambulance) that it occurred to her that if Mr. Ironweed had been poisoned and if that poisoning had occurred during the Halloween party, the murder might have been a case of mistaken identity.

The killer thought he was poisoning Father Felix.

FORTY-FOUR

"Have you heard?"

Mrs. Hopwood had heard nothing except that Alexander had gotten an A on an essay entitled "Why God Created Hell." Upon reading it, Mrs. Hopwood found it most depressing and she was sorry that her son had such a dismal view of life, when she, herself, had always tried so hard to be bright and cheerful.

Nevertheless, an A was an A.

"Mr. Ironweed is dead!" Mrs. Johnston said very dramatically.

"What?" Mrs. Hopwood collapsed on the bed.

"And this time I found the body!" Mrs. Johnston said this with a great deal of satisfaction in her voice as though she was in some sort of competition with Mrs. Hopwood and the death of Mr. Ironweed had evened the score.

"You're kidding!"

"Have you ever known me to kid?"

The answer to that was no, Mrs. Hopwood had never known Mrs. Johnston to have a sense of humor at all. "What happened?"

"I was supposed to clean up with my eighth graders." Mrs. Johnston was relating the details with breakneck speed. "They were very bitter and I can't say I blame them. Just because they're the oldest class doesn't mean that they should get stuck with all the grunt work. Anyway, I was feeling rather resentful myself, because really, shouldn't Mr. Ironweed be helping? After all, that's what he gets paid for. But, of course, I didn't realize that he couldn't help not helping. Because he was dead. Anyway." Mrs. Johnston stopped for a much needed breath. "I went into the boiler room and I couldn't open the door because his body was pushed up against it and I got a student to help me, and there he was, just lying on the floor, minus his teeth. Mr. Ironweed, I mean."

Mrs. Hopwood thought that most peculiar, Mr. Ironweed having no teeth, but she knew that Mrs. Johnston did not like to be interrupted.

"Several of the girls started screaming, well, almost all of them did. At first we thought it was Father Felix because he was dressed in a priest's habit. Well, when Father Felix came running down the stairs, I guess he heard the scream, I swear people on the other side of the park heard the screams, we knew that the dead man was poor Mr. Ironweed."

"Oh my!"

"And that's not the worst of it. The phone was on the floor and so was—are you ready for this?"

Mrs. Hopwood wasn't really ready for any of it, but she answered in the affirmative anyway.

"There was a puddle of spilt soda on the floor, like he dropped dead while he was drinking it. What does that tell you?"

Mrs. Hopwood was just about to answer. It told her that Mr. Ironweed's fate was similar to Miss Pinkerton's, too similar for comfort, but the moment she opened her mouth, Mrs. Johnston cut her off.

"Do you know what I found on top of his desk? Your Educational Evaluation papers. So." Mrs. Johnston took another breath. "What do you make of that?"

"He was poisoned," Mrs. Hopwood said thoughtfully.

"I believe he was. And I also think it has something to do with the Educational Evaluation."

"But if that were the case, then why didn't the murderer take the papers from Mr. Ironweed?" Mrs. Hopwood wondered.

"Because he was probably planning to come back after Mr. Ironweed conked!" Mrs. Johnston snapped.

"You said he," Mrs. Hopwood said. "But if Mr. Ironweed was dressed like Father Felix then…"

"Then maybe the murderer was really after Father Felix," Mrs. Johnston interrupted.

"You took the words right out of my mouth," Mrs. Hopwood said.

"Well, I'm sure you have plenty of other words. At any rate, that thought crossed my mind almost immediately. Then I decided against it. First of all, you didn't see Father Felix when he spotted the body. He didn't look surprised that Mr. Ironweed was dead. No siree. What seemed to shock him was that I was the one who discovered the body. And he was angry, very angry. I think he planned on finding Mr. Ironweed and then taking the Educational Evaluation papers. Then he said, in front of all the students, that poor Mr. Ironweed had a heart attack, as if he didn't want anyone to even entertain the thought that it was murder. No, I don't think this excuses Father Felix at all. In fact, I'm more convinced than ever that he is the guilty party."

Mrs. Hopwood was not at all convinced but she wasn't about to protest. "What happened to my Educational Evaluation papers?" she asked.

"I managed to grab them. I have them home right now. I'm going to look them over very carefully. There must be something in these papers that Father Felix is ready to kill for. Then I'll call you back and we can decide what to do next."

Mrs. Hopwood hung up the phone, feeling very unsettled. She hadn't known Mr. Ironweed very well. He seemed like an unhappy man, always living in the past. But to think he was dead—and to think he died during fun day—and to think he was poisoned—and to think that someone was walking around that party with the intention of murdering him… Why, anyone could have drunk that tampered soda.

One of the teachers, one of the students.

St. Polycarp was definitely not a safe place and if Father Felix didn't admit that and if he refused to do something about that, then maybe Mrs. Johnston wasn't so crazy after all.

FORTY-FIVE

SHE HADN'T WORN LIPSTICK in years. She didn't even like lipstick and especially a bright red color. But it was lying on the counter of the department store, like it was a tester.

She thought maybe she could give it to Mrs. Hopwood.

She picked it up and opened it as though she was going to use it. And then she looked around. There was only one girl at the counter and she was way over at the other side, trying to sell some expensive eye cream to a lady with a deep tan, who was, quite frankly, beyond the eye cream remedy.

Miss Danvers dropped the lipstick into her tote bag, right under the fifth grade spelling papers, and made her way to the door.

She stopped at the scarf counter and then at the watches. It had been her experience that if she left immediately, she would evoke suspicion. Not hurrying away from the scene of the crime was a better option.

Only this time it didn't work. Not at all. She had just stepped out of the door when she was stopped.

"Excuse me, miss." A big, African-American security guard stepped in front of her.

"Yes?" She had to act perfectly innocent, even if her heart was pumping so loudly she could barely hear him.

"I'm going to have to ask you to come this way, please."

Several customers stopped to stare at her. She glowered back at them and tried to assume an innocent posture. "What is this about?" she snapped.

"I'd rather not discuss it here. If you'd come into the back room..."

"I demand to know!"

"Ma'am, you've been caught shoplifting."

A small circle of people, mostly women, mostly middle-aged and older, were gawking at her as though she had committed a murder and not merely pinched a lipstick, which was nothing but a tester and something that couldn't be sold anyway.

"That's ridiculous!" Still she proclaimed her innocence.

"I'm afraid," the man said in a serious, grim tone, "that I'm going to have to ask you to empty out your tote bag. Now, you can do this here or in the back. It's up to you."

She was not going to do it there. Not in the center of the store, with all these strangers examining her as if she were a character in a Patriot's Day play. She walked behind the guard and muttered to no one in particular, "It's a mistake."

But it wasn't a mistake and the security guard, whose name tag said Bill Douglas, soon found the tester when he emptied out her bag.

"It must have fallen in," Miss Danvers said to the man who was sitting at the desk. He wore a suit and looked like he just walked off the set of one of those *Law & Order* shows.

"We have you on tape." The man at the desk had a raspy voice. "So don't waste your breath."

Meanwhile Bill Douglas was examining her tote bag, her spelling tests, her plan book, her progress reports. He even peeked into her lunch container and opened her Tupperware container of tuna fish. Then he started on her handbag, emptying it out on the desk. She had stashed candy from the Halloween party inside with her pill container, with vitamins and aspirin, and her address book, and her wash and dries in case of a spillage in the classroom. And finally he opened her wallet and looked at her identification.

Miss Danvers did not protest. She didn't think it would matter if she did. She could only hope that they wouldn't charge her. She said the Hail Mary privately, although she wondered if it was all right to pray to escape punishment when you were clearly guilty.

"Okay," Bill said and he paused and exchanged looks with the man at the desk. "I see that you're a Catholic school-teacher. I'm going to tell you what we're going to do. We're not going to charge you. But we don't want you in this store again. Not for at least a year. If we see you on the premises—"

"I won't be back," she said.

But then the man at the desk, who hadn't even glanced at her, looked again at her wallet and took down her name and address. Miss Danvers did not like that. All of it seemed like an invasion of privacy which, of course, it was, but having committed a criminal act, she was hardly in a position to complain.

"You can go now."

Miss Danvers practically flew out of the store. The wave of relief that swept over her was exhilarating. She had gotten away with it. Well, not quite. She had been caught, but if they weren't going to press charges, who would care?

Besides, Mrs. Hopwood didn't deserve that lipstick. She hadn't been very nice to Miss Danvers. She tended to stick by Mrs. Johnston, who could be quite nasty.

Miss Danvers had a feeling that everything was going to turn out all right.

FORTY-SIX

THERE WAS LITTLE DOUBT in Father Felix's mind that Mr. Ironweed had been murdered. The coroner didn't even bother with an autopsy. The janitor was old and perhaps the heavy lifting at St. Polycarp had contributed to his death.

Father Felix knew differently.

After Mrs. Johnston had left with her rambunctious students, Father Felix had performed the last rites. He looked around at the room, at the spilled soda and the half eaten food. He went upstairs to wait for the ambulance. He watched, with half the students of St. Polycarp, as they carried Mr. Ironweed away with a sheet over his face. Then Father Felix decided to return to the boiler room.

He remembered seeing the empty cup of cola on the floor while he was performing the sacrament and he wondered if maybe there was a trace of something else in that cup, something besides the soda.

But the cup was gone.

He searched in the trash bin and even in the cafeteria, where the students had made some progress straightening up. Nothing.

Someone else had been in the school. Someone else had taken away that cup.

And it wasn't Mrs. Johnston, because Father Felix had seen her sitting in her car. Besides, the doors were locked. She couldn't have gotten back in. It was someone else, someone hiding.

The cup was taken because the murderer knew what would have been discovered. And if poison had been added to that cup and it had occurred during the party, it was also possible the killer believed he was murdering Father Felix.

Again Father Felix pictured Miss Mooney, with her bony finger outstretched, cursing the school, cursing the teachers and cursing him.

He wished that he had the nerve to call her, to plead with her to remove the curse. But what if she made it worse? Was that possible?

Somehow on his own, he'd have to find a way to turn the situation around. And he'd have to do it without the help of Mrs. Johnston or Mrs. Hopwood or Sister Scholastica or Sister Augusta, because if the police got even the slightest suspicion that not one, but two murders had been committed at St. Polycarp, they wouldn't even wait until June to close the doors of the school.

It was after Mr. Ironweed's funeral Mass when Father Felix was sitting inside his office, wondering how he was going to find another janitor and how soon it would be before Sister Augusta and the diocese began to wonder why so many people at St. Polycarp were having heart attacks, he heard a knock on his door.

Ms. Morningstar poked her face in and said that Mr. Brewer, Bruce's father, wanted to speak to him.

"This is not a good day," Father Felix said. "Tell him to wait until parents' night."

"He says it's urgent."

"I just finished a funeral Mass and really—"

The door burst open and a rather intimidating Mr. Brewer stood in the threshold. "I just need a minute of your time, Father," he demanded, barreling his way in.

"It's all right, Ms. Morningstar," Father Felix said to his secretary as though there was some way she might have stopped Mr. Brewer.

"Would you like to have a seat?" Father Felix asked, although that would mean that he'd have to get up and clear off a chair.

Mr. Brewer shook his head. "I come here on a matter of great importance."

"So you said." Father Felix could only hope that the bump Bruce had received weeks ago hadn't grown and, in the meantime, Mr. Brewer had spoken to his friends and relatives and they had all advised him to sue St. Polycarp.

"Your son Bruce is doing so well." Father Felix decided to start in the affirmative.

"This isn't about Bruce."

Father Felix released a sigh of relief, which lasted about a half a second.

"This is about my credit card."

"Your credit card?"

"That's right, my credit card," Mr. Brewer continued in a slightly hostile tone. "Someone is using it."

"Isn't this a matter for the police?"

"I've been to the police and they told me to come here."

Father Felix stared down at the Educational Evaluation from St. Jude, focusing on its bright purple cover. "I don't understand."

"These purchases, they are all made through the computer."

"All right…" Father Felix was trying hard to find a connection.

"You have a computer room."

"That's true."

"Someone here has gotten hold of my credit card number and they are using your computers to make all sorts of purchases."

Father Felix was not a computer whiz—in fact, he was afraid of them. His heart pounded every time he saw a message with an X in the box. So perhaps there was a way to trace the computer used to make the purchases, and that trace led straight back to St. Polycarp. Somehow, though, that sounded rather involved, and Father Felix thought the police probably had more pressing matters to attend to.

Like the murders of poor Mildred Pinkerton and Mr. Ironweed.

If they had known.

"You're not listening to me, Father Felix."

"Yes, I am." He was a priest who lied. "Just because we have a computer room doesn't mean—"

"I was against getting this credit card. I want you to know that. But my wife insisted. She said in case of emergency. I put it in my drawer and I never used it. All of a sudden I get a bill for five hundred dollars!"

"That's very disturbing. So the card wasn't stolen?"

"The numbers were!" Mr. Brewer snapped.

"But how would someone at St. Polycarp know those numbers, and, Mr. Brewer, it's not only the numbers that they need. The thief would have to know the expiration date, and there's a little code on the top—"

Mr. Brewer leaned over Father Felix's desk, causing Father Felix to tip back on his chair, almost falling. "You think that we don't know what's going on in this school? You think just because we don't have a lot of fancy degrees, we're not worried?"

Father Felix shook his head.

"That teacher dying of a heart attack, and then the janitor croaks a few weeks later, that's no coincidence. My credit card number being stolen, while it's still in the drawer, my little boy being trapped behind a sofa, almost smothered to death? Well, we know exactly who is to blame."

Father Felix was wishing that Mr. Brewer would share the information with him.

"This is not normal stuff, not stuff that human beings can do. There is a presence in this school, like a fog that's sweeping over the area." Mr. Brewer began to gesture feverishly.

"Aliens?" Father Felix asked.

"I'm not saying aliens." Mr. Brewer backed off. "All I'm

saying is that it's not a normal force, not something we can fight in the usual ways. So me and the parents, we're going to get together and think about how we can rid the school of this evil presence."

"That's a good idea." Another lie from a priest.

"In the meantime, Father, I'd advise you to do a lot of praying."

As though he hadn't been doing a lot of praying. "Well, thank you for bringing this matter to my attention." Father Felix stood and Mr. Brewer got the hint. He actually winked at the priest as he exited.

Father Felix sank down in his chair again. Hadn't Ms. Morningstar said something about her credit card number being used by a stranger? Maybe Mr. Brewer wasn't so crazy, after all.

He hoped that it was aliens who had invaded the school.

That would be so much simpler.

FORTY-SEVEN

MRS. HOPWOOD'S CLASSROOM was a mess. Papers littered the floor, the wastebasket was overflowing, and she saw a roach scurrying in the corner. Mr. Ironweed had only been dead for a few days and the entire school was sinking under. There was no telling when Father Felix would be able to find a new janitor, if he was even looking.

Mrs. Hopwood suspected he was not. The poor man had plenty of other things to worry about, especially with someone like Mrs. Johnston breathing down his neck, convinced that he was a murderer.

It was snack time in the second grade and Mrs. Hopwood was devouring her peanut butter crackers greedily. She was afraid to eat anywhere but her classroom, and she guarded the food she brought from home.

Father Felix marched into her classroom and looked around, rather discouraged. Well, it wasn't up to her to clean the classroom, was it?

"Did you get the book?" he asked her.

"Excuse me?"

"Did you get the Educational Evaluation book?"

She shook her head. She could not believe that with everything that had happened, with two staff members suddenly and permanently checking out, Father Felix was still going ahead with this Educational Evaluation—as though it mattered.

"I handed it to Mr. Alabaster. He said that he'd drop it off in your classroom."

"I have a prep coming up," Mrs. Hopwood said. "I assume that the gym teacher is here."

"He's here but he's strained his arm so all he can do is point."

Mrs. Hopwood didn't care what he could do as long as he disappeared with her children.

Father Felix drew a deep breath and prepared to say something. But just as he was opening his mouth, Harold came running up to report that he had spilled his apple juice on the floor.

Which meant Mrs. Hopwood would have to make a half-hearted attempt to wipe it up.

Father Felix rolled his eyes and left.

MR. ALABASTER WAS NOT in his classroom and, when she attempted to find him, she learned that he was taking his students for a walk around the block. He hoped to get rid of their excess energy.

There was no sign of the Educational Evaluation book in his classroom.

Mrs. Hopwood found that she had fifteen minutes of free time. She could use it to change her bulletin board from ghosts and goblins to turkeys and thankful prayers, or she could correct the math quiz, or she could create a thematic unit for the upcoming faculty meeting or she could snoop.

She chose to snoop.

She snuck down into the basement, with every intention of searching the boiler room. If Mrs. Johnston had found the Educational Evaluation folder in Mr. Ironweed's desk, there was no telling what other secrets Mr. Ironweed was privy to.

Perhaps he was the one who had taken the folder from her desk. But why and for whom?

When she reached the janitor's door, she found that it had been bolted with a padlock.

So much for that, she thought.

SHE ENTERED the teachers' room with lunch—her tuna sandwich and her potato chips, all brought from home and carried in her handbag. Mr. Alabaster was there with Miss Danvers, Miss Crossover and Mrs. Belgrave. Mrs. Hopwood sat down, looked at the full pot of brewing coffee and decided to pass.

"So I said to the mother—" Mrs. Hopwood assumed that Mr. Alabaster was telling one of his convoluted tales "—I'm not giving your son an A if he doesn't deserve it. Math isn't like literature, there's no latitude. Either you got the problem right or you didn't. Her son didn't get the problems right. I offered to help him after school, but he has to go work in their bodega. Then the kid tells me, on the QT, that his parents are planning to burn down the bodega in order to get insurance money. What am I supposed to do with information like that?" Mr. Alabaster was using his teeth to break open some red pistachio shells.

"Nothing," Miss Danvers said. "Don't get involved. First of all, you don't know that it's true. And if it is true, it makes them dangerous people."

Mrs. Hopwood couldn't help but wonder if more dangerous people were sitting right there beside her.

"Could I have some more of those?" Miss Crossover asked.

"Sure, be my guest." He shot the bowl across the table and Miss Crossover picked up a handful, examined her pink palms and then looked down at her pale tan cashmere sweater.

"I'll have some too." Mrs. Belgrave took a handful. "Be careful of that beautiful sweater, Bonnie. It would be a shame to stain it. Where did you get it?"

"It's a Ralph Lauren. I bought it in three colors. Beige and—"

"Mr. Alabaster, do you have my Educational Evaluation book?" Mrs. Hopwood interrupted.

"Oh yeah. Father Felix asked me to give it to you and I

was planning to but then some fourth graders were fighting in the hall—"

"What fourth graders?" Miss Crossover was using her French manicured nails to break open the shells.

"Two little boys. One of them is missing his teeth, probably from other fights. One of them has a nasty cowlick."

"Anthony and Andrew. Troublemakers," Miss Crossover commented thickly as she chewed.

Mr. Alabaster rose from his chair, went over to the sofa, picked up Mrs. Hopwood's Educational Evaluation book and then promptly dropped it on the floor. He retrieved it, then shoved it across the table. It landed at Miss Crossover's place. She shoved it toward Mrs. Hopwood.

Mrs. Hopwood took the book. She supposed at some point she'd have to at least scan it.

"You want a ride home tonight?" Mr. Alabaster offered.

The door opened and Mrs. Johnston walked in. "She does not," Mrs. Johnston spoke for her.

Mr. Alabaster did not seem bothered by her rudeness. Instead he extended the bowl. "Want some nuts?"

Mrs. Johnston looked at him with some disdain. "No, thank you," she said in a rather snippety voice. "I'm not staying. Mrs. Hopwood, may I speak to you privately?"

"Amelia," Mrs. Belgrave said in a trembling voice, "when you have a minute do you think you could put that water bottle on the cooler? We're all rather thirsty and you're the only one who can lift it."

"When I have a minute," Mrs. Johnston said briskly.

Mrs. Hopwood rose, left her sandwich, her chips, and her book but grabbed her open can of Sprite and followed Mrs. Johnston into the corridor.

"I was up all night." Mrs. Johnston lowered her voice to a whisper.

Mrs. Hopwood looked for circles under Mrs. Johnston's eyes but her brown skin was even and smooth.

"I'm faced with a moral dilemma. That's what kept me

up. That and the twins' teething, whimpering and whining. I almost poisoned them with all the whiskey I put on their gums. How old do kids have to be before you can sleep through the night?"

Mrs. Hopwood thought for a moment. "I'm not sure. I think about twenty-five."

"Thanks. You're a great help. Anyway, we have to do the right thing."

"The right thing?"

"It's up to us because no one else seems to care. Either that or they're not smart enough to make the connection. Not that I want to cause trouble. But I really need to know what side of the fence you're on."

"What side of the fence?"

"The matter cannot be handled within these walls. We have to seek outside help."

"Outside help?"

"What is wrong with you?" Mrs. Johnston said irritably. "Are you deaf? You keep repeating everything I say. I'm going to make an appointment with Sister Augusta and tell her our suspicions."

"But Sister Augusta is such a serious person."

"Murder is a serious business."

"You mean you're going to go in there and just accuse Father Felix without one shred of proof?"

Someone was climbing up the stairs.

Mrs. Johnston's big, round, black eyes flickered around. "No, I'm just going to tell her what's happening. She can draw her own conclusions. Father Felix is doing nothing to protect us."

"Well, maybe he is," Mrs. Hopwood argued, "and we just don't know about it."

"He certainly didn't do a very good job protecting Mr. Ironweed!"

Mrs. Hopwood could not argue that point. "Where're my papers? The ones you took from Mr. Ironweed's desk?"

"Shh! I am still looking them over."

Father Felix sneaked up behind them. Mrs. Hopwood released a slight scream.

"Are you ladies having a problem?"

"Nothing we can't handle." Mrs. Johnston pasted a fake smile on her face.

"Let me know what you decide tonight," Mrs. Johnston said, as she walked away, leaving Mrs. Hopwood with Father Felix.

"What was that all about?" Father Felix asked.

"She wants me to join Amway," Mrs. Hopwood lied.

FORTY-EIGHT

"I'D LIKE TO SPEAK to Sister Augusta."

"She's in a meeting. May I take a message?"

Mrs. Johnston hesitated. She didn't want to leave a message, but she knew that she could play phone tag all day. "This is Mrs. Johnston. I'm calling from St. Polycarp Elementary School. I have a matter of great importance to discuss with her."

"If you leave a name or number, I can have Sister Augusta call you back."

"I really would like to meet with her."

"If you leave a name or number, I can have Sister Augusta call you back," the mechanical voice repeated.

"It is very important that this remain confidential," Mrs. Johnston said.

"If you leave a name or number, I can have Sister Augusta call you back."

Mrs. Johnston left her cell phone number. And then, against regulations, she left her cell phone on all during class.

But Sister Augusta did not return her call.

MRS. JOHNSTON WAS leaving for the evening when she noticed Mr. Alabaster in the computer room, working busily on one of the computers. At first, she assumed that he was merely typing a math test.

She was walking down the hallway when she saw him rise and leave the room briefly. She watched him as he strolled down the corridor and went into the faculty bathroom.

Then Mrs. Johnston sneaked into the computer room and looked at what Mr. Alabaster had been working on.

He was on that gambling website again, a site called youareawinner.com. It offered to place casino bets, basketball bets, poker and blackjack bets. Offers of big money kept flashing before her very eyes and, if Mrs. Johnston had been the type of woman to take risks, she might have been lured by all the promises.

Her eyes traveled down to the bottom of the page, where the owner's name and e-mail address were prominently displayed. She was horrified to learn that the website belonged to none other than Albert Alabaster.

When she heard someone approaching the room, she leaped up and dashed over to a computer in the corner, pretending to be absorbed.

Mr. Alabaster didn't even notice her, which was a good thing, because Mrs. Johnston was trying to figure out what all of this meant.

It was not against the law to operate a website. But Father Felix certainly wouldn't approve. But then again, if Father Felix was a murderer then it hardly mattered whether or not he would approve the actions of any of his teachers.

But what if Mr. Alabaster was somehow using his website in the classroom? And what if—what if—Mr. Ironweed happened to stumble upon this little secret (although Mrs. Johnston was willing to bet, if she were a betting woman, which she was not, that Mr. Ironweed was probably quite computer illiterate). Besides, it would not explain poor Mildred Pinkerton's passing, since she had died *before* Mr. Alabaster came on the scene.

It wouldn't even explain the cookie money, because that was missing before Mr. Alabaster had been found.

It was all very confusing.

Mrs. Johnston could call Mrs. Hopwood after school to

discuss the matter with her, although Mrs. Hopwood was quite useless when it came to support.

Nevertheless, Mrs. Johnston had a feeling that this information was going to come in mighty handy.

FORTY-NINE

SHE WANTED THAT DANISH PASTRY. And she didn't want to break her twenty-dollar bill. Besides, every time she handed the clerk a big bill, he scowled at her.

The clerk was busy with someone behind the counter, trying to explain to the person that flavored coffee was more expensive than regular and it was wrong to take a sip before paying. "Pay first!" the clerk kept insisting. But the customer was pretending that he didn't understand.

Miss Danvers didn't understand either. She didn't understand why the teachers at St. Polycarp Elementary School had supported this deli for so long. The coffee was never fresh, the fruits were bruised, the sandwiches skimpy, and even their chips often had an expiration date that had come and gone.

But there was nothing wrong with the cheese Danish.

So she took it. She lifted it up from the glass container and pretended she was searching for her wallet. Instead, she just dropped the Danish into her handbag, tissue paper and all.

And then she walked out of the store. She stood on the sidewalk and took the pastry out of her pocketbook and devoured it. And while she was enjoying all that sugared cheese, she turned around and she saw Mrs. Hopwood, carrying a cup of coffee, exiting the store.

Mrs. Hopwood didn't say anything. She just stared at Miss Danvers. Miss Danvers knew by the expression on her face that Mrs. Hopwood had seen what she had done.

Well, what had she done really? She had taken a two dollar item. All the business that Miss Danvers had given the deli, she was entitled to a lousy two dollar piece of pastry. They should be giving her something for free now and then.

But Mrs. Hopwood didn't look like that's what she thought. Not at all. She walked right by Miss Danvers with a sick, odd expression on her face.

Miss Danvers knew exactly what was going to happen. Mrs. Hopwood would go straight home and call Mrs. Johnston and reveal what she had witnessed. Everyone knew that Mrs. Johnston was a notorious gossip and the fact that Miss Danvers had pinched a piece of pastry would be all over the school.

The memory of two people dead of heart attacks would fade like a first grader's voice singing solo in the Christmas play. Everyone would be abuzz with Miss Danvers's petty crime.

Miss Danvers wondered what she could do put a stop to Mrs. Hopwood's big fat mouth.

FIFTY

"Is this Father Felix?"

Father Felix hated conversations which began in that manner. He felt that the caller should always identify himself first.

"To whom am I speaking?" he snapped.

"This is Bill Douglas from Mayfair Department Store. Is this Father Felix?"

"It is." Father Felix's first reaction was bewilderment. He could not imagine why this gentleman was calling him. He hadn't been in Mayfair Department Store in months. Had he entered some sort of raffle and now they were calling him to claim his prize?

Yeah, right.

"Do you employ a teacher by the name of Hilda Danvers?"

"Yes. Is she looking for some sort of a part-time job? I can tell you that she always comes in on time, well, mostly always. And she doesn't make a practice of taking days off, like some of the other teachers, especially around the holidays."

"This is not about a job."

Father Felix was mute.

"I think that you should know that your reliable Hilda Danvers was caught shoplifting in our store a few days ago."

"I think there must be some sort of a mix-up." Now Father Felix was really befuddled.

"She was seen pocketing a lipstick tester."

"Miss Danvers doesn't even wear lipstick," Father Felix

argued. "She's a middle-aged woman, a little on the heavy side, with bulging eyes, bushy hair and protruding teeth."

"Father, I know what she looks like. I saw her school ID. I'm talking about the same woman."

"But why would she do such a thing?" Father Felix wondered aloud. "It's not as though the woman is poor. She gets a decent salary, although she is taking care of an aging father and maybe—"

"Father, I am not a psychiatrist. I'm a security guard. My cousin went to St. Polycarp. Of course, we're going back about twenty years. Out of respect for the school and because I'm a Catholic myself, I've persuaded the store not to press charges. But I think you should know the sort of people who are teaching at your school. Aren't they supposed to be examples to your students? Don't you—"

"Yes, of course," Father Felix interrupted him, because the last thing in the world he needed now was a lecture from some lapsed Catholic. "I will certainly speak to Miss Danvers and I appreciate your telling me this. God bless you."

Father Felix hung up the phone, not giving Bill Douglas the opportunity to utter another word.

Hilda Danvers was a shoplifter. That piece of news was astonishing itself. But then Father Felix began to wonder...

Maybe Hilda Danvers was having some sort of financial problems and maybe somehow she had gotten hold of Ms. Morningstar's and Mr. Brewer's credit card numbers. It was a reach, but Father Felix was of the opinion that if you broke the law in one area, you might very well break it in another.

Maybe Miss Danvers was afraid that the Educational Evaluation would uncover something about her past. Maybe she had a police record and had somehow managed to keep it hidden. And if Mrs. Johnston took a real good hard look (and Mrs. Johnston was just the type of individual to take a real good hard look), there was no telling what would turn up.

Poor Mildred Pinkerton had been the first one to take a good hard look.

And maybe Mr. Ironweed.

No, he could not see Hilda Danvers as a cold-blooded murderer. She had been with the school going on three years and he certainly would have picked up on something somehow.

His thoughts were interrupted by a loud knock on the door. Ms. Morningstar burst in and announced in a rather gloomy voice, "Sister Augusta is waiting outside for you. She says that she has to meet with you. Right now."

FIFTY-ONE

"MRS. JOHNSTON, I'd like to speak to you."

Mrs. Johnston did not like to speak to parents during class time and especially so early in the morning. Mr. Knell was interrupting her class and it wasn't always easy to restore order after even a minor upset.

"I'm rather busy right now," she said as she stood at the door and watched her students, just itching to misbehave. "Parents' night is next week. At that time—"

"This won't take long."

Mrs. Johnston supposed it was about Meredith's C in English composition. But really it was about time Meredith learned to use paragraphs. The entire essay (which consisted of three pages) was written without one single break.

"This isn't about your teaching," Mr. Knell said suddenly. "In fact, it's not even about you."

Now Mrs. Johnston was interested.

"All right, class," she instructed. "You may read the chapter on your own. No talking!"

She knew that was a sheer impossibility but she had to say it anyway as she stepped into the hall, all ears.

"I want to issue a complaint."

The person to issue a complaint to was not Mrs. Johnston, but Father Felix. But Mrs. Johnston wasn't about to say that. She was too curious.

"I am very unhappy about Miss Pinkerton's replacement, Mr. Alabaster. I think he is teaching our children how to gamble!"

Mrs. Johnston tried her best to act utterly shocked.

"My Meredith is very interested. She goes on these websites and she practices. I swear if she could find a way, she'd place bets herself. And it's not just me who's not happy. Mr. Brewer actually got the number of his credit card stolen. I don't know how that happened, but I swear that it has something to do with this Alabaster fellow. Mr. Brewer…he thinks that there is an extraterrestrial being roaming the halls of St. Polycarp, but I think it's just a thief, plain and simple!"

Mrs. Johnston was thinking about how to respond but there was no need to do so, since Mr. Knell had not finished. "I pay a lot of money, work two jobs so Meredith can come here. I send her to Catholic school so she'll know the difference between right and wrong. What's she learning in seventh grade math? That's what I'd like to know."

"Probably not a lot." Mrs. Johnston found herself agreeing.

"That's what I thought," Mr. Knell said with some satisfaction.

"I promise you that this will get solved," Mrs. Johnston said.

"You're a good teacher," Mr. Knell told her. "You taught Meredith how to speak English good and how to write nice. I think she should have a good math teacher too."

"She will," Mrs. Johnston promised.

When Mrs. Johnston returned to class, she found bedlam. Students were out of their seats, arguing and throwing papers. Meredith remained at her desk, her eyes cast downward.

"If everyone is not in his seat at the count of three," Mrs. Johnston threatened, "there will be no recess."

After a great deal of scurrying, order was restored. The students began to read aloud one by one, but Mrs. Johnston was hardly paying attention. Instead she was thinking.

Mr. Alabaster was definitely up to no good. But whether that had anything to do with the dead people and the poison was doubtful. She was just about to write a note to Mrs.

Hopwood about the dilemma when there was a knock on the door.

Ms. Morningstar called her out of the classroom and again the class went wild. But this time Mrs. Johnston didn't care.

"Father Felix and Sister Augusta are in the faculty room waiting for you."

"Now?"

"Now. I'm supposed to watch your class. Do they have something to do?" Ms. Morningstar asked in a testy voice.

"They're supposed to be reading a short story. They can read it by themselves."

The students were almost finished reading the story and Mrs. Johnston knew in less than five minutes they would be idle. Idle children were trouble. But that wasn't Mrs. Johnston's problem.

Her problem was much bigger than idle children.

SHE HAD REQUESTED a meeting with Sister Augusta by herself. The fact that Father Felix was present was very unsettling. How could she possibly speak with him sitting right there?

Couldn't she at least ask Mrs. Hopwood to be present—for moral support?

She guessed not, because who would watch her class?

With a rather heavy heart, she made her way to the teachers' lounge and spotted Father Felix at the head of the table beside Sister Augusta. Both of them looked rather grave.

"Please come in, Mrs. Johnston, and have a seat," Sister Augusta said tersely.

Mrs. Johnston situated herself at the other end of the table, as far away from them as possible.

"You phoned my office and told me that you have a matter you wish to discuss with me and it needed to be in complete privacy," Sister Augusta said. "But as you, no doubt, realize there is a chain of command. You cannot go above Father Felix's head and go straight to the superintendent. It's just not done. And even if the matter concerns Father Felix, then he should have, at the very least, a chance to defend himself. Do you understand?"

Mrs. Johnston nodded her head.

"The matter you wish to discuss—does it concern Father Felix?"

"No."

Father Felix looked startled.

"Then whom does it concern?"

"It concerns…" Mrs. Johnston hesitated for a moment. "It concerns another teacher."

"This is a faculty problem?" Sister Augusta clearly saw this as something minor and she seemed very annoyed.

"In a manner of speaking," Mrs. Johnston said. She waited for either Father Felix or Sister Augusta to say something, to help her along. But both of them stared at her and waited.

Mrs. Johnston drew a deep breath. She looked at her hands, which were trembling. She felt intimidated, sitting there while a priest and a nun glared at her. But she had never been a woman to back down.

And she wasn't about to start now.

"It's come to my attention that the new teacher, the seventh grade teacher, who came to replace Miss Pinkerton, is not teaching math in the traditional manner."

"Who is this new teacher?" Sister Augusta spoke.

"His name is Albert Alabaster." Father Felix spoke for the first time. "He came straight from the diocese."

"He did not," Sister Augusta said firmly.

"Well, that's what he said." Father Felix seemed extremely flustered.

"I don't care what he said," Sister Augusta argued. "I never heard of him and I know all the teachers we employ."

Father Felix paled and shot a nasty look in Mrs. Johnston's direction. Mrs. Johnston was thinking that Father Felix should consider himself lucky that she hadn't told Sister Augusta her real reasons for requesting the meeting.

"And how is he teaching math?" Sister Augusta asked.

"He has a website, his own website. It's a gambling website. He's teaching the children to how to bet, how to figure out odds—"

Sister Augusta gasped.

"Several parents are complaining. Some of them have had their credit card numbers stolen—"

"Do you have any proof of this?" Father Felix suddenly turned aggressive.

"I saw it with my very own eyes."

"Then why didn't you come directly to me?" He actually rose from his seat.

"Yes, why didn't you go directly to him?" Sister Augusta demanded.

"Well, because…" Mrs. Johnston was trying to think of a plausible excuse, but with the two of them staring at her that way, it was quite difficult. "It's because Father Felix never does anything," she said to Sister Augusta. "Two staff members have died of heart attacks at this school, weeks from one another, and he doesn't even think it's mysterious."

"I'm afraid that Mrs. Johnston has a histrionic personality." Father Felix sank down in his chair. "She sees trouble at every corner and if she doesn't, she will frequently manufacture it."

Mrs. Johnston thought that was rather a low blow, but since she had just called Father Felix incompetent to his superior, she could hardly complain.

"He does nothing," she muttered. And then much to her surprise, the door to the faculty room opened and Mrs. Hopwood came in, carrying a sandwich. She looked around at the grim scene and then said, "Is it okay if I put this in the refrigerator?"

Mrs. Johnston was not about to waste an opportunity. "Tell her," she demanded.

Mrs. Hopwood looked very confused.

"Tell Sister Augusta that Father Felix doesn't take us seriously. That when we brought our concerns to him, he got very irritated and practically threw us out of his office. After insulting your blinds and your bulletin boards."

Mrs. Hopwood started to sway in a most annoying manner. Mrs. Johnston wanted to get up and shake her, but she thought that action would only lend credence to the fact that she was melodramatic.

"Both of you listen here." Sister Augusta pointed her stubby finger.

"I just wanted to put my turkey in the refrigerator," Mrs. Hopwood said.

"Catholic schools are not a democracy. Teachers don't get to elect the principal and then vote on his performance. Father Felix was chosen to lead St. Polycarp because he has the experience and the education to do so. If you want to criticize him, then you must speak to him first. Although I must admit—" her voice softened "—you have some serious concerns."

Mrs. Hopwood began to back up towards the door. Mrs. Johnston would certainly have words with her tonight. "I'll keep my sandwich," she said as she made a grateful exit.

"You can leave, Mrs. Johnston," Sister Augusta said. "Right now Father Felix and I need to discuss this matter between ourselves. We'll call you if we have any questions."

Mrs. Johnston didn't like being dismissed and she especially didn't like the fact that they didn't seem in the least bit appreciative.

But, although she hadn't come right out and accused Father Felix (how could she?), she had at least planted a seed in Sister Augusta's mind. And she had reported Mr. Alabaster, which really was the right thing to do.

She had done something.

Which was more than she could say about the rest of the staff.

Especially her good friend, Mrs. Hopwood.

FIFTY-TWO

Mrs. Hopwood could not believe that Mrs. Johnston had actually contacted Sister Augusta. She had to give credit to her friend. She certainly had a lot of nerve. Mrs. Hopwood would never open her mouth. For one thing, she wasn't convinced of Father Felix's guilt. And second of all, she actually felt sorry for Father Felix. He certainly had his hands full. Two staff members dead within weeks of one another.

One teacher convinced that he was a murderer and one teacher who was a shoplifter.

So far Mrs. Hopwood hadn't said a word about what she had seen. Unlike Mrs. Johnston, Mrs. Hopwood didn't believe that it was her place to report people. Sooner or later Miss Danvers would get caught unless she stopped doing what she was doing. And for that she would need professional help. Maybe Mrs. Hopwood should recommend it to her.

But Mrs. Hopwood preferred to mind her own business. Although she was sure she'd get a vicious call from Mrs. Johnston that night because Mrs. Hopwood hadn't run to her defense in the teachers' lounge.

Mrs. Hopwood was packing up her schoolbag when she heard the rain lashing against the window panes. It was like a typhoon out there. The wind was actually howling. It would be impossible to hold an umbrella steady and her raincoat didn't have a hood.

And just when she was thinking about how horrible her situation was, Mr. Alabaster stuck his face in her doorway.

"You need a ride home?" he offered.

Mrs. Hopwood hesitated. While the weather was atrocious,

Mr. Alabaster's driving was abhorrent. Still, waiting for a bus in the middle of a hurricane was no class trip to the park.

"I'll take you to your door," Mr. Alabaster offered.

Mrs. Hopwood was immediately suspicious of the good deed. "May I be honest with you?"

Mr. Alabaster frowned.

"I appreciate the offer, I do. But your driving is a little—" she paused looking for a kind way to say dangerous and deadly "—a little erratic."

She had insulted him anyway. "I don't know what you mean. I get where I have to go and I've never been in a major accident."

Mrs. Hopwood thought it was just a matter of time. "You drive much too fast and you hit other vehicles and you keep right on going."

"Okay, okay." He put his hand up. Mrs. Hopwood was certain he would turn around and leave the room in a huff. But instead he promised to slow down.

"Well, that's very nice," she agreed, "but why would you want to go out of your way?"

"I guess you're not used to the staff at St. Polycarp being nice."

"Some of them are quite nice," Mrs. Hopwood said, "when they're not dead."

Mr. Alabaster ignored the comment. "I just hate to see you waiting in the rain. I'll meet you at the front door in about three minutes."

Mrs. Hopwood nodded, gathered the rest of her things and said an Act of Contrition as she prepared for the journey home.

They walked out of the building together and Mr. Alabaster, being somewhat of a gentleman, held the car door open for her.

She was just about to stoop down and climb into his sports car, when she heard a window fling open behind her.

"Julia!"

She turned around and saw to her amazement that Mrs. Johnston was hanging out the office window on the second floor. Her large bulky body was extended, her neck was stretched and she was calling out Mrs. Hopwood's name in a rather panicked voice. She was quite oblivious to the pelting rain.

Mrs. Hopwood thought that she had forgotten something and Mrs. Johnston was about to hurl an object at her. Instead Mrs. Johnston screamed, "Don't get into that car!"

It was nice of Mrs. Johnston to be so worried, but when a bolt of lightning struck, Mrs. Hopwood yelled back, "He promised to drive slowly."

"Don't get into that car!"

Mr. Alabaster, who had no umbrella himself, was getting soaking wet. "What's her problem?" he asked Mrs. Hopwood, as though she knew.

"Do not get into that car. Think of your son, Alex. Think of your husband. Think of your mother."

"He's going to go slow."

"I'm going to go slow," Mr. Alabaster bellowed as he walked over to the driver's side.

"He's a criminal!" Mrs. Johnston shrieked.

There was a clap of thunder and Mrs. Hopwood thought perhaps she hadn't heard correctly. She looked at Mrs. Johnston and then at Mr. Alabaster as she decided what to do.

"A dangerous criminal!" Mrs. Johnston yelled.

A dangerous criminal, Mrs. Hopwood wondered, although Mrs. Johnston hadn't said anything about Mr. Alabaster being a murderer. A gust of wind almost blew her off her feet and Mrs. Johnston's torso was yanked back from the window.

And just when Mrs. Hopwood had decided to risk all, and actually had one foot into the passenger's side, holding on to the seat for support, Father Felix stuck his head out the very same window. "Do not get into that car," he ordered Mrs. Hopwood.

Mrs. Hopwood was definitely confused but she knew one

thing. Father Felix was not prone to exaggeration and the thought that Father Felix and Mrs. Johnston were suddenly saying the same thing from the same office was rather disconcerting. She prepared to disembark her left side from the car.

"And as for you, Mr. Alabaster." Father Felix was attempting to be heard above the clamoring wind. "I must speak to you immediately. Sister Augusta is waiting for us in the teachers' lounge."

Mr. Alabaster started the car.

"If you would just come inside—"

But Mrs. Hopwood could plainly see that Mr. Alabaster had no intention of coming inside. Instead he moved the car forward with Mrs. Hopwood's calf still on the passenger side. The force of the speed threw her backward and she fell hard on the pavement.

"Are you all right?" Father Felix asked her.

"What happened?" Mrs. Johnston's head was bobbing outside the window.

"I want an explanation," Mrs. Hopwood said, "and it better be good."

FIFTY-THREE

MISS DANVERS WAS sneaking around the corridor.

It was important that she leave the school without being seen. She knew exactly what was happening. Mrs. Hopwood had gone straight to Father Felix and told him about the shoplifting. And, if that wasn't enough, she had dragged Mrs. Johnston with her.

This was just the sort of thing that Mrs. Johnston would love. Why, an incident like this would be worth hours of conversation between the three of them.

What was Miss Danvers to do?

She could quit her job, but that wasn't a viable option. Who would support her father? Who would buy the groceries and pay for the cable television he enjoyed? Who would be responsible for the taxes on the house and the vet bills for Sinbad, the twelve-year-old mutt he loved? Who would pay for the home health aid?

Well, if Miss Danvers quit her job she could become her father's home health aid, but she'd rather scrub floors.

No, Miss Danvers knew exactly what she was going to do. Tomorrow when Father Felix called her into his office, she would make certain that he was alone. And then she would accuse Mrs. Hopwood of being a liar and Mrs. Johnston of being a troublemaker.

She would deny the entire thing. After all, Mrs. Hopwood had no proof whatsoever.

And then she would steer clear of Mrs. Hopwood for the rest of the year.

But June was a long time away.

FIFTY-FOUR

FATHER FELIX SAT DOWN in his living room with a tumbler of brandy. He was hoping that the alcohol would calm him enough so that he'd be able to think clearly.

There was no question of keeping this from the diocese. Mrs. Johnston had already seen to that. Although why she had gone to Sister Augusta and not to him was still a mystery. She claimed that he hadn't acted, but she hadn't even given Father Felix a chance. Not where Mr. Alabaster was concerned.

If Mrs. Johnston was referring to the cookie money, Father Felix was bound by the seal of the confession so he couldn't confide in Mrs. Johnston even if he wanted to. But really it wasn't any of her business.

Father Felix was going to have to fire Mr. Alabaster first thing in the morning. That was assuming Mr. Alabaster returned to school.

Then there was the matter of Miss Danvers. So far no one knew about her shoplifting. He wouldn't fire her but he'd have to plead with her to get help. Although maybe he wouldn't renew her contract for next year.

But it wasn't the gambling site and the shoplifting charge that weighed heavy on his shoulders like the eighth graders' backpacks.

It was something far more serious.

After Mrs. Johnston and Mrs. Hopwood had left (Mrs. Hopwood had been attended to by Nurse Abby because she was quite battered and bruised when she had been dragged by Mr. Alabaster's car for a half a second), after Father Felix was sure that the school was empty, he went down to the boiler room and unlocked the door.

He emptied out Mr. Ironweed's desk and found the usual things, pencils, pens, magazines (and not ones he could share with the student body). He found something that gave him the willies: love notes to Miss Crossover. Father Felix doubted if Mr. Ironweed had ever given them to Miss Crossover. She certainly would have complained more bitterly to Father Felix if he had.

In the letters Mr. Ironweed admitted that he had let the rats loose in the school in an attempt to impress her. It was just his bad luck that Bonnie Crossover wasn't even in school that day. He promised to prove himself to her because he wanted to create a life together, and he vowed to get to know her in as many ways as possible.

Father Felix guessed that he was a stalker and it was Bonnie Crossover's good luck that Mr. Ironweed had died. Well, it was really Father Felix's good luck also because Father Felix would have had to fire Mr. Ironweed right alongside with Mr. Alabaster.

It made sense that Mr. Ironweed had a heart attack. The man was in his early seventies and carrying a torch for a thirty-year-old woman was bound to be frustrating and futile, especially for a man in Mr. Ironweed's position.

Except that Father Felix was doubtful that the heart had taken its own natural course.

It wasn't only the missing cup that worried Father Felix. It was something else. Something that Father Felix had found underneath the girlie magazines in the bottom drawer.

A list of credit card numbers and their expiration dates. Even the small codes.

Where had Mr. Ironweed gotten such a list and what had he intended to do with it?

Father Felix took another swig of brandy.

He supposed that it was possible that somehow Mr. Ironweed had found the list in Mr. Alabaster's classroom and was attempting to blackmail him. And Mr. Alabaster had murdered Mr. Ironweed in order to keep him quiet.

But then who had killed poor Mildred Pinkerton? Mr. Alabaster hadn't even been on the scene at the time of her death.

Maybe Miss Pinkerton hadn't been murdered at all. Maybe she just happened to have a heart attack and maybe Mr. Alabaster was using her demise to tie the deaths together, even though they weren't related.

Or maybe Mr. Alabaster operating a gambling website from St. Polycarp was just another crazy coincidence and Mr. Ironweed having the credit card numbers, yet another coincidence.

And what about Miss Danvers? Just because she happened to take a tube of lipstick from a department store didn't necessarily mean that she stole credit cards and murdered janitors.

And eighth grade teachers, who might have stumbled upon her dirty little secret.

Just another coincidence.

But as Father Felix finished the last of his brandy, he realized that there were too many coincidences for comfort.

FIFTY-FIVE

MRS. JOHNSTON ARRIVED at the crack of dawn on the following morning.

Mrs. Hopwood had some sort of school meeting the night before for her son and Mrs. Johnston was not able to get her on the phone. She left a message suggesting they have breakfast together in Mrs. Johnston's classroom, where they could discuss the situation behind closed doors.

But Mrs. Hopwood was running late, which really annoyed Mrs. Johnston, because after all Mrs. Hopwood only had herself to get ready and Mrs. Johnston had to worry about two two-year-old twins.

Mrs. Johnston finally went down to the office, hoping to catch Mrs. Hopwood coming in, and much to her surprise she saw Mr. Alabaster waiting on the bench. Her astonishment must have been obvious because he actually snickered at her. "You didn't think I'd come back, did you?"

"I didn't think you'd have the nerve."

"I didn't do anything wrong," he defended himself.

"You encouraged our students to gamble."

"I did not. I merely introduced them to a way of calculating the odds, as a math problem. They caught on right away. And, as far as I'm concerned, it's a more interesting way to teach than a lot of useless figures."

"Not if they're using their parents' credit cards."

Mrs. Johnston had to admit that Mr. Alabaster looked genuinely confused. "I don't know what you're talking about."

"Well, if you're waiting for Father Felix, you'll find out soon enough."

Mrs. Johnston looked up as Mrs. Hopwood came strolling down the hall, wearing a ridiculous pair of multi-striped rain boots and a bright pink slicker. She was carrying a lime-green umbrella.

It wasn't raining.

Mrs. Hopwood also looked stunned at seeing Mr. Alabaster sitting there complacently on the bench. She suddenly stiffened, opened her mouth, as though she wanted to say something, and then shut it quickly and turned away.

"You are so late," Mrs. Johnston accused her.

"I'm sorry, but there was a crazy person on the bus and we all had to get off."

"Do you want a ride home today?" Mr. Alabaster offered.

"You won't be here to be giving her any rides home," Mrs. Johnston said. "Besides, she won't go with you."

Mrs. Johnston looked at Mrs. Hopwood, who remained silent.

"Next time she accepts a ride home, she'll want it to be with a person who waits until she's out the car before taking off. But I suppose her not being with you was a blessing in disguise."

Someone was climbing up the front staircase. Mrs. Johnston hoped that it was Father Felix. She would like to see the expression on *his* face when he saw Mr. Alabaster waiting for him, as cool as could be. As though he had done nothing wrong. As though this were just another chilly November morning.

But it was only Miss Danvers, who had a furious expression on her flat face. At first Mrs. Johnston thought the anger was directed at Mr. Alabaster. Perhaps Mr. Alabaster had gotten hold of *her* credit card number also, which would certainly add fuel to the already raging fire.

But instead Miss Danvers turned towards Mrs. Hopwood, pointed her finger and said, "Thanks a lot for telling everyone."

Mrs. Hopwood immediately became defensive. "I swear to you, I didn't tell a soul. Why would I?"

Mrs. Johnston stood transfixed, curious and annoyed that she had no idea what was going down between them.

When Miss Danvers walked away, Mrs. Johnston shoved Mrs. Hopwood into the second grade classroom and demanded an explanation.

"She thinks that I went to Father Felix about something I saw."

"Yeah?" Mrs. Johnston leaned over Mrs. Hopwood as Mrs. Hopwood uncapped her coffee.

"But I didn't."

"I don't care if you did or you didn't," Mrs. Johnston said impatiently. "What I want to know is what you saw."

Mrs. Hopwood seemed very uncomfortable, which really angered Mrs. Johnston. "I would tell you," she said.

"And probably everyone else." Mrs. Hopwood took a sip of coffee.

"And what's that supposed to mean?"

Mrs. Hopwood took a deep breath. Mrs. Johnston could tell that she was about to give in. "I was at the deli..."

"Yes?"

"And I saw Miss Danvers take a piece of Danish without paying for it."

Mrs. Johnston sank down on one of the little second grade chairs. She heard a slight crack and then she rose again. "Is that all?"

"That's it. I swear. She put it in her pocketbook."

"She probably didn't want to stand in line. Still, it's not right. You didn't tell Father Felix?"

"I didn't want to be a snitch." Mrs. Hopwood opened her own handbag and took out a coffee cake muffin. She split it in half and handed a portion to Mrs. Johnston, who did not refuse.

"It seems to me that there's a lot of people here with secrets," Mrs. Johnston said. "And two of them are dead."

"I don't think that Miss Danvers would murder someone just because she steals food now and then." Mrs. Hopwood was getting crumbs all over her floor, which wasn't a good thing because since Mr. Ironweed's demise, St. Polycarp didn't have a janitor and, from the looks of things, Mrs. Hopwood was not taking his place. "And if Mr. Alabaster was a murderer, he probably wouldn't be sitting on that bench, trying to proclaim his innocence."

"Of course, he would," Mrs. Johnston argued. "Guilty people always try to claim they're innocent."

"Well, he can't be a murderer." Mrs. Hopwood finished her muffin and took another sip of coffee. "Because he wasn't even here when poor Mildred Pinkerton was killed."

"Unless he had a partner."

"And they decided to murder Miss Pinkerton so Mr. Alabaster could get a position at St. Polycarp because that's the only way you can get a teaching job in a Catholic school?" Mrs. Hopwood suggested sarcastically. "Or maybe he wanted to teach here because our parents are so wealthy he could use their credit cards to gamble away millions."

"Well, you're certainly in a mood," Mrs. Johnston said. "I'm going to tell you something I know for certain." She looked around and then started to whisper in a scandalized tone. "It's not over yet. I feel it in my bones."

"I hope you're wrong," Mrs. Hopwood said. "Because all this drama is beginning to affect my teaching."

"Yeah, like you can really teach," Mrs. Johnston commented as she left the second grade.

FIFTY-SIX

"MRS. HOPWOOD, you have a phone call."

Mrs. Hopwood was right in the middle of teaching the difference between a hard vowel and a soft vowel, something she didn't quite understand herself, when Ms. Morningstar strolled into her classroom.

The thought that someone was calling her in the middle of class felt as though a heavy pancake from the cafeteria had been dropped into her stomach.

Alex was in some sort of trouble.

"Can you take a message?" Her voice came out all squeaky and scared.

"If I could have taken a message, I wouldn't be here," Ms. Morningstar snarled. "They said it's important. I'll watch your class, but please, be quick. I have my own work to do."

"What's the matter, Mrs. Hopwood?"

"Where's she going?"

"Are we going to have a substitute?"

Mrs. Hopwood didn't even bother giving Ms. Morningstar instructions. Let her figure it out herself, Mrs. Hopwood thought, as she walked into the office and picked up the receiver.

"Mrs. Hopwood?" A voice she didn't recognize. Had Alex skipped school and been caught doing something illegal? Was she speaking to the police?

"Yes?" she whispered.

"This is Sister Santina from St. Jude School."

Mrs. Hopwood released a sigh of relief.

"Mrs. Hopwood, are you all right?"

"I'm fine. Just fine."

"I asked Father Felix to have you call us."

"Well, I never got the message." And then because Mrs. Hopwood didn't want Father Felix to look bad, she quickly added, "There's been a lot happening in our school. We lost our seventh grade teacher and our janitor died right on the premises—"

"Yes, I know all about the seventh grade teacher," Sister Santina said in a very non-sympathetic voice. "And I'm sorry about the janitor. Miss Pinkerton was very good about following up. But you're supposed to visit our school in January."

"I'll be there." It sounded like there was an argument going on in Father Felix's office.

"Well, it's less than two months away. And I need to know if you've had a chance to look at our Educational Evaluation book."

"Your what?"

"I never did it!" Mr. Alabaster was using quite a loud voice.

"The book we sent you."

Mrs. Hopwood thought about lying.

"I am not lying," Mr. Alabaster protested. "I never used those credit card numbers."

"No, I didn't," Mrs. Hopwood admitted. "And I'm very sorry about that. I promise that I'll read it in the next few days."

"This is just too much of a coincidence," Father Felix said. "Those students who gave you the credit card numbers have all had problems."

"I'd appreciate that," Sister Santina said. "I'll give you our phone number. And when you have had a chance to read it, will you please call me? I'd like to go over a few things before your visit."

"Yes, Sister, I will. And I do apologize."

Mrs. Hopwood found a pen and a scrap of paper on Ms. Morningstar's rather disorganized desk. She scrawled the number and promised again to be in touch. Then she hung up the phone and edged closer to Father Felix's closed door.

"All right," Mr. Alabaster said. "Some of the students did write down the credit card numbers and bring them to class. They wanted me to place bets. I refused. You can ask them. Ask Bruce Brewer and Gregory Morgan. I wouldn't do it."

"Well, maybe you used the credit card numbers for something else," Father Felix suggested. "Like maybe a flat screen television set or a new computer."

"I did not! The only person I placed a bet for was Ms. Morningstar. Her son talked her into betting on the NBA championships. She lost the bet and that was the end of it."

There was a long silence.

"Let me ask you another question." Father Felix was clearly unhappy. "How did you find out about the job opening in seventh grade?"

"I read the obituaries."

"You told me that the diocese sent you."

"No, Father Felix, I did not. You merely assumed the diocese sent me and I didn't correct you."

Mrs. Hopwood heard footsteps coming down the corridor.

There was another long pause.

"That piece of paper with the credit card numbers on it," Father Felix said. "Where is it?"

"I lost it."

"You lost it?" It was obvious from Father Felix's tone that he didn't believe Mr. Alabaster.

"I don't know what happened to it. I think I threw it away. I had it in the teachers' room and when lunch hour was over, I put my Subway wrapper in the trash. Maybe the paper was there too. I don't remember."

"What's going on?" Mrs. Hopwood jumped as she whirled around to face Miss Crossover.

"Oh, nothing. I—I had a phone call from the Educational Evaluation trip I'm supposed to go on. It never ends."

Miss Crossover ignored her complaint. "How's it going in there?"

"I think he might get fired."

"That's too bad," Miss Crossover said. "That means more work for all of us. Especially if Father Felix decides to split the class up until they find a sub."

"Mrs. Hopwood." She looked up to see Lydia coming down the hall. "Ms. Morningstar said that if you're finished with your phone call, she really needs to get back to work."

"I'm coming."

Mrs. Hopwood figured that the conversation between Father Felix and Mr. Alabaster was ending anyway. Miss Crossover stayed behind on the pretext of using the copy machine, but Mrs. Hopwood could plainly see that she had one ear to Father Felix's door.

As Mrs. Hopwood hobbled back to her classroom (her purple and black heels with the very pointy toes were crippling her), she wondered...if Mr. Alabaster hadn't used the credit cards, than who had? Miss Danvers?

She could discuss it with Mrs. Johnston but she knew that she would be opening a can of wiggly worms.

While the children colored in the welcome mats for parents' night, Mrs. Hopwood made a halfhearted attempt to flip through the Educational Evaluation book from St. Jude.

It was then that she discovered that page thirteen was missing.

FIFTY-SEVEN

MISS DANVERS RECEIVED the note during social studies. It was sent up by Ms. Morningstar, who was grumbling about the lack of an intercom system.

"This has been my morning," she said. "Watching classes while Father Felix meets with the teachers. And then he expects me to get out letters to parents about tardy children. As though that's the worst of his problems."

Miss Danvers thought that if Father Felix was meeting with all of the teachers then that meant that this meeting was not personal. Maybe he just wanted to give the teachers a pep talk because of everything that had happened.

So Miss Danvers was fairly optimistic as she approached his office.

The expression on Father's Felix face dashed her confidence.

"Please take a seat, Miss Danvers, and close the door behind you."

Her heart thumping much too fast (leaving her to wonder if she would be the third member of the staff to have a heart attack at St. Polycarp), she perched on the edge of the chair across from Father Felix.

The seat was quite warm, which told Miss Danvers that just minutes ago, Father Felix had spoken to someone else.

Mrs. Hopwood?

"This is a little awkward," Father Felix said quite slowly and deliberately, "but it has come to my attention that you have a shoplifting problem."

"I can't believe she went running to you. She has such a

big mouth. It was only a piece of Danish. And the deli was crowded. I had to get home and no one was waiting on me."

"To whom are you referring?"

"Mrs. Hopwood, of course. I also think you should know, Father Felix, that she hardly does any teaching in her classroom at all. Her children are always coloring."

"I appreciate your telling me that. But, Miss Danvers, this has nothing whatsoever to do with Mrs. Hopwood."

Miss Danvers was momentarily stunned. She realized then that everything that she had tried so hard to hide was about to come crashing down. And, in a way, it was a vast relief.

"Miss Pinkerton found out, didn't she? When she was doing the faculty checks, she learned that I had a record for a misdemeanor. But it was only Victoria's Secret. And only a pair of thong underwear—"

"Enough." Father Felix held up his hand. "This is too much information."

"It was only twice, I swear it. The Danish and the underwear. I was embarrassed to buy the panties. I thought the saleswoman would laugh at me. She was a skinny blonde and here I am, a middle-aged woman with a big backside—"

"It wasn't Miss Pinkerton," Father Felix interrupted her.

Now Miss Danvers was thoroughly confused and thoroughly angry with herself. She had confessed to crimes that Father Felix had been blissfully unaware of. Then how *had* he found out?

She didn't want to know.

He told her anyway. "The security guard at Mayfair Department Store phoned me. He said you were caught taking a lipstick tester."

"I thought it was free!"

Father Felix stared at Miss Danvers for a few moments. Miss Danvers hung her head low and tried to look humiliated.

"It's obvious that you have a problem. And it's also obvious that you need some kind of professional help."

"And I'll get it, honestly, Father. It's just that I have so much pressure at home with caring for my dad and all. But I swear I'll go into therapy."

"Yes, well, considering that you just swore to me a number of times a few minutes ago, and then turned around and told me bald-faced lies, you can understand why I'm dubious."

"Please, Father." Miss Danvers managed to bring a few tears to the surface. "Don't fire me. I have to support my dad and if I don't work, he'll have to go into a public nursing home."

"Miss Danvers, I'm going to ask you another question. And I need for you to be completely honest with me. Do you understand?"

"I couldn't lie to a priest."

He glared at her. "You have a problem with shop-lifting—"

"It's a compulsion, Father, but with help I think I'll be able to beat it."

"Do you also have a problem with credit cards?"

"Oh no. I only have American Express and you have to pay that at the end of the month so you can't get behind, not really."

"I mean—" Father Felix cleared his throat "—do you have a problem stealing them?"

Miss Danvers was appalled. "Just because I take a lipstick tester or a piece of pastry now and then doesn't mean that I'm guilty of credit card fraud. I wouldn't even know how to do that if I wanted to."

"Supposing you were to find some credit card numbers…"

"You mean, like a slip on the street? But wouldn't you have to know the name and the address? And wouldn't you need the actual card?"

Father Felix shook his head. "You can go back to your class now."

Miss Danvers stood, slightly relieved. "Thank you, Father. And I promise you, I'm going to take care of my little problem. You won't say anything about this, will you? I mean, you *are* a priest."

Father Felix seemed rather surprised at her question. "I'm afraid, Mrs. Danvers," he said, "it's a little late to be silent."

As Miss Danvers walked back to her classroom, she was sure that Mrs. Hopwood was already smearing her reputation. If Mrs. Hopwood had told Mrs. Johnston, then Father Felix was right. It was all over the school.

Well, as long as they could keep it from the students.

But really, she thought, you'd think that Father Felix would have more important things to deal with. At least I'm not teaching my children how to gamble.

FIFTY-EIGHT

SHE WAS LYING.

Father Felix realized that Miss Danvers couldn't be trusted. But then again, he was hardly a competent principal. He'd managed to hire a shoplifter and a compulsive gambler.

And a murderer.

The question was—who was the murderer? Miss Danvers was right about one thing. Just because she pinched a few items (really nothing of value, but he supposed that wasn't the issue) it didn't mean that she stole credit card numbers. And even if she had used the credit card numbers for her own benefit, it didn't mean she was a murderer.

But the problem was that he couldn't believe Miss Danvers. If she had lied to him a few minutes ago, then chances were she'd lie again. In a heartbeat.

He couldn't keep her at the school but right now he couldn't replace her either. He had to replace Mr. Alabaster and the janitor. The parents were in an uproar.

He couldn't blame them.

The school was turning into an insane asylum and he was the gatekeeper.

Maybe he could find someone else to take Mr. Alabaster's seventh grade, someone relatively dull and normal. And maybe he could find a substitute for Miss Danvers while she worked on her problem. And maybe someone had an uncle who needed a job and could keep the school clean without managing to get killed.

And then maybe things would go back to normal.

Then maybe he could forget about Mr. Ironweed and the

missing cup and the stolen credit card numbers and everything would just die down...

Die down. Two people down already and he was just going to let it go? Not even make an attempt to find out why?

He couldn't do that. He owed it to Mr. Ironweed (although it was beginning to look as if Mr. Ironweed wasn't the man he appeared to be). But Father Felix certainly owed it to Miss Pinkerton. He owed it to the school, to the diocese. To the students. To the faculty.

To God.

But unless God helped him with a miracle, he didn't see how he was going to solve this.

FIFTY-NINE

"WELL, TELL ME WHAT you heard," Mrs. Johnston demanded as she cut a Mars bar into tiny pieces for her two boys.

"Father Felix confronted Mr. Alabaster. Mr. Alabaster admitted to teaching the kids how to gamble but he swears that he never encouraged it nor did he take any credit card numbers."

"Liar," Mrs. Johnston spat. "Jeffery James, this is your candy. That's your brother's. Eat your own candy."

"You're giving them candy?" Mrs. Hopwood asked over the phone. "It's almost supper time."

"It keeps them quiet while I make macaroni and cheese."

"He sounded pretty convincing," Mrs. Hopwood said. "He said he had a list of credit card numbers, which he claims to have lost in the teachers' room. I guess, if that's true, any teacher could have picked it up. And another thing—"

"Okay, that's it. No one is getting any candy!" The boys started to wail. Mrs. Johnston had to resist the temptation to slap them. "If you can't eat nicely—"

"Do you want to hear this?" Mrs. Hopwood asked rather impatiently.

"Of course I want to hear it," Mrs. Johnston snapped. Mrs. Hopwood didn't understand the first thing about being a mother, the constant distractions. Perhaps Alex had been an ideal toddler, but he was making up for it now. "I wouldn't have called you if I didn't want to hear it."

"Ms. Morningstar asked Mr. Alabaster to place a bet."

"No!"

"Yes, but according to Mr. Alabaster, when she lost, that was that."

"I knew it!" Now Justin Joseph was throwing his candy at his brother and a tiny piece hit Mrs. Johnston smack in the jaw. "So help me, God, both of you boys are going to time out! Didn't I tell you right from the get-go that there was something not right with that woman?"

"Just because she placed a bet doesn't make her a murderer," Mrs. Hopwood said.

"How do you know all of this, anyway?" Mrs. Johnston was feeling rather prickly. Between Mrs. Hopwood's constant challenging of her and the twins' never ending screeching, it was hard to keep an upbeat attitude.

"I told you. I got a call from the principal of St. Jude. She wanted to know if I had looked over their Educational Self-Evaluation."

"And had you? All right, that's it. Hold on." Mrs. Johnston picked up both of the twins, one in each arm. They were screaming as though she was beating them with a stick. She opened the door to the playroom and dropped both of them in the playpen. They continued to holler.

She slammed the door behind her, removed a piece of sticky candy out of her hair and returned to the phone. "Are you still there?"

"I'm still here," Mrs. Hopwood said in an exasperated voice, as though she had something to be exasperated about. "I did look over their evaluation and discovered something strange."

"Really?" Now that she had put the twins in the other room, Mrs. Johnston could barely hear their shrieks. She could concentrate on the conversation at hand. "How was it strange?"

"There was a page missing."

"You mean that the fool who was collating it left something out?"

"I'm not sure. I think that the missing page was actually torn out," Mrs. Hopwood said.

"Why?"

"Because I can see some rough edges. And pages twelve and fifteen, they have these queer red stains on them."

Mrs. Johnston gulped. "You mean like blood?"

"No, more like food coloring." Mrs. Hopwood stopped and then said suddenly. "I know what it is! Mr. Alabaster actually handed me the book in the teachers' room and he was eating some red pistachio nuts. He must have gotten the dye on the pages."

Mrs. Johnston didn't think that was very likely. "Was the book open?"

Mrs. Hopwood had to admit that it wasn't.

"You have to call Sister Susan tomorrow and find out about that missing page."

"Her name is Sister Santina."

"Whatever."

"I'd feel kind of silly," Mrs. Hopwood said.

"Why? You have a perfect right to know what was on that page. It could be something important. Before she died, poor Mildred Pinkerton left us two clues. She said the cookie money was missing. We still don't know who took the cookie money and the fact that Father Felix won't tell us is highly suspicious. She also said that someone is not who they appear to be. I think Miss Pinkerton stumbled on something while she was researching our Educational Evaluation…" The twins were now screaming at the top of their lungs. Mrs. Johnston was afraid that the neighbors would call the police, as they had done in the past.

"But this is someone else's Educational Evaluation," Mrs. Hopwood argued.

Mrs. Johnston found Mrs. Hopwood's constant need to argue as tiring as raising her two terrible twins. "Didn't Miss Pinkerton have a copy of that Educational Evaluation?"

"Yes."

"And didn't it disappear?"

"It did."

"So call. I have to go." Mrs. Johnston hung up the phone and went inside to deal with her children. How could it be that Mrs. Hopwood, a reasonably intelligent woman, couldn't see that it was necessary to follow up every lead, no matter how unimportant it seemed?

Two people had already been killed.

And Mrs. Johnston had every reason to believe that the murderer still had unfinished business at St. Polycarp.

SIXTY

MRS. HOPWOOD WAS anticipating a long day. For one thing, it was pouring out, which meant no recess for the children. For another thing, it was parents' night, an evening when parents and guardians would pick up their children's report cards from three to five and from seven to nine. The teachers had to hang around the school and wait and then explain to befuddled adults why their precious children were not performing up to par.

It seemed to Mrs. Hopwood that all parents had the same reaction to poor marks. "My child can do better," they all claimed. "He's just not trying hard enough." No one ever wanted to admit that perhaps their child was not academically inclined. It was easier to claim that he was lazy.

Was that Alex's excuse? Was he just not smart enough to get the Bs that Mrs. Hopwood had been demanding of him?

"DID YOU CALL Sister Santina?" Mrs. Johnston demanded at two forty-five, after the children were dismissed.

"I forgot." And Mrs. Hopwood *had* forgotten. There was an outbreak of chicken pox in her class and three children had already gone home. The parents were behaving as if someone had let loose the black plague. It was only the beginning of November and already Mrs. Hopwood had faced head lice and chicken pox.

She couldn't wait until flu season.

"Call her now." Mrs. Johnston was eating a chocolate ice cream bar with a crunchy coating.

"It's almost three. She's probably not there."

"You have to try," Mrs. Johnston insisted. "You don't know what this might mean."

What Mrs. Hopwood knew was that Mrs. Johnston was quite bossy and quite determined. And, so far, with all of her meddling, all of her suspicions had come to nothing. But, nevertheless, with Mrs. Johnston standing right behind her, Mrs. Hopwood had no recourse but to pick up the office phone and dial the number for St. Jude Elementary School.

The secretary answered and when Mrs. Hopwood asked for Sister Santina, she was told that Sister Santina was not available.

"She's not available?" Mrs. Hopwood repeated blankly.

"Ask her," Mrs. Johnston ordered.

"Maybe you can help me. My name is Julia Hopwood. I have a copy of the book you put together for the Educational Evaluation and I was wondering—"

"Can I put you on hold for a minute?"

"She put me on hold," Mrs. Hopwood told Mrs. Johnston.

"Would anyone like to order some sandwiches?" Father Felix came out of his office. He looked at Mrs. Hopwood. "Who are you calling?"

"She's calling St. Jude Elementary School. She's missing a page from the Educational Evaluation Book," Mrs. Johnston answered for her.

"I'll have a sandwich." Miss Crossover stepped behind Ms. Morningstar's desk. "I'll have a tuna on rye."

"Yes, thank you," Mrs. Hopwood said. "I am missing page thirteen from your booklet and I—"

"I'm afraid I can't help you," a bored, indifferent voice responded. "I'm just the secretary and I don't know anything about that booklet. If you leave your name and number, I can have Sister Santina call you."

"Okay, my number is—"

"Tell her you'll be here until late tonight," Mrs. Johnston said. "You can give her the school number. And, Father, I'll have a BLT with an order of onion rings and a piece of chocolate cake."

Mrs. Hopwood gave the useless secretary the information and then ordered a ham and cheese sandwich with a cup of coffee.

"Do we have to pay for this?" Mrs. Johnston said.

"Probably," Mrs. Hopwood answered as she went to get her purse.

IT WAS EIGHT O'CLOCK at night and Mrs. Hopwood was utterly exhausted. She was busy trying to explain to Thelma Lou's mother why her daughter was having problems in math.

"I think it's because she's not neat," Mrs. Hopwood said. "And then she gets her columns all mixed up. She's adding from the tens and hundreds together. She forgets where the carry over number is."

"I know what you mean." Thelma Lou's mother shook her black curls. "I love my daughter but she is a terrible slob."

"Well, if we could just help her become neater, I'm sure her marks would improve."

"Thank you, Mrs. Hopwood, for giving me hope."

"I enjoy Thelma Lou. I really do." And that was the truth.

"And I just want you to know, Mrs. Hopwood, that no matter what they say about you, I think you're a darn good teacher."

Mrs. Hopwood felt her heart drop like a textbook on the floor. She could barely find her voice. "What are they saying about me?"

"A fine teacher, not like that horrid Mr. Alabaster."

A sharp peel resounded through the building. "Parents and teachers—" Father Felix's voice crackled through the intercom "—the conference time is over. Please vacate the building. If you want to discuss your child's progress in greater detail, make an appointment."

"As you know my son, Adrian, was in his seventh grade

class. Talk about not knowing how to teach math. Adrian actually took our credit card numbers to school. Now, I can't prove that Mr. Alabaster placed any bets but do you know—"

"We will be locking up the school in five minutes," Father Felix said. "Last call."

"Do you know anyone who lives on Maple Grove Drive?"

"Maple Grove Drive…" Mrs. Hopwood repeated thoughtfully. That did sound familiar but she was still wanted to know who said what about her teaching ability.

"Someone used my husband's credit card to purchase a beige cashmere coat to the tune of twelve hundred dollars. I never spent that on a coat. I never even spent that on an entire wardrobe. Did Mr. Alabaster have a girlfriend?"

"I don't know."

"Well, I'd like to find out. Some of the parents are talking about suing St. Polycarp but I would rather not go that route. I know that you're trying to get that certificate to raise the standards of the school, and I'm not a troublemaker…"

The lights were flashing on and off.

"I think you better go," Mrs. Hopwood said. She was not feeling kindly towards Thelma Lou's mother. She thought it quite cruel being told people were talking about her. Mrs. Hopwood didn't know who or what they had said, so how could she possibly defend herself?

"You're right, but please try to find out." Thelma Lou's mother continued talking.

"Try to find out what?" Mrs. Hopwood asked. Right now there was only one thing she wanted to find out.

"Who lives on Maple Grove Drive. You would think that the credit card company would do that. They are issuing us another card, but we have to wait and my husband needs it for gas. He drives a truck, you know."

"I know." The halls were darkened.

"I'm going, I'm going," Thelma Lou's mom said as she grabbed her Thanksgiving tote bag from one of the little desks. "I'll see you tomorrow morning in about twelve hours at prayer time."

Mrs. Hopwood was just about to utter "don't remind me" when she bit her lip and yawned.

Who had said she wasn't a good teacher?

She wondered if everyone had already left. Usually the janitor stayed around but, obviously, Mr. Ironweed wouldn't be staying around anymore. She switched the light off in her classroom and closed the door.

Ten to one, Amelia Johnston had already gone. She always used the excuse of her twins to duck out early on parents' night.

Was Mrs. Hopwood supposed to sign out? She approached the office and stopped, looking around for the sign out sheet on Ms. Morningstar's messy desk.

The phone rang.

She was not picking it up. It was late and she was tired and in no mood to take a message.

The machine clicked on.

"This is Sister Santina. This message is for Mrs. Julia Hopwood. I understand that you are missing a page from our book. I don't understand how that could have happened."

Incompetence, Mrs. Hopwood thought.

"We were so careful putting it together. At any rate, Mrs. Roacher told me that it is page thirteen you're missing. That's extremely unfortunate because that page is our dedication to a longtime teacher."

Not very important, Mrs. Hopwood thought, and then she decided that she was not going to bother signing out. It wasn't her fault if she couldn't find the sign out sheet. She walked out of the office.

"A teacher who had dedicated years to St. Jude School and died suddenly of a heart attack."

Mrs. Hopwood stopped.

"Her name was Bonnie Crossover."

Mrs. Hopwood felt as though a student had poured iced fruit punch on a brand-new outfit.

She turned around and raced to grab the phone.

"Sister Santina," she said breathlessly, "this is Julia Hopwood."

"Oh, Mrs. Hopwood. I didn't think—"

"What did you say the name of that teacher was?"

"Bonnie Crossover."

Mrs. Hopwood, dazed and confused, sank down in Ms. Morningstar's creaky chair.

"It was all very sudden. She died—"

"Bonnie Crossover," Mrs. Hopwood said. "Dead."

"Yes, I just told you that." There was a touch of impatience in Sister Santina's voice.

"You see, Sister, we have a Bonnie Crossover teaching here. And she is very much alive."

"Well, obviously, it can't be the same person."

"What did your Bonnie Crossover look like?"

"She was an older woman. A woman in her sixties, and so close to retirement."

"And her background?"

"She had a BA from Mount Holyoke College and a Masters from Notre Dame."

Mrs. Hopwood wanted to ask another question, but her chest had constricted and she was having a hard time breathing.

"What is this all about?" Sister Santina seemed very suspicious.

"Just one more quick question, Sister. After Miss Crossover died—"

"Mrs. Crossover."

"Did anyone else disappear around the same time?"

Sister Santina was silent for so long that Mrs. Hopwood thought that they had gotten disconnected or that someone had cut the line.

"Funny you should ask," she finally said. "There was a woman. It was horrible, really. She was a teacher's aid in the lower grades. She had been accused of killing her husband because they had a fight over her credit card bill. She claimed it was self-defense but before the police could arrest her, she disappeared. I don't know if she was ever caught."

"And what—" Mrs. Hopwood gulped "—what did this teacher's aid look like?"

"She was a nice-looking woman. She had a scar over her left eyebrow. I believe she got it when her husband threw a leg of lamb at her. So you see, Mrs. Hopwood, St. Jude Elementary School has been through quite a bit and we really do want this certification. We want to raise the standards of our school in order to gain the parents' confidence."

Mrs. Hopwood heard footsteps in the distance. "Thank you, Sister."

"Do you want me to fax you the missing pages?"

"That would be good."

"What is your—"

Mrs. Hopwood hung up the phone. The footsteps were getting closer now. Clickty—clack, clickty—clack...

Mrs. Hopwood ducked under Ms. Morningstar's desk and waited.

SIXTY-ONE

EVIDENTLY MRS. HOPWOOD had already flown the coop. Mrs. Johnston was planning to give her a ride home, even though it was out of her way. But she didn't like the thought of her friend waiting in the dark on such a cold night for a bus.

Well, maybe Mrs. Hopwood got lucky and caught a cab.

Was Mrs. Johnston supposed to sign out or not? She decided to skip it. It was late enough. She should have left a half an hour ago but she was trying to talk Mr. Brewer out of suing the school and naming Mrs. Johnston as a party. All because she had tried to extract Bruce's head from the sofa.

Talk about making an enemy by doing someone a favor.

Mrs. Johnston heard a slight movement—like someone breathing—and it seemed as if it was coming from behind Ms. Morningstar's desk.

It could be a mouse. It could be another rat. It could even be a killer.

Mrs. Johnston was not going to stick around and investigate. Especially by herself.

Just when she was about to flee, a loud thump startled her. She jumped and then saw Mrs. Hopwood leap from underneath Ms. Morningstar's desk.

"Oh my God!" Mrs. Johnston put her hand to her chest. "You don't need to drink poison to have a heart attack around here. What are you doing?"

"I was hiding. But then my high heel caught on the phone wire and it crashed."

"I hope you didn't break it."

Mrs. Hopwood looked down at her chartreuse pump. "No, it seems all right."

"I'm talking about the phone! I don't think Ms. Morningstar will take that lightly. I suppose it's stupid of me to ask why you're hiding."

"We've got to break into Father Felix's office."

"What?"

"I know who the murderer is!"

"I told you it was Father Felix."

"It's not Father Felix."

"Then who?"

"You were right."

Mrs. Johnston was surprised. "I was right?"

"Sister Santina called me back. The missing page was a dedication to a dead teacher. She died of a heart attack."

"No!"

"Her name was Bonnie Crossover."

Mrs. Johnston was completely lost. "What are you talking about?"

"Our Bonnie Crossover is not Bonnie Crossover at all. I think she's an escaped murderer."

Mrs. Johnston could not comment. She was too shocked.

"Don't you remember we were talking about it in the teachers' room? She's the woman who killed her husband over credit cards. Of course, her husband did hit her in the face with a lamp chop."

"What?"

"Her scar."

"Let's call the police," Mrs. Johnston insisted. "Why are we wasting time trying to break into Father Felix's office? What's in there?" Mrs. Johnston thought for a moment. "You don't mean that she's killed Father Felix and he's just lying there—"

"I want to look at her file. I want to find out if she lives on Maple Grove Drive. I also want to see if her credentials match the dead Bonnie Crossover's. And I'm sure that Father

Felix has already gone home. I don't think we should wait until tomorrow. Do you know how to break a lock?"

That question really miffed Mrs. Johnston. "You think just because I grew up in a tenement I know how to break and enter?"

"I didn't say that." Mrs. Hopwood was silent for a moment. "Do you?"

"No!"

"Well, at least do you have a bobby pin?"

Mrs. Johnston touched her tightly braided hair. "Do I look like I have any use for a bobby pin?"

Mrs. Hopwood looked around and grabbed the scissors on Ms. Morningstar's desk. "Maybe I can pick the lock with this."

"I think you're making a big mistake here," Mrs. Johnston said. "We should call the police and tell them what we know. They'll send television cameras right over to the school and you and I will be heroes."

"And what if we're wrong?"

"How could we be wrong? You said yourself—"

"It's possible that there's a second Bonnie Crossover. She could just share the same name with the dead woman. It could be an unfortunate mistake."

"Yeah, sure. It's a good thing you don't teach logic. We have two murdered people here and it's just a coincidence that an escaped killer is on the loose with another murdered woman's name." Mrs. Johnston watched Mrs. Hopwood approach Father Felix's office and stick the point of the scissors in the door's keyhole. "You don't know what you're doing."

"You want to try?"

Mrs. Johnston gave her a shove. "I don't feel good about this." Mrs. Johnston soon discovered that the scissors were nowhere near the right size for the tiny keyhole.

"And she seemed like such a nice person," Mrs. Hopwood said. "And so classy with all those expensive outfits. I always feel rather tacky next to her."

"You are tacky next to her."

"Thanks a lot."

Mrs. Johnston put down the scissors. "This isn't working. Maybe we should try a paper clip. Go look on Ms. Morningstar's desk. What's with Maple Grove Drive?" Mrs. Johnson asked.

"One of my parents told me, Thelma Lou's mother, actually, that her credit card number was stolen and merchandise was delivered to Maple Grove Drive. Do you know what else she said? That all the parents were talking about me."

"What are you doing over there? How long does it take to find a paper clip?"

"She doesn't have any. Unless I open this package—"

"Open the damn package!" Mrs. Johnston stopped. She could hear someone racing down the stairs. She looked at Mrs. Hopwood. "Now what?" She swallowed.

"Do you think there's room for both of us under Ms. Morningstar's desk?" Mrs. Hopwood asked.

SIXTY-TWO

MISS DANVERS SAW IT right away. And her blood turned cold.

She was talking to Miss Crossover, sitting inside her room and complaining about an unreasonable parent, when Miss Crossover did a very unusual thing. She reached into her designer handbag and removed her compact to refresh her lipstick. She opened the compact and examined herself.

The compact was gold and had the initials MMM on it.

Miss Crossover painted her lips a glossy pink, snapped the compact shut and then put it inside her bag. She did this without uttering a word, which was a good thing, because Miss Danvers was finding it hard to locate her voice.

"So I guess we should call it a night." Miss Crossover rose and stretched.

Then Miss Danvers did a dumb thing. She asked Miss Crossover where she got her compact.

Miss Crossover shrugged and answered as though it was the most natural thing in the world. "I bought it."

"With those initials?"

The moment Miss Danvers said that, she realized that she had made a major mistake. Miss Crossover's face got all funny and then she muttered, "I don't know what you're talking about."

But she did. And so did Miss Danvers. That compact belonged to Myrtle and it was stolen with her makeup bag. With her heart pills. Which may have been used to kill poor Mildred Pinkerton.

And like the rumor circulating, maybe to murder Mr. Ironweed.

"It's nice," Miss Danvers managed to mutter. "I'd like to get one for my mother."

Another dumb thing because everyone knew that Miss Danvers's mother had died when Miss Danvers was a teenager.

Miss Crossover switched off the light in her room, plunging them both into darkness. Miss Danvers felt a path of sweat running down between her breasts and all she could think of was how to get out of the school.

"I was thinking," Miss Crossover said, and it seemed to Miss Danvers that her voice was tight and strained, "maybe you'd like to go for a drink. I could use a nice cold glass of wine right about now. What about you?"

"I don't think so," Miss Danvers said as she edged towards the stairs.

"How about a cup of coffee and piece of apple pie at the diner?"

She's going to kill me, Miss Danvers thought. *She's going to drop something in my drink and then I'm going to have a heart attack also and even though it's suspicious, what will they be able to prove?*

But why? Why was she doing this?

"How about the cup of coffee then?"

"Okay," Miss Danvers said, and then she thought that once they were outside she could run for help. The important thing was that she had to make it out of the deserted building alive.

The woman was obviously crazy and crazy people were unpredictable.

Miss Danvers heard voices and they seemed to be coming from Father Felix's office—women's voices, but that was quite all right.

"I just want to sign out," she said.

"I don't think you want to do that."

"You mean we're not expected to sign out?" Miss Danvers was trying to make it sound like a routine question.

But suddenly Miss Crossover was in front of her, and she had never realized until that moment how big a person Miss Crossover actually was. Not that she herself, Miss Danvers, wasn't somewhat large, but Miss Crossover was muscular and strong. Still, Miss Danvers thought that there was nothing to prevent her from giving Miss Crossover a gentle shove. Maybe down a flight of stairs.

Nothing but the needle in Miss Crossover's hand. A hypodermic needle aimed at Miss Danvers's arm.

"What are you doing?" Miss Danvers asked another stupid question. Because it was perfectly obvious what she was doing. Miss Crossover was trying to kill her.

"I can't take any chances. I've come too far."

"And that's going to give me a heart attack?" Miss Danvers asked in a hoarse voice. But all the time she was thinking that Miss Crossover really didn't have to do that. She was going to have a heart attack all on her own.

"Why?"

"Because—because I'm not who you think I am."

"Who are you?"

Miss Crossover looked extremely agitated. Miss Danvers was afraid to move. She was afraid to turn around. One inch and she could be stuck.

Even though she was a Catholic schoolteacher, she was not a praying sort. It didn't matter. She was praying now, plenty. Although she wasn't even sure of the words that were coming out of her mouth.

And just when she thought everything was lost, she heard a loud voice scream, "What is going on?"

Father Felix was still in the building.

SIXTY-THREE

FATHER FELIX WAS ON his way out of the school when he heard voices coming from the main office.

At first he thought it was some of the parents, who had ignored his warnings about the building closing. He figured he'd better check.

He stumbled on a most unusual sight. There was Mrs. Hopwood, bent over, inserting something into his lock. And there was Mrs. Johnston standing right alongside of her, egging her on.

They didn't seem upset to see him. On the contrary, they seemed relieved.

"We have to get into your office." Mrs. Hopwood spoke hurriedly. "It's very important."

He stared at them, too astonished to speak.

"Bonnie Crossover is a murderer," Mrs. Johnston burst out and then Mrs. Hopwood looked extremely annoyed, as if she was the one that should have broken the news and Mrs. Johnston had stolen her thunder.

"Well, actually," Mrs. Hopwood broke in. "That's not quite true. Bonnie Crossover is dead."

"Bonnie Crossover is dead?" Father Felix repeated, dazed.

"The real Bonnie Crossover is dead," Mrs. Johnston said in a rushed tone of voice. "The woman teaching upstairs is an imposter."

"Who murdered her husband and is fleeing from the law. But her husband was abusive and hit her with a lamp chop."

"How do you know all this?" Father Felix asked, puzzled.

"I called St. Jude School," Mrs. Hopwood answered quickly. "You know I'm supposed to go there and observe."

"One of the pages in the book they sent her was torn out," Mrs. Johnston interrupted. "And I told her that she'd better call and find out what was missing, although I have to tell you, she was very reluctant to do so."

"It was a dedication to a dead teacher. Bonnie Crossover. And at the same time Miss Crossover died a teacher's aid disappeared. One that was about to be arrested for murdering her husband."

"The way we figure it," Mrs. Johnston said, "this woman upstairs teaching those unsuspecting fourth graders assumed Miss Crossover's identity. Then somehow poor Mildred Pinkerton found out about it—"

"She actually left a note for us, saying *someone is not who they appear to be*."

"You didn't tell me *any* of this." Father Felix collapsed into Ms. Morningstar's chair.

"Like you'd really believe us," Mrs. Johnston huffed.

"And Mr. Ironweed, he must have discovered something," Mrs. Hopwood said.

"He was in love with her," Father Felix said thoughtfully. "I think he knew she was stealing credit card numbers."

"Well, there you go!" Mrs. Johnston said triumphantly.

"What did you expect to find in my office?"

"We wanted to see her file," Mrs. Hopwood said. "Just to see if it matches the dead woman's. Did she say that she went to Mount Holyoke and has a Masters from Notre Dame?"

Father Felix knew that she had.

"And does she live on Maple Grove Drive?" Mrs. Johnston asked.

Father Felix knew she did.

"Then the heck with your office," Mrs. Johnston said. "We should call the police right away."

"Maybe we're being a little hasty," Mrs. Hopwood said.

"Hasty?" Mrs. Johnston shouted. "I don't think we're being hasty at all. What do you think, Father Felix?"

He didn't have a chance to answer. The bloodcurdling scream coming from a floor above them told Father Felix that they had not been hasty enough.

SIXTY-FOUR

FATHER FELIX SHOT OUT of the chair like a kindergarten student who had just won a box of stickers. Mrs. Hopwood stepped back in fear.

No one was paying particular attention to Mrs. Johnston, which was quite all right. Because, instead of taking the front staircase, where the scream had erupted from, she walked quickly along the narrow corridor, through the double doors, and ascended the back staircase.

Whoever was up there would not expect anyone to come from behind.

The second floor hallway was dark and Mrs. Johnston did not think it would be a wise decision to switch the overhead lights on. That would alert whatever-her-name-was. She had obviously screamed in an effort to bring Father Felix running.

And he had fallen right into her trap.

Mrs. Johnston looked around for a weapon, but being an elementary school, weapons were few and far between.

Then she saw it. The water bottle she had never gotten around to inserting into the cooler. If she could slip behind and hit whoever it was over the head, that would throw her for a loop.

It was the water cooler or the Bible.

The water cooler was heavier than Mrs. Johnston thought. Of course, lifting it in the past had consisted of hurling it on top of the cooler, never carrying it down a school hall. She was huffing and puffing, drenched in sweat. She was afraid tha she was making so much noise that someone would certainly hear her.

Someone like whatever-her-name-was.

Mrs. Johnston followed the sounds and saw to her amazement that the pandemonium had moved to the first floor landing. She could see from up above that whoever-it-was had poor Miss Danvers by the neck and was holding a hypodermic needle, pointing it at the terrified woman.

Father Felix was standing in front of both women and he was obviously trying to appease whoever-it-was, which was a complete waste of time. "Let her go," he said. "Take me instead."

Mrs. Johnston thought that sounded like a line from a bad movie. Because it was quite clear that if whoever-it-was let Miss Danvers go, she could easily be overtaken by Father Felix and Mrs. Hopwood. Well, maybe not Mrs. Hopwood, who was standing ashen faced and paralyzed in the corner.

"Don't do it, please," Father Felix said. "God will forgive you those other deaths."

Whoever-it-was actually started to laugh. Even Mrs. Johnston thought Father Felix sounded rather absurd.

Mrs. Johnston stepped forward and raised the water container.

The movement alerted Mrs. Hopwood, who bobbed her head up and stared straight at Mrs. Johnston. And she didn't do it unobtrusively either. She actually gave a small gasp of surprise, which, of course, meant everyone, including whoever-she-was, craned their necks to look at Mrs. Johnston, bent over the banister with the water bottle in her hands.

There wasn't time to think. There wasn't even time to aim. Mrs. Johnston let go of the water bottle (actually, her arms could no longer support it) and she sent it hurling to the first floor landing.

Her intention had been, of course, to hit whoever-it-was. Instead it smashed straight into Mrs. Hopwood's shoulder.

She promptly collapsed on the floor beside a startled Fathe
Felix (who had managed to duck just in time).

But when the plastic water bottle crashed to the floor, i
cracked wide open. Gallons and gallons of water poured ever
which way, flooding the area. Whoever-it-was (probably afrai
to get her shoes wet) stepped aside. Just an inch. But enoug
for Miss Danvers to flee.

Once Miss Danvers started to run, she didn't stop. She ra
straight to the front door, shrieking as though she had alread
been murdered.

And whoever-it-was was busy looking at her shoes a
though she couldn't understand how she had managed to ge
them wet.

"Call the police," Mrs. Johnston screamed down at a use
less Mrs. Hopwood, who was just opening her eyes, daze
and confused.

"I'm way ahead of you," she yelled.

And then Mrs. Johnston heard the sirens.

SIXTY-FIVE

THE ENTIRE FACULTY assembled inside the art room where Father Felix was to make an announcement. Mrs. Hopwood situated herself beside Mrs. Johnston in strict disobedience of Father Felix's orders.

It had been over a week since Ruth Milheiser, AKA Bonnie Crossover, had been caught and arrested. Father Felix had already hired two new teachers, Faith Ferran, an odd-looking woman who was wearing a pillbox hat (to replace Ms. Milheiser), and Kenneth Olegin, a rather hefty man (to replace Mr. Alabaster). Mrs. Hopwood thought that Mr. Olegin had probably been hired to scare the seventh graders and, although that was a rather difficult task, Mrs. Hopwood thought he just might be able to do it.

"Okay, I'll be brief," Father Felix began.

Mrs. Johnston huffed in disbelief.

"We're gathered here just to set the record straight. I know a lot of you have been receiving questions from the media and parents, and I caution you not to answer them. What we say can be twisted. The good news is thanks to Mrs. Hopwood—"

"What did she do?" Mrs. Johnston, who had been leaning back in her chair, popped up, like a piece of burnt toast.

"What do you mean, what did I do? I called the police."

"The police might have come too late. If I hadn't dropped that water container on Ms. Crossover...or Ms. Milheiser—"

"You didn't drop it on her. You dropped it me."

"All right, ladies." Father Felix put his hand up. "I'd like to thank both Mrs. Hopwood and Mrs. Johnston, who worked well together, to catch a brutal killer and to solve the murders at St. Polycarp Elementary School."

Mrs. Hopwood shot Mrs. Johnston a smug look.

"I also wanted to tell you another piece of good news," Father Felix continued. "I got a call from Sister Augusta. She feels very strongly that because of everything we, as a staff, have had to cope with at St. Polycarp, we shouldn't have a problem getting our Educational Evaluation."

Everyone in the room breathed a sigh of relief.

"This morning I had three calls from prospective parents. As unbelievable as it seems, the publicity surrounding the unfortunate deaths of poor Mildred Pinkerton and Mr. Ironweed seemed to have increased our enrollment. Hopefully, that will continue. And lastly, I got a letter from Penny Northstar."

Mrs. Johnston groaned. "Is she the lady that fixes up libraries?"

"That's exactly what she does. She obtains grants for schools and she helps to build and organize libraries. She wants to come and talk to us about the possibility of redoing our library. This, of course, would go a long way to help us to obtain our Educational Evaluation certification."

"I thought that was in the bag," Mrs. Hopwood said.

"I didn't say it was in the bag. What I did say was the ghastly events of the last few months will not stand in our way. I'd like to dedicate our new library to Miss Pinkerton. We need a committee to meet with Mrs. Northstar and work with her."

Miss Danvers's hand shot up.

Father Felix ignored it.

"What about you, Mrs. Hopwood?"

"I'm sorry," Mrs. Hopwood said firmly, "but I'm already chair of the Educational Evaluation Committee and really—"

"She's easily overwhelmed," Mrs. Johnston interrupted.

"Why don't you do it?" Mrs. Hopwood challenged her.

"That would be nice," Father Felix said.

"I'll do it," Mrs. Johnston said, "if she'll help me."

Mrs. Hopwood nodded. But she wasn't planning on actually *doing* anything.

"Thank you all for showing up," Father Felix said, "and I'm counting on your continued support." And then he beamed.

Mrs. Hopwood hadn't seen him beam for a long time.

"See you all tomorrow." Father Felix turned towards the door.

"Excuse me." Miss Ferran stepped up to Mrs. Hopwood, and then adjusted her pillbox hat (and all Mrs. Hopwood could think of was wherever did Father Felix find her and why did he insist on hiring such an eccentric staff?). "May I talk to you for a moment?"

Mrs. Hopwood nodded because she certainly didn't want to appear snobby.

"I know you've been here quite a while so I'd like to talk to you about a few things. I don't want to bother Father Felix and I certainly don't want to be known as a troublemaker."

Mrs. Johnston edged closer.

"There's a leak in my classroom and the drip, drip, drip is most annoying. And I don't understand why the microwave in the teachers' room turns off midway through the cycle. Also, the door to my room doesn't lock and yesterday when I asked the cafeteria lady for French fries, she actually counted them out! In my last school…"

Mrs. Johnston walked away.

"In my last school, things were very different."

Mrs. Hopwood looked Miss Ferran straight in the eye and then she said, "Welcome to St. Polycarp."

REQUEST YOUR FREE BOOKS!

2 FREE NOVELS
PLUS 2 FREE GIFTS!

W(●**)RLDWIDE LIBRARY**®
Your Partner in Crime

YES! Please send me 2 FREE novels from the Worldwide Library™ series and my 2 FREE gifts (gifts are worth about $10). After receiving them, if I don't wish to receive any more books, I can return the shipping statement marked "cancel." If I don't cancel, I will receive 4 brand-new novels every month and be billed just $4.99 per book in the U.S. or $5.99 per book in Canada. That's a saving of 17% off the cover price. It's quite a bargain! Shipping and handling is just 50¢ per book.* I understand that accepting the 2 free books and gifts places me under no obligation to buy anything. I can always return a shipment and cancel at any time. Even if I never buy another book, the two free books and gifts are mine to keep forever.

414/424 WDN E9NE

Name _____ (PLEASE PRINT)

Address _____ Apt. #

City _____ State/Prov. _____ Zip/Postal Code

Signature (if under 18, a parent or guardian must sign)

Mail to **The Reader Service:**
IN U.S.A.: P.O. Box 1867, Buffalo, NY 14240-1867
IN CANADA: P.O. Box 609, Fort Erie, Ontario L2A 5X3

Not valid for current subscribers to the Worldwide Library series.

Want to try two free books from another line?
Call 1-800-873-8635 or visit www.ReaderService.com.

* Terms and prices subject to change without notice. Prices do not include applicable taxes. N.Y. residents add applicable sales tax. Canadian residents will be charged applicable provincial taxes and GST. Offer not valid in Quebec. This offer is limited to one order per household. All orders subject to approval. Credit or debit balances in a customer's account(s) may be offset by any other outstanding balance owed by or to the customer. Please allow 4 to 6 weeks for delivery. Offer available while quantities last.

Your Privacy: Worldwide Library is committed to protecting your privacy. Our Privacy Policy is available online at www.ReaderService.com or upon request from the Reader Service. From time to time we make our lists of customers available to reputable third parties who may have a product or service of interest to you. If you would prefer we not share your name and address, please check here. ☐
Help us get it right—We strive for accurate, respectful and relevant communications. To clarify or modify your communication preferences, visit us at www.ReaderService.com/consumerschoice.

WWL10